Praise for Russell Rowland's work

Fifty-Six Counties: A Montana Journey:

"*Fifty-Six Counties*, a book I read with pleasure and admiration, is a great companion for those who already love Montana and for those anxious to get a real sense of the place without the salesmanship."

– Tom McGuane, *The Cadence of Grass* and *Gallatin Canyon*

"Russell Rowland is fiercely devoted to the atonement and beauty that are the hallmarks of all great works of art. This is a book for Montana, for the nation, and for the world."

– Shann Ray, *American Masculine, American Copper*

"I can't wait for others to discover this book. Thoughtful, wise, funny, sincere, and *deep*: those are the words that come to mind when reading this treasure. This book is utterly unique. A gorgeous accomplishment."

– Laura Pritchett, *Stars Go Blue*

"Everything about Montana is big: its proverbial sky, its mountains, its wide open spaces. If you have room for only one book about Montana on your shelf, make it this one.

– David Abrams, *Fobbit, Brave Deeds*

In Open Spaces:

"This heartfelt exploration of the lives and hard times of a prairie ranch family fairly pulses with the intrigues of existence. Russell Rowland has given us a vivid and distinctive piece of homespun to take its proper place in the literary quilt of the West."

– Ivan Doig, *A Trip to Wisdom* and *This House of Sky*

"Charged with dramatic tension -- a joy to read."

– Ha Jin, *Waiting*, winner of the National Book Award

"[An] outstanding debut...Rowland's examination of family dynamics is poignant and revealing...."

– *Publishers Weekly* (starred review)

"A family epic that has a muted elegance...A gracefully understated novel."

– *New York Times Review of Books*

"*In Open Spaces* is sage, humane, and immensely readable."

– C. Michael Curtis, senior editor, "The Atlantic Monthly"

"A heartfelt debut...[An] unpretentious, involving story told with unfaltering authority."

– *Kirkus Reviews*

"As a lifelong reader of books written about the west, particularly those about Montana, Russell Rowland's *In Open Spaces* is as good as it gets...a powerful book."

– C.J. Box, author of *Open Season* and *Savage Run*

"Like Norman McLean's *A River Runs Through It*,...Rowland...brings [Montana's] unique beauty alive...."

– *Denver Post*

High and Inside:

"Richly and intimately told, *High and Inside* is a raucous tragicomedy, infused with the desire we all feel in the face of our greatest mistakes: to somehow win redemption, no matter how large our flaws."

– Kim Barnes, *In the Kingdom of Men*

"At times funny, at times tragic, often wise and always moving, this wonderful novel is a grand slam of indelible characters and infectious drama, and a flat-out great read."

– Alan Heathcock, *Volt*

Arbuckle:

This book is humble and deep, like the author himself. Part love story, part frontier mystery, Russell Rowland's latest novel is a heartbreaking, heartwarming journey that's meant to be savored.

--Jamie Ford, New York Times bestselling author of *Hotel on the Corner of Bitter and Sweet*, and *Love and Other Consolation Prizes*

ARBUCKLE

R⦶

A Novel

Russell Rowland
Author of *In Open Spaces* and *Fifty-Six Counties*

This book is dedicated to the homesteaders

56 Counties Press
939 14ᵗʰ Street West
Billings, Montana 59102
www.russellrowland.com
rowlandrussell@gmail.com

Book Layout © 2018 BookDesignTemplates.com
Cover by Allen Morris Jones (http://allenmorrisjones.com)
Cover Art by ZZ Wei (http://zzweiart.com)
Author photo by Alexis Bonogofsky (http://eastofbillings.com)

Arbuckle/ Russell Rowland. -- 1st ed.
ISBN 978-0692778395

BOOK ONE

BOLAND

I HAVE NEVER BEEN A SHY GIRL. From as far back as I can remember, my father told me, "Catherine, don't you be afraid to speak your mind." And I wasn't.

My father was afraid I would turn out like my mother. Not that he didn't adore her. But he never got used to the way she went through life sideways, worrying that the worst was going to happen. He wanted better for me. He wanted me to be my own person.

That's what I was thinking about as I stood in the lobby of the Deadwood Bank. I couldn't stop staring at the manager's Adam's apple. The marble in his throat jumped with every word he spoke, to the point that I almost lost track of what he was saying. But I caught the gist of it.

And I cut him off. "You are making a mistake, sir."

His mouth curled into a smirk. "Pardon me?"

"You heard me...you're making a mistake."

"Well..." The bank manager raised his brow, making no effort to hide his amusement. "You do realize, Miss Boland, that a woman of your..." He paused, fingering the knob in his neck as if it needed to be adjusted.

"Age?" I identified a faint whiff of something unpleasant, something sour. Cabbage, maybe. And it made me that much firmer in my conviction. "Sir, for one thing...I am not nearly as old as I appear, and for another, the fact that you would think that's important...well, it just makes me that much less interested in working for you."

The man puffed air through his nose. "That's interesting, Miss Boland...because I see you don't have a wedding ring, either. Considering how few women there are around here, it says a lot about you that you haven't found a husband *or* a job."

I stood looking at this man...this hideous man with a throat like a turkey. And I thought about telling this man about the business I had started and operated for the past few years. I thought about telling him just how hard I had worked to avoid having to depend on men like him...men who thought women needed to have the world explained to them. And more than anything, I considered slapping this man's face. But I had not been raised that way. So instead I lifted my chin an inch, took a deep breath in through my nose, and made a slow, deliberate turn.

"Good luck, Miss Boland," the man called out, and his tone nearly made me forget how I was raised.

Outside, I walked around the corner from the bank and pressed my thumb and forefinger to my eyelids. I fought back a quiet flow of tears, wishing that a simple encounter like this wouldn't affect me so much. A few years ago, it would not have affected me at all. A few years ago, I had a clear idea of how things worked, and how I fit in this world.

I remembered something else my father used to say, often to himself, when something had gone wrong. It was one of those sayings he'd probably heard from his own father through the years, until it became a part of his worldview. "Opportunity knocks most for those who extend an invitation," he'd mutter in his thick Scottish brogue. I decided I wouldn't let this man slow me down, or discourage me. I would take that man's stupidity and use it as motivation.

I stalked across the dusty main street of Deadwood and strode up the wooden steps to the only other bank in town, the First National Bank of Deadwood. I was so focused on my destination that I nearly head-butted a man exiting the bank. This skinny cowboy with a beaky nose was stuffing something in his pocket as he stepped out onto the boardwalk.

"Pardon me, ma'am." He tipped his hat.

"It's quite all right...I wasn't paying attention." I felt my skin turn pink.

"Well good day to you." The young man was so unnerved he could barely speak.

"Good day to you too, sir." I watched him walk away, pushing his hand deep into his pocket. I was amused by how nervous he seemed. Almost scared.

Inside the First National Bank, I noticed an immediate difference. While the tellers in the first bank had appeared anxious

and serious, especially when the manager emerged from his office, the tellers in this bank made no effort to hide their laughter
as I approached the tiny window.

"May we help you, ma'am?" The teller who spoke was at least
thirty, which made me smile to myself. Too old, indeed.

"Is the manager in?" I asked.

"Yes of course," the teller responded before retreating to a
back office.

I smiled at the younger teller while I waited. She was a pretty
young woman, with dark hair and cheeks that looked to be
smeared with red jelly. She had stacked a tower of gold coins in
front of her and was breaking it up into smaller towers.

"Are you looking for a job?" she asked in a whisper.

I nodded.

She held her hand to the side of her mouth, palm out. "Good,"
she whispered. "We need someone!"

I smiled, my heart lifting.

A ringing laugh echoed from the back office and a moment
later a man ducked through the doorway. He had almost no hair,
and what he did have was wispy, nearly yellow, drooping in thin
streams to his shoulders. His scalp was shiny and red, and he
wore a black suit with a delicate string tie that looked insignifi-
cant in the midst of his wide chest. He smiled broadly when his
powder blue eyes met mine.

"So..." He threaded his fingers and bowed slightly. "Are you
looking for employment?"

"Yes I am."

He nodded. "Your timing couldn't be better." He stepped back toward the office. "Let's go back here and talk in private, away from these two busybodies." The two women laughed. "I'm Lars, by the way. Lars Larson."

I raised my eyebrows.

"I know...don't laugh." Lars held a hand out, inviting me into his office. "I'm very sensitive."

This made me laugh.

"See now, that lack of respect is going to make it very difficult for you to find a job, young lady." And he winked.

Lars asked me my name, and once we were seated, he propped his elbows on the desk, and rested his chin on his fore-finger. A large jar of black licorice sat on his desk next to a green ink blotter and a pad of paper. The office even smelled of lico-rice. "Have you worked in a bank before?"

"No sir, I haven't...but for the past five years I had my own hat shop in Belle Fourche."

Lars' eyebrows rose. "You were the owner?"

I nodded.

"What was the name of it?"

"It was called 'Boland's.' Not very creative, I'm afraid."

Lars chuckled. "I thought your name was familiar. I've actually heard of it. I think I bought my mother a hat there once. So what happened to the shop?"

I squirmed. Although Lars' questions were perfectly reasona-ble, and he obviously wasn't prying, it was still an uncomfortable subject. And it was a reminder that perhaps leaving my recent past behind wouldn't be so easy. I could provide distance from Lonnie Spicer and his betrayal, but the hurt was going to follow me everywhere. "Well, I had to leave Belle Fourche, for personal reasons, so I ended up selling the shop."

Lars nodded again. "I see." A long pause followed. I tried to contain my emotions and keep my expression as blank as possible. But I could feel the tears well up in my eyes.

Lars let his hands fall to the table and he leaned forward slightly. I could see the concern in his face. He looked as if he might reach out and put a hand on mine, and I prayed he wouldn't, thinking that this show of kindness would push the tears right out of me. I straightened my back and looked him directly in the eye, forming a convincing posture of composure.

"Catherine?"

"Yes, Mr. Larson?"

"When can you start?"

RO

George Arbuckle knuckled Jacob Poplar's front door and stood up straight, trying to stretch out his back after a long afternoon of branding. Poplar himself answered the door, and once inside, George stood in front of Poplar's buffalo hide chair, his hand deep in his pocket. Poplar fiddled with his pipe, tamping the tobacco with his finger, then lighting a match against his thigh.

"I have your money, Mr. Poplar." George wriggled his fist from his pocket and held a wad of bills toward Poplar.

Poplar nodded. "You go ahead and keep that money, George."

George frowned, his hand still extended. "But sir...you told me..."

Poplar nodded, then turned in his chair, facing George, who was baffled by the bemused expression on Poplar's face. "Do you remember what you said when I asked you to pay for those cattle, George?"

George thought for a minute. "No sir, I'm sorry...I don't remember."

"Of course you don't remember, George. That's because you didn't say a word. That's why I don't want your money, George. I just wanted to see whether you had the kind of character I thought you do."

George couldn't help but be annoyed that he'd ridden all the way into town to get to the bank before they closed. Wasted hours. His hand had still not moved. "Well I don't feel right about this, sir. Those cattle were my responsibility."

Poplar now turned his whole body toward George. His bulbous nose emitted a puff of smoke. "George, just take the money. And make sure it doesn't happen again."

George tucked the money back into his pocket. "Thank you...I promise I'll do everything in my power..."

"I know you will. Good night, George."

In the bunkhouse, the other hands hunched over a pile of pennies in the middle of the weathered table. They studied their cards. None of them acknowledged George. He ducked into the sleeping quarters, a tiny room filled with roughly constructed bunks, fingering the bills in his pocket, scanning the room for a hiding place. The sparsely furnished room provided few options. Two bunks on each side...a trunk for each ranch hand for his clothes. No locks.

George returned to the front room. "Who's on watch?"

The others didn't answer at first, so George did a quick head count. "Is it Bones?"

"Yeah, Bones."

George sat across the room, took off his boots, and pulled a large sheet of paper and a pencil from the cupboard. "How was it out there, Chester?"

"I didn't see nothing."

"Good." George unfolded the paper, and spread it out on the floor, where he studied the drawing. It was a rough map of the land around them, complete with plans he'd been mulling over for irrigating and gathering water in the various pastures. It wasn't something he'd ever be able to use, since this wasn't his land. But he liked thinking about it. It was good practice for the day he had his own ranch. He felt the eyes of the others on him as he propped the map on his knees and thought about changes. George had ordered another book about irrigation weeks before, and he wondered why it hadn't arrived.

"I can't believe you drew into that straight," one of the cowboys muttered. "Lucky SOB."

"You got the last watch tonight?" Chester asked, turning to George.

George nodded. After erasing one of the dikes on his map and re-sketching it fifty yards to the east, he studied the map and refolded it. Then he stood. "Well, I'm gonna hit the hay."

Nobody responded.

George shook himself awake, reaching down into the back of his underwear and pulling the folded bills from inside. He drew his dungarees on, then buried the bills back into his front pocket, slid his feet into his boots, and donned his duster. Outside, the cold air brought a gasp, and George quickly ducked back inside, took off his duster and pulled on a wool sweater. One of the other hands muttered in his sleep.

George's horse Puck protested the early hour, shaking his head and snorting every few paces. The late spring air smelled fresh, rich with the scent of new grass. The sky was slate grey, and the Black Hills hunched like buffalo in the distance.

"I know, boy...I'd just as soon be in bed myself." He patted Puck's muscular neck.

As George neared the cattle, he peered into the darkness, scanning the perimeter of the herd for the orange glow of Bones' cigarette. When he couldn't spot an ember, he called Bones' name. There was no answer, but George wasn't worried. The herd covered a large area, and Bones was probably on the opposite side, out of earshot. George heeled Puck into a trot, and they circled the herd, with George calling out Bones' name every few minutes. The cattle were mostly quiet, with only an occasional moo. Twenty minutes later, when George was as far from the barn as he could get, he started to worry. Bones would know it was time for his relief. He studied the herd, trying to gauge whether there were more missing cattle. He hated to think about it, but the herd looked a little light.

He nudged Puck into a gallop. Three-quarters of his way around the herd, he spotted Bones' horse thirty yards away, standing regal but riderless.

"Oh no," George muttered.

He pushed Puck toward the horse, and as they got closer, George could make out a man-shaped figure lying on the ground.

"Damn it!" George swung down from Puck's back and rushed toward the prone figure. And even ten yards away, he could tell that Bones was dead. Still, George drawled Bones' name as he crouched next to him. Bones stared goggle-eyed into the darkness, a bag of tobacco resting in an open palm on his chest. A closer look revealed a mark. A hole as round as a peppermint right in the middle of Bones' forehead. And a trickle of blood from one corner of his mouth, as if his last words had also been murdered. George stared at the wound in Bones' forehead, thinking about how little it takes to kill a man. A tiny hole, not even as big around as a dime. And he covered Bones' eyes with one hand.

Just before sunup, George rapped on Jacob Poplar's front door again. The minute Poplar's face appeared, he started shaking his head. "You gotta be kiddin' me," he muttered.

George looked at his boots. "There's more this time, sir."

"More cattle?"

"No sir...more news. Bad news."

"What do you mean?"

"We lost a man...Bones. They shot him."

"God dammit." Poplar slammed his hand against the wall. He stood in silent thought for a moment, staring beyond a spot on the floor. And then he looked up at George. "I'm sorry...come on in, George. Come in." He grabbed George's upper arm and guided him to the sofa, where George sat. Poplar sank into a chair perpendicular to the sofa. He put a palm to his forehead, and he was silent for a long time.

George wondered whether Poplar remembered he was there. "Would you like me to do something, Mr. Poplar? You want me to ride into town and tell the sheriff?"

Poplar shook his head. "I'd rather not get him involved just yet."

"Well what are we going to do?"

With that, Poplar stood. "What did you do with Bones?"

"He's in the barn."

Poplar thought, fumbling with his chin. "He doesn't have family around here, does he?"

"No sir...I think he's from Texas."

"Did you tell the others yet?"

George shook his head.

"Well, let's start by getting him buried."

As George and Poplar approached the bunkhouse, a cool dread filled George's chest, thinking of the reaction of his fellow ranch hands. The glow of the sunlight was just beginning to leak into the eastern sky, bringing an orange/yellow tint to the clouds.

They entered the bunkhouse, where the men milled around, drinking coffee, pulling at their clothes, scratching their rumps.

"Boys, we got some real bad news," Poplar announced. "The rustlers cut down Bones last night...shot him."

The men went quiet, and still. One of them sat down. A few looked at George from the corners of their eyes.

"We need to get him buried...he's out in the barn," Poplar said. "So get your share of grub and meet me out there." He started for the door, then turned. "Chester, come here a second."

Chester Bonefield gave George a funny look, a slight frown, then trotted outside, and the men didn't see him again for the rest of that day.

I SAT ON A ROUGH WOODEN BENCH on Main Street in Deadwood, my purse resting like a poodle on my lap. For my first day at the new job, I had worn my favorite dress, made from forest green satin. I made this dress for last year's Christmas pageant, and people complimented me all night long about how good it looked with my red hair. The dress made me happy. I could actually feel a difference in the way I moved in this dress, as if I could somehow internalize its beauty. I'd worn it to every important occasion since.

I studied my new town. Deadwood was squeezed into a narrow wedge between two mountains, as if a mythical axe had been pounded into the mountain range and left its impression. The houses that were not on the main streets teetered precariously on these steep inclines, many of them propped up with lodge poles formed from the surrounding forest.

Along the main street were more saloons than I'd ever seen in one town. A hundred yards away, I could make out the balcony of the Gem Theater, known as the most notorious of Deadwood's many brothels. I would have never considered moving to Deadwood a few years before, when the town was a musty swamp of murder and rampant lawlessness. According to rumor, every outlaw in the Black Hills trickled into Deadwood, like pebbles rolling down those steep mountainsides. Just days after the most recent sheriff arrived in Deadwood, Wild Bill Hickock had been shot in the back and killed. That was big news, and it was also the final straw. Sheriff Pierre LeFont informed everyone that he wasn't going to tolerate having the locals living in constant fear for their lives. LeFont recruited good deputies, and the turn-around had been dramatic.

But I worried about my decision. Despite the stories that the town had been transformed, I knew it was still a lot more dangerous than most towns in the area. And now that I was here, I could feel it. It was the way people avoided looking at each other. The way they walked with their bodies slightly turned. Away.

But not all of them. I watched Lars Larson stroll up the sidewalk, his lanky stride slow and rhythmic. He greeted everyone he passed.

"Well well...someone who loves their job as much as I do." Lars smiled at me.

"I hope so," I said.

"Well I trust you will." Lars winked while he slid the key into the door.

"What would you like me to do this morning?" I asked once we were inside.

Lars adopted a thoughtful pose, a finger to his lips. "I thought I'd have you start by painting my office."

I stopped, thinking about my dress, and the probability that even the slightest bit of paint would ruin it.

Lars turned and looked me in the eye. A slow smile came to his face. "You don't think I'm serious, do you?"

My concern erupted as laughter.

"Oh boy," Lars muttered. "I always forget that it takes a while to get used to my sense of humor. I'm sorry."

I waved his apology away. "I'd much rather work in a place where people laugh."

The younger teller entered the building talking—just jabbering away about whatever came into her head—how much her feet hurt, how beautiful it was outside. After she introduced herself as Allison Ingram, Lars interrupted her monologue to request that she teach me the basic duties of the job. After rolling her eyes dramatically, which made Lars laugh, Allison had me sit just behind her and watch as she counted and recorded the money in her drawer. We hung the OPEN sign in the window, unlocked the cage in front of her window, and I observed as Allison assisted the customers.

I asked questions when I wasn't following. And between customers, Allison showed me where they kept the various forms, and how to keep records. And finally, when we weren't covering that information, we talked about what *really* mattered. The people.

In a whisper, she explained, "With Lars, all you have to do is make sure the numbers match at the end of the day. And be nice to the customers. He has no tolerance for rudeness, no matter what they do. He bawled me out once for arguing with a customer...and this costumer was horrible. So rude!"

I thought I detected something in Allison's voice when she talked about Lars. A warmth. Allison's already ruddy cheeks took on a slightly darker shade when she said his name.

"And you need to watch what you say around her," Allison whispered, tilting her head toward the teller to her right. I tried to remember the woman's name but couldn't think of it. There was something less than memorable about every facet of this woman. But I had especially noticed her tendency to look at me from the sides of her eyes.

"She's the worst gossip in town!" Allison continued.

"Shhh." I held my forefinger to my lips. "She'll hear you."

"She's also kind of deaf," Allison said.

I laughed, covering my mouth.

Lars emerged from his office, a stick of black licorice hanging from one side of his mouth.

"Oh no, he's eating his licorice already," Allison announced, and the other teller giggled.

"I will not have you filling this girl with your false impressions about my licorice consumption on her first day!" Lars declared.

Allison shook her head. "There's no telling what Lars will do when he's under the influence of licorice."

Lars shook his head. "She's exaggerating."

I studied Allison as Lars ducked into his office, and I had to hold my tongue to keep from saying, 'You're in love with him.'

It was while I was thinking this that the front door opened and the same cowboy I had almost run into the day before entered. He approached Allison's window with his head down, then dug deep into his pocket and pulled out a wad of bills. He laid them on the counter.

"How are you today, Mr. Arbuckle?" Allison asked.

The cowboy simply nodded, his face reddening.

"Did you want to deposit this money?" Allison turned to me as she asked, raising her brow and trying to hide a smile.

Mr. Arbuckle nodded again. The poor guy could barely look at us.

"I guess you didn't need the money after all?" Allison asked.

Now Mr. Arbuckle's face turned crimson. His eyes shifted from side to side. I was amused by how he struggled to bring himself to speak. "There was a misunderstanding," he muttered.

"Okay, Mr. Arbuckle, we'll just get that back into your account then," Allison said, and she started to fill out the paperwork.

But Mr. Arbuckle apparently felt a sudden need to explain further. "I thought my boss wanted me to pay for some cattle that were stolen, but it turned out..."

I studied the troubled expression on this man's face. He was desperate that we understand. "It's okay, Mr. Arbuckle," I assured him. "We don't need to know."

And it seemed as if the whole shape of his face changed. He nodded, and his shoulders dropped a bit. He took a deep breath, and after the transaction was finished, he smiled at me and said his thanks.

When he left, the other teller turned to Allison and said, "Well that's the most we've ever heard from Mr. Arbuckle."

Allison nodded. "Catherine smiled at him. That did it."

I felt my face redden. "Oh shush."

"No, really," Allison said. "The poor man never talks. That's the most I've ever heard him say."

"Lord, I feel like this day is never going to end!" Allison pulled a handkerchief from her sleeve and dabbed her forehead. The grandfather clock struck three, the melodic 'bong' filling the tiny bank.

I smiled. It was just the opposite for me, of course. The excitement of my first day. It seemed as if we'd just arrived.

Allison fanned herself with her handkerchief. "This heat doesn't help."

I had just started toward Lars' office to ask him a question when the front door burst open and five men rushed inside, their faces wrapped in flour sacks. Allison started screaming. I dropped to the floor, scooting under the counter. I felt the fear in my knees.

"Where's the manager?" one man shouted.

Lars ducked through the door of his office, a stick of licorice hanging from the corner of his mouth. "What can I do for you gentlemen?"

"Oh come on now," the leader of the gang said. "You know what to do."

Lars nodded, calmly raising his hands to ear level. "I'll open the safe." He turned around, but before he took another step, the back door opened, and the third teller stepped inside, just returning from an errand. She screamed, and Lars yelled at her to get down, but the roar of a gunshot filled the room. Lars shouted, and the stick of licorice fell to the floor. He grabbed his elbow. Then another shot rang out, and the third teller fell with a thud.

"Why did you do that?" Allison screamed.

"Give us the damn money!"

I saw this as the time to act, and I stood, pulling my hand from my boot. I held the derringer my father had given me, pointed it at the robbers, and announced "Drop your guns!"

The men all froze, a row of burlap faces showing nothing but wide eyes. And then they started laughing.

Their attitude infuriated me, and I shot to prove I was serious, aiming at the legs of one of the men. But my nerves affected my aim, and the bullet buried deep into the wall. This just made them laugh that much harder.

One of the robbers stepped toward me and reached for the gun. "Come on now...why don't you just drop that slingshot and nobody will get hurt."

I aimed at his chest and pulled the trigger again. But nothing happened. The gun was jammed. One of them cringed in mock fear. "We're gonna die, boss!" he squealed.

His attitude made me so angry that I wound up and threw the derringer as hard as I could.

The derringer bounded off his head with a loud whack, and he fell to the floor, out cold. The laughter stopped just as quickly, and a brief silence followed, broken only by the quiet moans of Lars lying in the doorway of his office. The other teller didn't make a sound, and I feared she was dead.

"Listen here, Annie Oakley," the leader of the gang muttered, walking toward me. My nose started running, but I didn't want to make a move, so the moisture gathered on my lip. "Have you ever heard of desperadoes?"

"Of course I have."

"Did you ever take the time to think about that that word means?"

I didn't answer right away. "It's not that hard to figure out."

The man continued toward me, his boot heels clunking against the wooden floor. Lars had gone silent now, and I was afraid of what this meant.

"Every one of these men here has killed someone." He stopped just a few feet from the counter between us. I could hear his breath behind the flour sack. "We got nothing to lose. We're just waiting for someone to either shoot us down or string us up. And until that happens, we have to make a living. We got to feed our families and pay for the whiskey that helps us forget about what we done."

I couldn't help myself. "Oh come on...that's just an excuse. There are better ways to make a living than scaring the hell out of people and taking what they have!"

He pointed. "We don't care whether you're a woman or not. We'll kill you if you step in front of what we want." Now he leaned across the counter and pushed his masked head right up against my face. I couldn't breathe. But I could smell his breath. It was foul, tobacco and whiskey-flavored. "Now...do you still want to be a hero?"

"I'm not trying to be a hero," I said. "And it's got nothing to do with me being a woman. I wouldn't like you even if I was a man."

He stared at me, and his arm rose, pulling the gun from beside his leg until the barrel stared at me like a steely black eye. I thought about the fact that they'd already killed one person, maybe two. There was no reason to spare me. But I held his gaze and was surprised to see the expression in his eyes change, as if without the flour sack, I'd see a big smile on his face. "Aren't you scared?" he finally asked.

"Are you kidding? I'm scared to death. But I talk when I'm scared. I talk and I throw things."

He lowered his gun, and the flour sack muffled a quiet chuckle. "If we ever consider letting women join our little gang, I'm going to come looking for you." And then he turned. "Okay, boys, let's get this over with before somebody comes."

Lars had crawled to the safe and opened it, so the men gathered the money, and my knees wobbled as I held my hands up by my shoulders.

As soon as the men were gone, I rushed toward Lars' office. "Lars?"

"Yes?"

"Oh thank God you're still alive."

"Yeah, you're not rid of me yet."

Then I thought of the other teller, still lying on her back just a few feet away. "What about her?"

"She's dead," Allison said.

I studied the woman, whose eyes were wide and glassy. I felt guilty about how Allison and I had just been gossiping about her a few hours earlier. The three of us were silent for a time, looking at her body as if waiting long enough would give us some idea of what we might do to prevent what just happened. And I wondered again whether I'd made a smart move, choosing this town.

"I don't even remember her name."

CHAPTER 3

I REMOVED EACH ARTICLE OF CLOTHING from my satchel and stacked them carefully in my bureau. From the bottom, I pulled out the final item, which was wrapped in towels. I sat on the bed and folded back the towels and was relieved to see that the china serving platter was still intact...no cracks or chinks. The platter had a pattern of tiny blue flowers surrounding the edge...I always thought they were baby's breath. That's what I wanted them to be anyway.

I glanced around the room, which was warm, homey, with framed pictures on the wall and a beautiful oval mirror opposite the doorway. A writing desk cozied up in one corner. The bed-clothes were good quality cotton, with lace trim. The room was so much better than I expected. I saw no sign of previous tenants, and it made me wonder about the lives that had passed through here. How many people had cried over lost loved ones, cradled someone in their arms, watched an electric storm from this window? I found some strange comfort in the fact that this room had a history. That others had experienced their own brand of life in this room.

When Allison mentioned that there was a room available at her boarding house, I followed her home with the idea that I'd give it a look but not make any quick decisions. The hotel where I was staying would be fine until I found a place where I felt safe. Especially after the robbery. But from the moment we approached the big Victorian, I began to change my mind. And when I met Mrs. Tilford, the warm, gregarious matron of the house, I knew this place was perfect. I returned to the hotel and gathered my things, and now I placed the platter on top of the wooden chest, then stepped back to see how it looked. Across the room, the platter appeared in the oval mirror, which provided a perfect frame. I smiled.

A knock sounded.

"Catherine, are you ready for dinner?"

"Come in, Allison."

The door cracked open, and Allison's shining smile peeked through the narrow gap. "Do you love it?"

I sighed and nodded. Allison entered, sat next to me on the bed, and wrapped an arm around my shoulders. "Are you okay?"

I nodded again. "A little shaky. What about you?"

"I can't believe Mabel is dead." We sat quietly for a few minutes, our faces blank with the blunt realization that we had barely escaped death. And although it was a subject worth contemplating, we didn't seem to have a word to say about it.

Allison looked different somehow, and I realized that she was wearing more makeup than she did at the bank. Her lips were already full, but they were now colored such a bright red that her lower lip looked like a wet piece of hard cinnamon candy. I couldn't stop staring at it.

"Let's go eat," she finally said.

Sitting up to the table, I took inventory of the tenants. Ten people sat tucking napkins into their collars or spreading them across their laps. The faces reflected an interesting mix of age and occupation. There were a couple of young cowboys, but next to them was a man of about thirty who wore the clothes of a businessman—black suit with starched white shirt, and a paisley bow tie. A very old woman sat at the end of the table, and I wondered where her people were. How could she be alone at this stage in her life?

Once Mrs. Tilford served the food, the conversation turned to the robbery, with people discussing the details and asking Allison and me questions over the clink of silverware. Mrs. Tilford turned to me and said, "I hear you tried to stop the robbery, Miss Boland!"

I coughed, wiping a spot of gravy from the corner of my mouth. "Oh, hardly. I mostly gave those awful men a bit of cheap entertainment."

"They think it was the rustlers, right?" someone asked. Others confirmed this.

"But didn't you knock one of the men out?" Mrs. Tilford asked.

"She did!" Allison said. "It was impressive."

"You punched him?" someone asked.

I had to laugh. "No...I threw my gun at him."

This drew a round of laughter, and I couldn't help but laugh myself at the absurdity of it all.

The young man in the suit then asked, "Where did you move here from, Miss Boland?"

"Just down the road, in Belle Fourche."

"And what were you doing there, in Belle Fourche?" he asked.

"I had a hat shop."

"You owned it?"

I nodded. As the young man's questions continued, I felt the tension building in my shoulders, which bothered me. I'd always enjoyed getting to know new people. A good discussion had always been welcome. This discomfort felt wrong. Unnatural.

"Mr. Smalls, if I didn't know any better, I'd say that you were getting very nosey," Allison said to the young man in the suit.

"Am I?" Smalls blushed.

"Allison, leave the poor guy alone. He hasn't had a date in four years."

This was the first time any of the cowboys had spoken, and Allison responded by laughing long and hard. Smalls excused himself, and I felt badly for him. But I was more focused on the way Allison looked at the cowboy who'd made the comment. Her eyes shone, and her eyelids fluttered. That lower lip almost seemed to swell.

"Bernie Sanford, you're awful," Allison said.

"Hey, it's the truth," Bernie said. He was a handsome man, no doubt, in the same way that many of the local cowboys were...his face round and colored by the sun, except halfway up his forehead, which was white as flour. A large mustache flowed down both sides of his mouth like molasses.

"That doesn't mean you should say it." But despite her scolding, Allison's cheeks burned red.

I thought about how I'd been convinced earlier that day that Allison was in love with Lars. Now I wondered whether my friend was simply smitten by whichever man happened to be standing closest to her. It was almost too easy in Deadwood, with the ratio of men to women at seven to one. Someone who looked like Allison could draw attention wherever she went, and I wondered whether Allison had gotten a little too accustomed to the ease of it all.

RO

George woke up to the sound of whispering mixed with stockinged feet shuffling along the floor.

"Who's going to wake up the farmer?" someone muttered.

"I told you I'd do it." George recognized the voice of Chester Bonefield. "You guys going to help me if he won't go?"

"He'll go," the first voice said, and sounds of assent followed.

George felt a nudge to his shoulder. "George. Hey, George."

George opened his eyes. "What's wrong?"

"We're havin' a meeting," Chester said.

"A meeting?" George lifted himself to his elbow. "What time is it?"

"I don't know...about midnight. Come on, George...they're waiting on us."

George sat up, rubbing his eyes with the back of his hand. He thought about asking what kind of meeting, but it really wasn't necessary. He knew.

Half an hour later, George dismounted his horse and joined a circle of cowboys standing with their hands in their pockets, cigarettes dangling from the corners of their mouths. George drifted off to one side, trying to avoid the circle. Trying not to be part of this. The other cowboys all stood facing one man. George didn't recognize the tall, distinguished-looking leader, but he had a feeling he knew who it was. If the rumors were true.

"All right, men…I think we're all here," the man announced, ticking off heads with his index finger. "First of all, no names. You all know why we're here. We're going to go after these fellas, and the less said, the better."

"Do we know where they are?" someone asked.

"We have a pretty good idea."

"What about our jobs?"

George was glad someone brought this up…what was Poplar going to think about half of his crew being gone?

"If you're here, your boss knows about it," the man said, and his tone made it clear that he didn't want to hear any more questions. "We have plenty of food for all of you, and if everything goes as planned, you'll be back to work tomorrow."

Just as they were about to break up, a shout sounded from the east, and all the cowboys jumped, some grabbing for their guns.

"Don't shoot!" someone shouted, and from the darkness two figures emerged, both holding their hands in the air, surrender-style.

One of the men looked vaguely familiar, and both were decked out in clothes that would have cost most of these men a year's salary. The taller man wore a huge black felt hat with a leather band, fastened with a shining silver buckle. His mustache featured carefully waxed points jutting out in either direction, the kind of luxury most cowboys couldn't maintain without too much free time.

The shorter man was the one George thought he recognized but couldn't place. His suit looked as if it had been spun that afternoon, shiny and pressed. He approached the leader as if they were old friends.

"Sanford! We're here to help." George somehow found some comfort in knowing he was right about the leader's identity. Preston Sanford.

Sanford adopted a kind of reverential demeanor that was dramatically different from what they'd seen, and pulled the two men to one side.

"The governor," George heard someone mutter.

That was it, all right. George had heard the governor was in the area, doing something or other, but what the hell was he doing here? How would he have possibly known about this?

Sanford talked quietly to the two men, and the governor seemed to argue with him, quietly, but eventually he and the taller man shook Sanford's hand and started to head off in the direction they came. But the governor stopped and turned.

"We believe in what you men are doing. Keep up the good work!" he cried. "You're all good patriots."

George was surprised to feel himself swelling a bit, despite his reservations.

George stayed toward the back of the pack of galloping horses, wondering how on earth he'd become part of this fiasco. Who put him up to this? It couldn't be Poplar's idea, could it? Considering all the men on their crew, what would make Poplar think that George would want to be part of this? George considered himself a pretty good judge of character, but could he be this wrong about the man for whom he'd worked the past two years? Besides, it was unheard of to give up part of the crew for a whole day.

More than anything, George noticed how different this ride felt from the hundreds of other times he'd ridden in a group. From the time he was strong enough to pull himself up into a saddle, this had been his favorite thing in the world...being in the middle of a roundup, or any gathering of men on horseback. The sounds of the leather creaking, horses snorting, the jangle of spurs. He even loved the smell of horses and cattle. And the motion of it all...the way a group of cowboys knew what needed to be done and did it without having to talk about it. But this...this just didn't feel the same. While he usually felt as if he was working with the men around him, this felt like a solitary journey.

Each of these men exchanged glances as if they hardly knew each other, as though they expected someone to turn on them at any moment.

They rode for a couple of hours, careful not to push their horses too hard. George fought the pull of sleep, occasionally slapping his cheeks. A man passed out dried apricots and some biscuits smeared with pemmican, and George was relieved to get some food in his belly. Chester drifted back and rode next to him for a time. George didn't feel like talking to anyone but decided that it might help him stay awake.

"You know anything about what we're up to here, Chester?"

"No more'n you."

"You know if Poplar had any say in getting us involved in this?"

"I have no idea."

"What about when he pulled you aside yesterday morning, and you took off for the day?"

Chester shot him a look but didn't answer. "It's the right thing to do, George. These bastards won't stop until somebody stops them."

"It's not exactly our job, though." George regretted saying this as soon as the words left his mouth. If Chester passed along this sentiment, and Chester was just the type who would, it wouldn't take long for word to spread that he wasn't onboard. Just one more reason for them to look at him as an outsider.

Finally, just about the time George wondered whether they would ever stop, a man rode up to Sanford, talking excitedly, pointing north. Sanford raised a hand, and the posse slowed their horses, gathering in a circle.

"We found 'em," he said. "They're camped just over that ridge." He tipped his head to the south. "Our man here says there's five or six of them."

The horses pawed the ground, and a few murmurs shivered among the men. George wondered whether he was the only one who felt uncomfortable.

"So here's what we're gonna do," Sanford announced. He laid out the plan, pointing to each man as he explained their duties. His instruction for George was lookout, which sounded about as safe as he could expect. George nodded, and followed the posse as they moved in a quiet pack, nudging their horses into a steady trot. The air smelled so fresh and clean, with just a hint of sage. George sucked the scent deep into his lungs, trying to capture the same feeling of confidence the scent usually brought, when he was out working with cattle and knew exactly what needed to be done.

Sanford signaled with his hands, and although everyone else seemed to know what these signals meant, many of them made no sense to George. He assumed someone would eventually tell him where to position himself.

But as they got closer, something occurred to him. And although the realization scared him, he couldn't help but smile at the fact that he hadn't even thought about it. What kind of cowboy was he, anyway? Well, that was just the point, wasn't it? He was the kind of cowboy who was only interested in cows. In ranching. He hadn't made his way to this country because of the stories he'd heard about gunfights and vigilante justice. He'd made his way here despite those stories. He'd left Johnson County, Wyoming just before the war between the cattlemen and sheep men got out of hand for precisely this reason. That's why it hadn't even occurred to him when his compadres woke him from a sound sleep that if he was going to join them on this adventure, he should probably be carrying a gun, something he didn't even own. George's breath raced. He kept seeing movement from the corner of his eyes and was embarrassed to look over each time and see nothing.

"Hey!" someone shouted.

George dug his heels into Puck's flank until he was next to the guy. They looked down from a small bluff onto a tidy encampment, where several figures lay huddled around a smoldering fire.

"You all right?" the cowboy asked. "You look a little spooked."

George adjusted his expression, trying to appear calm. "Of course I'm all right. What's next?"

"You just wait right here. We're going to come in around that way." The cowboy pointed across to the other side of the little gully. "So there's a chance they could try and go this way, but we're gonna try and take 'em by surprise, so they probably won't be going anywhere."

George nodded, and the cowboy rode off. But George realized from the instructions that their plan meant pushing the rustlers right toward him. He took a deep breath and tried to settle his nerves as he watched the clan ride off toward the opposite side of the camp. They split into two groups, with about six men going in each direction. He was surprised that they didn't leave anyone else to stand watch with him, and he tried to adopt their confidence about taking the rustlers by surprise. If all went well, they would capture them without incident. Maybe he could even sneak off in the midst of the chaos.

There was just enough moonlight to see blue outlines of the posse slowing their horses to a walk, then gathering in two spots, motioning frantically with their arms. But the horses sensed something. They tossed their heads, and their knees rose high with the urge to gallop.

And then a shout suddenly rose up from the small encampment. The six sleeping figures jumped to their feet, gathered their bedrolls, and hopped on their horses, all in a matter of seconds. They had clearly practiced this drill, as they rode off in the same direction without a word between them.

The posse responded, spurring their horses forward, rushing toward the camp. But the six men were already well ahead of them, riding straight up the embankment toward George. George sat frozen, realizing yet again that he didn't have a goddam gun. The grunts of the horses and the sounds of their hooves pounding against the dry ground got louder, and George realized he was about to die for a cause that he didn't even believe in. He braced himself. His breath stopped.

And for some inexplicable reason, he decided to fold his hands in front of him. He hadn't been to church in years, except for the occasional wedding or funeral, and he couldn't remember the last time he'd prayed. But there he sat, his hands folded like a child about to crawl into bed.

The rustlers crested the hill, and although they each held a gun, they looked at him as if he didn't register, as if he was some kind of apparition. The first rode past him, giving him a brief glance. The second pointed his gun at him, and George met his eyes with a solemn expression, ready to take the bullet. But the man seemed stunned for a moment, and just when George expected the blast of gunpowder, the man instead gave his horse an extra hard kick to the ribs, and the horse jumped forward. The next two men seemed content to follow whatever the men in front of them had decided and rode past him with hardly a look.

It was the fifth rider who pulled up short, jerking at the reins. His horse protested with a loud whinny and a shake of his head, and the last rider almost ran into them.

"Stupid son-of-a-bitch, what are you stopping for?" the last rustler shouted as he rushed past.

But the man didn't answer. He sat for a moment, the breath rushing through his nose and his mouth, which was slightly open. He held his gun in front of him, not really aiming at George, but prepared to aim. He looked George right in the eye. He was a young man, with a pathetic mustache, and a few days' growth sprinkled along each jaw. His felt cowboy hat was old and greasy, but he wore brand new clothes, perhaps a reward from their haul at the bank.

"Don't you have a gun?" the rustler asked.

George thought about lying, then wondered why he would lie, especially when the answer was obvious. The whole scene seemed completely absurd. He shook his head.

George thought the kid was going to laugh. The hint of a smile curled his mouth, and for a brief moment, they shared in the joke. Then a roar echoed across the prairie, and the rustler let out a shout. A spurt of blood flew from his upper arm, and his gun fell to the ground with a thud.

"God dammit," the young man shouted. He tried to spur his horse forward, but it seemed that the wound affected that entire side of his body. One leg was flailing in the air, and the other wasn't working at all. He bent forward, leaning over the horse's neck and shouting in his ear, "Move! Move, you stupid son-of-a-bitch."

Another shot sounded, this one ripping the flesh on his calf. He fell off his horse just as the posse hit the crest of the ridge. Their reaction to the scene was much as the rustlers' had been. They stopped their horses, studying George and the fallen man with slack jaws. George didn't realize his hands were still folded until he noticed one of the guys staring at them. He dropped them to his sides.

"What on God's green earth is going on here?" Sanford pulled up the rear of the posse, swung his leg over and dropped to the ground. "Why aren't you guys chasing the rest of them bastards. Move!"

Most of the men took off, their boots thumping their horses' ribs. A couple more shots popped the silence. Sanford studied

the guy on the ground, picking up the rustler's gun in a calm motion. He aimed it at the young man's chest and continued
contemplating him for a minute before shifted his eyes to
George. The injured man lay quiet, suffering his wounds without
a sound. He held one hand to his upper arm. His look was defiant,
but not threatening. George felt bad for him.

"Did you shoot him?" Sanford asked. George shook his head.

"Someone sure made a couple of nice shots then." Sanford
returned his gaze to the rustler.

"He don't even have a gun." The rustler tipped his chin toward
George, and Sanford's head jerked toward him.

"He's kiddin', right?"

George shook his head.

"You didn't bring a gun?"

George didn't answer.

"What did you think this was, some kind of tea party?"

"I don't own a gun...besides, nobody told me where we were
goin'."

Sanford fixed him with a look that was somewhere between
incredulous and amused. "What outfit do you work for?"

"I best not say," George said.

Sanford frowned. "You think I can't find out? Come on now."

George jerked his eyes toward the rustler.

Sanford scoffed. "A dead man ain't gonna track you
down...don't you worry about him."

A groan escaped the man on the ground.

"Why didn't you tell anyone that you didn't have a gun? Don't you think you might have served as a little bit better look-out...just maybe...if you had a gun?"

"Even if I had a gun, I wouldn't have stopped those men. I'd probably be dead."

Sanford glared at him, frowning. "Why *aren't* you dead? Why didn't they shoot you?"

George shrugged.

Sanford then walked slowly toward George, still aiming the gun at the rustler's torso. "Did I see your hands folded when we rode up here? Were you praying?"

George could hardly breathe. He couldn't imagine what these men might do to someone who joined a vigilante group armed with nothing but two folded hands. "I didn't mean to..."

"Do you realize what you've done?" Sanford asked, his voice nearly in a whisper.

George shook his head.

"You channeled the power of the Lord, my good man." Sanford spun around on one foot, and he now shouted into the air. "This man is cloaked in a coat that is stronger than any wind, or rain, or hailstorm. This man's faith has more power than a gun, men. You can learn from this man!"

CHAPTER 4

AS I PREPARED FOR BED MY FIRST NIGHT in my new home, I heard the shuffle of feet outside my door. My curiosity about the strangers in the house got the best of me, and I trotted toward the door and opened it a crack. Little did I know that my door needed oiling. A squawk echoed through the hallway and Mr. Smalls, the young man in the business suit, now replaced by a long nightshirt, turned his head.

"Oh, I'm sorry," I said.

Smalls started to walk away, but he stopped. "I'm afraid I'm the one who should be apologizing. I didn't mean to be so rude at dinner."

"I didn't think you were rude." I became conscious of my attire, and stepped back into the doorway, swinging the door shut just a little.

But Mr. Smalls paused, a thoughtful look coming to his face. I was struck by how slight he was, but he had lambchop sideburns that emphasized a strong jaw, which gave him a kind of presence. The muscle pulsed in that jaw as he lifted his eyes. "Miss Boland, would you mind if I ask you a favor?"

"Of course not, Mr. Smalls...what is it?"

"I wonder whether you'd be willing to join me in the parlor for a few minutes...to discuss something."

I held my face steady. It was an odd request from someone I'd just met. But Mr. Smalls had such a sincere expression, his face almost pleading. I didn't want to appear unfriendly, or mistrustful. Or afraid. I had been thinking too much lately about how Lonnie Spicer, and other men in my life, had disappointed me. I wanted to regain my trust in people.

"Well all right, Mr. Smalls...maybe for a few minutes."

"I would appreciate that. I'll be there shortly if you'd like to get your dressing gown."

I sat with my hands folded on my lap, watching the pendulum on a beautiful grandfather clock. I was still pondering the events of the day, picturing the lifeless body of Mabel, when Mr. Smalls entered the room. He tipped his head forward with a slight bow before settling into a stuffed chair perpendicular to the one where I sat. He seemed to need some time to gather his thoughts. He wriggled into the chair and plucked a pair of wire-rimmed glasses from his breast pocket, perching them on his nose.

Finally, he took a deep breath and turned to me. "Miss Boland, I'm troubled about something, and I have a feeling, well...that I might be able to help you."

I frowned, quite involuntarily. "Help me? What makes you think...we've just met."

Mr. Smalls began to nod vigorously. "Yes yes...I assumed you would wonder that. I know it seems odd. I know you must think I'm...well, it doesn't matter. But...well, I just have a strong feeling..." He fixed a steady gaze on me, and I found a tenderness in his deep chocolate eyes that touched me, but also made me slightly nervous.

"All right, Mr. Smalls. I'm certainly willing to listen."

It was then that Mr. Smalls reached inside his dressing gown, and there was something about the gesture that disarmed me. The way his thin hand slid between the folds of fabric seemed to suggest something sinister, or untoward, and before I could think, I started talking, my voice shaking. "I really should get to bed, Mr. Smalls. I didn't realize how late it is, and I'm awfully sorry I..."

"Oh. Well, all right then..." Mr. Smalls pulled his hand from his dressing gown, and it cradled a black book, the leather cover of which I immediately recognized. "I just wanted to offer you this bible. I'm sorry if I'm jumping to conclusions, but I had a feeling you might need some guidance...or maybe just some comfort."

My hand flew to my throat, where I gripped my collar, and began twisting the fabric. "Thank you, Mr. Smalls. I appreciate your concern." I reached out and accepted the book, wondering to myself what it was that he saw...was it something in my eyes? The way I moved? Did my voice show a weakness, or fear?

"Good night, Miss Boland. I'm afraid I've offended you one more time, and that was the last thing I wanted."

"Oh no, Mr. Smalls. That's not it at all. I just...well, it's not what I expected."

Mr. Smalls smiled, but I sensed a sadness behind the expression. "Good night, Miss Boland."

I sat in the parlor for a while, cradling the bible in my hands. This exchange had nudged the memories of my last days in Belle Fourche into my head, and the emotions now welled up inside me. Especially the anger. How could I let Lonnie Piper hurt me so deeply? Would I ever be able to be in the same room with a man again without these feelings of panic? Mr. Smalls was clearly as harmless as any man I'd ever met, and here I was jumping to horrible conclusions, all because of a simple gesture. I never wanted to become this fearful. Never imagined it was possible. I studied the bible. I had never been religious, although I had some kind of faith, I suppose. My parents were occasional churchgoers, but it was mostly for the social benefits. But as I held this small book in my hand now, and closed my eyes for a moment, I realized that just thinking about the idea of faith gave me a small measure of peace.

RO

Preston Sanford stood over the injured man while the last few members of the posse returned from their failed effort to capture the other rustlers. Loud complaints about their inability to formulate a better plan echoed across the night plains.

"You guys shut your traps," Sanford shouted. "We got us a rustler here...so it's not a complete waste of time."

"You don't know I'm a rustler," the rustler declared.

"Oh really?" Sanford said.

"How the hell do you know?"

Sanford crouched down, his feet right next to the man's head. "Well, okay...let's just say for the sake of argument that you're telling the truth."

"I am!" The man twisted his face toward Sanford. His expression showed considerable pain. He gripped his shoulder hard, and the blood that oozed between his fingers looked like oil in the gunmetal blue night sky.

"Uh huh." Sanford nodded. "Like I said, we'll pretend for a sec. So if that's true, then why in the hell were you boys ready to jump on your horses and take off like your hair was on fire?"

"Indians," the man said immediately.

"Of course...how did I know you were going to say that?" Sanford nodded thoughtfully. "And you know...that makes sense until you think about the fact that we don't look anything like Indians. So once you saw us, you had no reason to keep running."

"You're not going to listen to reason no matter what I say." The man winced in pain.

"I'm more than happy to listen to you. I just have to warn you that I probably won't believe you."

The other men laughed, but George found himself wondering whether this man was telling the truth. What if they really weren't the rustlers?

"You have no right to take the law in your own hands," the man said through gritted teeth.

Sanford grinned, his eyes squinting. "Damn, boy...you've either got some nuggets or you're one stupid son-of-a-bitch; you realize we got your life in our hands here, don't you?"

"What difference does it make?"

Sanford stood. "I guess that answers that question. You really are stupid, aren't you?"

The rustler shook his head, a wry smile on his face. "It ain't enough to kill an innocent man, huh? You gotta humiliate him first."

"Would you rather just get it over with?"

"Damn right. Get it over with...don't keep me in suspense."

Sanford smiled, then looked at the circle of faces around him. "What do you think, boys? Should we give him what he wants?"

Some of the men shouted in the affirmative. But George was silent, studying the man's face. He couldn't help wondering why he looked so calm in the face of death. Aside from the pain, he seemed at peace somehow.

Sanford chuckled. "You hear that? They want to grant your wish."

"Good."

"Well unfortunately for you, I don't agree with them."

The man spit. "You have no right," he groaned. "You have no regard for basic human decency."

"That's what you have to say?"

"What kind of outfit is this, anyway? You barge into a camp in the middle of the night, you have a lookout without a gun. Did you just plan this thing as you were riding out here?"

Yes, as a matter of fact, George thought to himself.

A sickening thud was Sanford's answer to this question. He had kicked the man in the head, the point of his cowboy boot colliding with the man's temple.

"You bastard," the man said, barely audible.

Sanford leaned over him. "Has it occurred to you that you might not want to make me mad...that I'm the last guy in the world you might want to piss off right about now?"

"Why the hell should I care? You're going to kill me anyway."

Sanford scoffed, and George felt himself wanting to intervene. He wondered how he and these other men—all of them— could stand around and watch someone treat another man this way. It would be one thing if they knew for sure this guy was guilty.

Sanford shouted over his shoulder. "Bernie, grab that rope and get it set up on that cottonwood over there."

A cowboy with a handlebar mustache unlaced a rope from the back of his saddle and hopped down from his horse. He trotted his horse over to the cottonwood tree and threw the rope with an underhand toss. The rope uncoiled and flopped over a thick branch. A noose had already been fashioned at one end.

"You're too stupid to live," Sanford muttered to the man. And then to George's surprise, Sanford planted another kick, right in the man's stomach. A deep, painful groan rose up as the man lost his breath and then began to choke on the lack of air.

"Get up," Sanford commanded.

The man looked up at him, a pleading expression, and when it was clear that Sanford was serious, he tried to push himself up to his feet. But he could barely move. His body had curled up like dried leather.

"Get up!" Sanford kicked him in the ribs again.

The man writhed, his body twisting like a snake. He mumbled something, but George couldn't hear him. But it infuriated Sanford, who bent down and jerked the man to his feet. The man's knees buckled. Sanford jerked him up again, wrapping his arm around the man's waist. He started walking him toward Bernie's horse. Although the kid could barely walk, he kept fighting, throwing an occasional elbow toward Sanford's chest. Sanford simply wrapped his arm more tightly around the man's shoulders. Each time the kid threw an elbow, Sanford punched him.

"Get up on that horse," Sanford told him. He pushed him toward the horse, and the man stumbled, his head smacking against the saddle. He nearly fell again, but he grabbed onto the saddle horn and held himself up. "Come on...get up there, you big tough cowboy," Sanford prodded.

"Yeah, listen to you...it's easy to be tough when you've got someone scared out of their wits, isn't it? When they know they're about to die?"

Sanford punched him again. "Get on that horse."

As George watched the scene, he felt a desire to rush forward and push Sanford away from the young man. He thought about the last time he'd seen another man die, a moment he'd hoped to never experience again.

"Do you believe in God?" Sanford asked.

The man looked puzzled. "Why?"

"Because if you don't, you might want to think again."

"What the hell?"

"God would have helped you avoid this fate, young man...the good Lord could have saved you from following a life of crime, and finding this noose around your neck."

"Who the hell are you to tell me about God...when you're about to kill a man? Who the hell do you think you are?"

Sanford started to help the young man lift his foot toward the stirrup, and at first it appeared that the young man was going to cooperate, but once Sanford slipped the man's boot into the stirrup, and started to lift him, the man kicked Sanford in the face, sending him flying onto his back. Sanford jumped to his feet, blood flowing from his nose, and started flailing away at the kid, punching and kicking, muttering invectives that didn't even seem to be real words...just angry sounds. George found himself rushing forward, and he wasn't alone. Several men grabbed Sanford and pulled him off the rustler, who was on the ground covering his face.

"String that sinner up before I kill him with my bare hands." Sanford strained to escape their grasp, jerking an elbow back into the chest of one of the men, who swore at him and told him to calm down.

"Don't tell me to calm down, god dammit...I got no good reason to calm down." Sanford kicked at the rustler, but missed, which just made his face turn a darker red.

"Get him up on the horse," someone else said.

Two men jerked the rustler to his feet, tied his hands behind his back and forced him up into the saddle. The man kicked at them every chance he got. Like Sanford, they responded by punching him, until the man's face was smeared with blood. One of his eyes swelled shut. A gash on one cheek folded out like a split chili pepper.

As George struggled to keep a grip on Sanford's straining limbs, he watched this scene take its course with the unpleasant knowledge that he had become part of a forward motion that could not be reversed.

Once the man was in the saddle, he did everything he could to propel himself from the horse, kicking his legs, flailing his bound arms around, and spitting on everyone within range.

"Somebody climb up there with him, goddammit," Sanford shouted.

Chester jumped up onto the horse, locking the rustler's thighs against the horse with his own legs. He wrapped his arms around the man's torso, pinning his arms to his side. Chester bit the kid's ear. Blood trickled down the man's neck, and George flinched.

"Is that rope ready?" Sanford asked.

"It's ready."

One of the men led the horse over to the twisted cottonwood and positioned it under the dangling rope. Chester reached up with one hand and secured the noose around the man's neck. He slid the coil up tight against the man's skin, pushing hard enough that the rustler's head began to turn red. He never stopped struggling. His legs strained, trying to kick. His arms wriggled beneath Chester's grip. George admired his determination to free himself.

"Don't hang him yet," Sanford said. "Give him a chance to think about what he done for a minute."

"I got nothing to think about," the young man choked out.

"Let me go," Sanford said to George and the other two men holding him. "There's nothing I can do to him now."

Once they released him, Sanford shook himself, then walked over to the horse and peered up at the rustler. "I'm gonna tell you why you're up there, you dumb son-of-a-bitch."

"I don't need you to tell me; it's because you don't give a damn about justice."

Sanford chuckled, but George could see the anger in the way he set his jaw, his teeth. "Here's the deal, kid. You killed one of our friends. Shot him for no good reason."

"I didn't shoot no one."

"You know what I mean. You were there. You might as well have pulled that trigger." Sanford jabbed at him with a finger.

"I don't have any idea who you're talking about. I wasn't there." The words were strangled by the noose, but the strength of feeling seeped through.

"There's just one thing you're not quite getting here, kid," Sanford growled. "We don't believe a word that comes out of your mouth."

"So I should just die with dignity? Is that it? Just shut up and take it like a man?"

"Something like that. God knows the truth, young man. God knows what you did."

"Then he knows I'm not guilty…"

"Just shut up." And with that, Sanford whacked the horse on the rump, and the horse took off with a start. Chester clearly wasn't expecting this, as he found himself hanging onto a dying man. The man's neck cracked, and he jerked, his legs bending and unbending like a bronc rider spurring his mount. Chester held on for a few seconds before realizing what had happened and dropping to the ground. Then they watched the rustler die, choking to death. A stench filled the air, and George had to walk away from the scene and hide behind a rock while he vomited. But he heard one last declaration from Preston Sanford before the man died.

"You're going home to the Lord, young man!"

GEORGE WAVED HIS HAND IN FRONT OF HIS FACE, trying to shoo a pesky fly. His neighbors fanned their faces with newspapers, pushing the heat around the room. George tried to focus on what the speaker was saying, but it seemed that every person who spoke stated some variation of the same speech. It was also hard to pay attention when the woman across the aisle kept glancing over at him.

"If it hadn't been for our fearless Miss Boland here," the speaker announced, "we might have lost one of the most respected members of our little community."

Everyone turned to look at the woman across the aisle, and one woman patted her on the knee. George caught her looking at him again.

"What did you do?" he whispered.

The woman shrugged, and a wonderful smile spread across her round face. She had dusty red hair, and a smattering of freckles across her cheeks. She held her hands folded on her lap, one on top of the other.

"Did you kill someone?" George whispered, and she covered her mouth to keep from laughing.

The next speaker droned on, and George smiled when Catherine rolled her eyes at him.

"What about this man who was hung?" someone asked. "Are we going to allow our citizens to take the law into their own hands like this?" His voice rose in volume, and George looked at his boots, hoping his face wasn't as red as it felt.

"Nobody knows who did that...it could have been Indians," the man running the meeting said.

"Oh come on, Pete...everyone knows what happened out there...we don't want another Henry Plummer on our hands. We've worked too hard to get past those days."

"What would you suggest?" someone else asked.

"There has to be a better way," the woman across the aisle said, with conviction, and there was a smattering of applause. George felt his face burning, wondering how she'd feel if she knew.

"What did you do?" he asked her again.

And her hands clapped together in a move so swift and surprising that George made a noise in his throat. At her feet, the fly lay dead, and the people seated around her chuckled in surprise and admiration.

After the meeting, George shuffled outside along with the crowd, and, glancing to one side, realized he was walking next to the same woman.

"Have I seen you somewhere?" George asked.

"Yes you have...at the bank. Just a few days ago. I work there."

Now George remembered. "I'm sorry I didn't recognize you."

"It's okay...you seemed a little distracted that day."

George thought about how much had happened since that trip to the bank. How could he have predicted where he'd be now, only a few days later? "Yeah, you could say that."

George looked at her from the sides of his eyes. Her skin was almost transparent, and the freckles danced across her cheeks like tiny cinnamon footprints. But it was her hair that was by far her best feature. It was almost pink, it was such a light red. And fluffy. Like the spun sugar he sometimes saw kids eating at the county picnics. She had it pulled back, but there were unruly feathers of hair jutting in every direction.

"So what do you think of all this?" she asked.

George sighed. "It's very complicated."

"You think? I don't think it is. We just need to give the sheriff all the help he needs to catch these guys. Maybe bring in some extra lawmen."

George nodded, feeling like a complete fraud.

"What do you think they should do about these vigilantes?"

George cleared his throat. "Well, I s'pose those fellas are doing what they think is right."

"Well of course they are." She stopped walking, and held out a hand, palm up, pounding it with her fist. "But nobody should take the law into their own hands. It's barbaric."

George nodded, looking at his feet. "So what exactly did you do, anyway?"

"Oh, it was nothing." Her blush was charming.

"Come on...it must have been pretty dramatic for them to bring it up."

"It was silly, really. I was trying to be a hero." As she told him the story of the derringer, her hands acting out each part of the story. They were like birds, flitting around each other and darting forward and back. When she got to the part where she threw the gun, she went through the entire motion, and nearly clipped him in the ear with her elbow. He ducked just in time.

"Oh, I'm sorry." She touched his forearm, laughing, and George felt a blip in his heartbeat.

"So you threw the derringer at them?" He started laughing.

"I didn't know what else to do!"

"I shouldn't laugh."

"So did they," she said. "The robbers laughed right in my face. It was humiliating."

"But you did save your boss's life."

"I don't know about that...I mostly just gave them something to laugh about. And it didn't stop them from killing that poor woman."

"Do you think it was the rustlers?"

"I'm sure of it...they said as much."

"Did you see any of them...their faces?"

"They had flour sacks over their heads."

"But they said they were the rustlers?"

"Well not right out, but it was clear."

"How many of them were there?"

"Six."

George nodded, feeling a little better.

Around them, others from the meeting drifted off to their homes or to the local saloons. George and Catherine walked down the streets of Deadwood and George gave little thought to where they were going. They passed Soapy Taylor, whose voice rang out across the crowd. "Win five dollars! Five easy dollars!" He had taken advantage of the meeting to attract a large crowd, and he plucked fifty-cent pieces from various hands, then gave each customer a small cube in return. They would unwrap it eagerly, hoping to find a five-dollar bill, or even a one-dollar bill. The winners held up their bounty proudly and sometimes shouted, but most of them ended up with cubes of soap.

Madame Mustache stood in front of her Wild West Theater, calling for visitors to her faro banks. George peeked into the windows of the Eureka Hall, where the large Keno wheel spun in a colorful whirl, and patrons held up their paddles, trying to will the number on their paddle to match that on the wheel.

"Hey Georgie Porgy!"

George's heart rose into his throat, and he tried to hurry his step.

"Georgie Porgy?" Catherine repeated.

George took a peek at her, and she was smiling at him, her head tilted to one side. Behind her, two women draped themselves over the balcony of the Gem Theater.

"Is that your nickname?"

George felt his face get hot. "I'm not sure where they got that." He started walking faster, but a hand on his forearm brought him to a stop. He turned to see Catherine's soft gaze.

"George, we all have to find our own way to get on in this life."

George nodded, but he couldn't look at her. "Where do you live anyway?"

"My house is just up the street."

George paused, wondering about the right way to address this situation. It was times like this that he often felt so out of tune with the world. As if there was so much that went on inside of him that words couldn't express. At least no words he'd ever learned. There were feelings deep in his heart that his tongue couldn't quite reach. "Um...would you like me to walk you home?"

Catherine laughed, and George was immediately taken in by the joy of the sound. "I think you already are."

"What's your name, anyway?" George covered his neck, which was burning up, with his palm.

Catherine told him her name with a shy tilt of her head. "And you are George," she said. "George Arbuckle, right?" After George confirmed this, she turned toward him, folding those expressive hands in front of her as if praying. And she said, "Mr. Arbuckle, are you planning to attend the dance this Saturday?"

"I didn't know there was a dance...I'm not much of a dancer." George identified the disappointment in her eyes from the moment the words left his lips. "But maybe I'll come by...they have sandwiches, right?"

And again she laughed. "Yes...as a matter of fact, they do have sandwiches. And cookies. And sometimes even a cake. And I'll try not to take it personally that you'd come for the food rather than the company."

George coughed. "Well you know, sandwiches don't make very good dance partners."

Catherine smiled. "Very true...so I hope to see you then." And she nodded definitively.

Then she held out her right hand, with authority, and they shook.

CHAPTER 6

WHEN I ENTERED THE BANK the next day, whistling echoed from the back.

"Lars must be feeling better," I said to Allison, who was counting the money in her drawer.

"He seems to be," Allison said.

Lars emerged from his office, his arm wrapped around his torso in a white sling. "Are you ladies talking about me again?"

"We have much more important things to discuss than you, Mr. Larson," Allison teased.

"Well, imagine that." Lars looked at me, propping his good fist on his hip. "Kicking an injured man while he's down."

I smiled. "I've tried telling you that she's a cold-hearted woman, Mr. Larson."

"Well I never!" Allison exclaimed.

Lars winked at me, and I caught a look from Allison.

"Well ladies...it's time for you to get to work, and time for my licorice break."

For the rest of the morning, I felt a chill from Allison, no matter how hard I tried to make her laugh. Even Lars couldn't seem to get a smile out of her, which confused me. Allison had been in such a good mood. One week had passed since the robbery, and although Allison had shown occasional moodiness, one of us was usually able to tease her out of it.

"Shall we go have some lunch?" I asked just before noon.

Allison nodded, but she didn't seem very enthused. We sauntered along the main street of Deadwood, our lunches tucked away in flour sacks.

"Are you planning to go to the dance this Saturday?" I tried to inject some cheer into my voice.

"I don't know...it all depends." Allison tipped her chin slightly to one side.

"Allison, what's going on?"

Allison's mouth formed a point. And she stopped. "I need to ask you, Catherine...what are your intentions with Lars?"

I stopped walking. "My intentions? What are you talking about?"

"I see the way he looks at you."

"Allison...wait a minute. Are you talking about the same Lars I think you're talking about...our boss?"

"Of course; who else would I mean?"

"Well, I just had to ask because I can't imagine what you could possibly mean. That man is madly in love with you, and you're asking me what my intentions are? I bet you anything that Mr. Larson couldn't even tell you what color my hair is."

Allison rolled her eyes to one side, then looked at me skeptically. "So you really aren't interested in him?"

"Allison, I've been dying all morning to tell you about the man I met last night. It's even someone you know...Lars Larson is the furthest thing from my mind."

Allison sighed. "I'm sorry. I just...well, I sometimes think I see him looking at you a certain way, and then this morning he winked..."

"Come on, Allison, you know he was just teasing. He winks at everyone!"

Allison nodded, and I was surprised to see a tear leak from the corner of her eye.

"You're really in love with him, aren't you?"

Allison looked down at her feet, and it was clear that she was too overcome with emotion to answer.

"Come on." I grabbed her upper arm. "Let's eat lunch."

R⦰

George wrapped his arm around a young heifer's neck and took her ear in his teeth, quieting her straining limbs. She bawled, and George drawled "Easy, girl" through his teeth.

"Arbuckle!" A voice echoed across the prairie, and George turned to see Chester walking across the corral.

George cut a notch from the heifer's other ear before he let her go. "What is it, Chester?"

"Poplar wants to see you." Chester looked out across the prairie.

George sighed. There was only one thing this could possibly be about, and he didn't want to talk to anyone about that. So he sauntered toward the main house with no urgency, even though he had a lot of work to do.

The smells of spring in Dakota surrounded him, thick and sweet. The grass was just turning green, its scent announcing the arrival of the season, as did the leaves that sprouted on the cottonwood, elm and oak trees.

George tried to imagine how he could possibly explain his presence at the lynching. He thought back to that night, and to Sanford's claim that the ranchers knew which of their hands were there. He knocked on the front door and was surprised when Sheriff Pierre LeFont answered.

"Come on in." The sheriff stepped to the side, and motioned George in with a dramatic sweep of his arm. His black, waxy mustache curled up and away from his thick upper lip. Poplar stood in the doorway to the kitchen, leaning his elbow against the door jamb.

"What's your name, cowboy?" the sheriff asked as George settled into the wooden chair he indicated.

George told him, noticing that Poplar was frowning at the sheriff. "What's this all about?" George asked.

Sheriff LeFont settled onto the arm of a thick leather armchair and folded his hands, resting them on one knee. "There's no use pretending, George. We know you killed this young man."

George tried to speak, but his voice caught. He sputtered, "I...what?"

"We have a whole passel of witnesses, George. We know you're the one who killed him."

"Killed who?"

Sheriff LeFont smiled, turned his head to one side, sighed deeply, and then dug in his pocket and pulled something out and studied it. After flipping the object between his fingers a few times, observing it at every angle, he reached his hand out to George. "Take a look at this, George."

George stood, reached for the item, and sat down, staring at his hand. It was a watch. A gold pocket watch. George looked up at the sheriff, who was now smiling at him.

"Do you know where we found that watch?"

George shook his head.

"We found that watch in your saddlebag, George. And it belonged to that young man who died."

George frowned. "Well, now you got me about as confused as I could get, Sheriff. I don't know what this watch was doin' in my saddlebag, but I've never seen it before. And what does that have to do with any of this? I'm a hard-working, honest man. You can just ask Mr. Poplar."

George looked at his boss, who turned his head away. George felt the gesture to his core. When he turned back, the sheriff was standing right in front of him, and LeFont bent down until George could smell the wax on his mustache.

"George...there's no use fighting this thing."

"I ain't fighting nothing, Sheriff. I got no reason to fight anything."

The sheriff reached out and plucked the watch from George's palm. "Why did you have this watch?"

"Sheriff, what the hell use would I have for another watch? I don't know where that watch came from."

The sheriff didn't move. He stood staring George straight in the eye. George wondered exactly what he knew. He apparently knew George was there. But what else? Was there any point in telling him the truth? George knew so little about the law. He didn't know whether he could be arrested for being there. But he didn't want to find out the hard way.

Finally, the sheriff stood. He turned and walked in a slow stagger to the couch, where he sat. "Where you from, Arbuckle? How did you end up here?"

"I'm originally from Iowa. But I moved to Wyoming for a while. I came up here because I wanted to get away from the Johnson County Wars. I left just before it got ugly. I've been a cowpuncher my whole life, sheriff. That's all I care about."

"Did they have vigilantes down there in Wyoming?"

"Hell, I don't know, Sheriff. We heard rumors, of course. But I never knew any. I don't like people poking their noses around in my business, so I don't poke mine in theirs."

"You got a family?"

"No sir...never been married."

"How old?"

"I'm twenty-six."

"You're twenty-six years old and you never been married?"

George shook his head, feeling somehow ashamed. What was this guy trying to get at?

"You too shy to meet ladies?" LeFont leaned forward, propping his elbow on his knee.

"No, not really...I'm just always workin', and I moved around a lot."

"'Cause you were running from the law? Is that why you moved around so much?"

George took a quick glance at Poplar, but he had disappeared, and George was overcome by the same fear he'd experienced when the rustlers came rushing toward him. He felt alone.

"Are you one of these guys that likes to watch people die, George? Does your flag run up the pole when you see a guy dangling from a rope?"

George knew that answering the question would implicate him. He knew that any sign of weakness would probably do the same thing. He held LeFont's eyes, although the inclination to look down, or up, or anywhere but straight ahead, was powerful.

"Answer me, George."

"The only man I ever seen die was my dad," George muttered, although this wasn't quite true. He had seen one other man die. "His horse flipped over on him, and no, I didn't like it one bit."

Now LeFont chuckled, backing away a couple of steps. He scrutinized George, squinting. "That's a sad story, George. I'm even inclined to think it might be true."

"You damn right it's true."

"Why'd you kill that guy, George? You can tell me...I know he deserved it. We all know that."

"I didn't kill nobody. How long do you plan to keep this up, because I got a lot of work to do."

"Why'd you kill him, George?"

George shook his head.

"He killed your friend. That's enough to piss off even the best of men."

"Listen, Bones wasn't a friend of mine. We just worked together."

"Is that right?"

"It is."

"So do you have many friends, George? Because you know...they say that's common among killers—tend to be loners. I heard you're not too popular among the hands here."

George rubbed his finger under his nose. "I don't mind being around people. And the only reason I'm not popular is because I have different ideas. I believe in different things."

"What kinds of things?"

George looked at his feet. "Nothing unusual...I just believe a man could make better use of this land if he learned to move the water around, and farm part of it."

LeFont now grabbed a kitchen chair, set it down backwards, with authority, just a few feet from George. He straddled it, resting his arms along the back. "George, can you see how I might think you could be involved in this?" LeFont held out one hand and grabbed his forefinger with his other hand. "One, you got a motive...these guys stole the cattle that were your responsibility and killed one of your hands." His second finger now buried itself within his fist. "Two, I got statements from several of your hands that you were gone that night." Now he held up three fingers. "And third, well...these guys you work with say you're kind of different...that you don't let people get too close."

George swallowed, looking down at his boots.

"So you see the problem I got here?" LeFont tilted his head, lowering it, as if he was trying to pry George's chin up with a look. "Plus, George...plus, we got a witness."

George swallowed. He heard footsteps and assumed Poplar had returned to the room. He was struck by the fact that this was no comfort to him, whereas it might have been an hour earlier. He couldn't remember feeling so alone.

LeFont waited for an answer. George finally looked up at him. "You know what I really think, George?"

George shook his head, not really wanting to hear the answer.

"I don't think you killed him."

George couldn't withhold his surprise. "You don't?"

LeFont shook his head.

"Then why the hell are you wasting my time?"

"Well I wasn't sure until now."

George held his tongue. He watched Poplar come into view, gliding across the room behind LeFont.

"You agree, Jacob?" LeFont asked, although he kept his gaze focused directly on George.

"I do," Poplar answered, to George's slight relief.

George waited; it seemed there was bound to be more. LeFont wasn't just going to let him go. He wouldn't waste this much time and just drop the subject. But LeFont didn't speak for a long, painful minute. Poplar cleared his throat. Someone was chopping wood just outside the house. The sound of axe on log beat away the seconds. The smell of something baking drifted through the house. Maybe a pie.

"So where does this leave us?" George finally asked.

"Give me some names, George." The answer came so quickly that George knew this was where LeFont had been going from the beginning. "Give me some names and you're off the hook. Your boss here says you're a good, reliable man. I can see that. You don't need to pay the price for these idiots."

George looked at Poplar, who had turned his back. So that was it? Poplar knew everything. What the hell was his role in all of this? It was impossible to tell.

But the choice was clear. Give up some names and walk away from this unpleasant situation into a life looking over his shoulder. He knew the other vigilantes would string him up in a minute if they found out. Or...keep his mouth shut and stay alive. But what was the price for that? What would it mean to remain loyal to this mysterious brotherhood? Would he be expected to take part in more...more what? George wasn't even sure what to call them. Executions? Acts of justice? One thing he knew. No matter what consequences came from keeping his mouth shut, it was better than the alternative. George Arbuckle didn't want to die.

He looked at LeFont and told him that with his eyes. Without speaking.

But LeFont wasn't going to give up that easily. "What's it going to be, George? You know I could haul you into jail right now based on what I do know."

George thought about this. If Poplar was part of this, would he really be willing to lose him for however long they decided to lock him up? He didn't think so. He told LeFont this, also without words. He looked at him and told him he wasn't going to say anything further.

LeFont stood. "I'll be back in a minute."

George nodded, and LeFont motioned with his head for Poplar to follow him. As they retired to the kitchen, the man chopping wood suddenly swore. George heard Poplar ask him if he was okay. And after being reassured, Poplar and LeFont talked in low tones for another minute.

When they emerged, they were both looking at the floor.

"You're a lucky man, George," LeFont said. "I'm not going to take you in. Your friend Mr. Poplar here said he's willing to vouch for you."

"Thanks, Mr. Poplar," George said, but part of him was thinking 'You better vouch for me after getting me into this, you son-of-a-bitch.'

"You can bet you're going to hear from me again, though," LeFont said. "I will be keeping a very close eye on you, Mr. Arbuckle."

"Well, Mr. LeFont, I think you'll find that to be a waste of your time."

"I hope you're right, George. I truly do."

When George returned to his work, Chester approached him immediately. "What happened?"

"Why the hell are you whispering, Chester? There's nobody within a half mile of us."

"Just tell me, George...what did he say?" Although he spoke in a normal voice, it was shaking.

"Probably the same thing he said to you, Chester."

Chester cleared his throat, and started pacing back and forth, leaving his boot prints in the mud. George twirled a lasso above his hat and tossed it over a heifer's head.

"You gonna give me a hand here, Chester, or are you waiting for an invitation?"

Chester jumped as if he'd just been scared out of deep sleep. "What did he say, George?"

"What did he say to you?"

Chester's breath started racing, flaring his nostrils. "He told me he was gonna arrest me for killin' that guy."

"Yeah? What did you tell him?"

"What do you think? I denied it."

"Well that makes sense." George tugged at his rope, trying to hold the heifer's head low. "Get her heels." Chester was avoiding his look, and this bothered George.

Chester adjusted his lasso and laid it just under the cow's bag. George gave his rope a tug, pulling the cow forward, and she stepped into Chester's lasso. Chester jerked the rope then pulled it tight.

"Was that all that happened?" George hugged the cow's neck, biting her ear, and took a notch out of her other ear with his knife. "Or did they want to know more?"

Chester shook his head, but George could tell he was lying.

"Yeah? Loosen that rope on her heels. You need to get your head back on the job here."

"Sorry…" Chester loosened the rope, and George slapped the cow's flank, sending her trotting back into the corral.

George was headed out to get another heifer, but he stopped and turned. "What did you do?"

Chester stood frozen for a minute, and then he turned and started toward the cattle, as if he suddenly remembered what they were doing.

"You gave him names, didn't you?" George said.

Chester crouched and shooed a heifer toward the gate. Chester's shirt had a wide band of sweat plastered down its middle.

George approached Chester from behind. "Did you tell them who was there?"

Chester turned around, and George was surprised to see tears. "I didn't know what else to do, George…that guy scared the hell out of me."

"What did Poplar say?"

Chester looked down.

"What did he say?"

"He said I'm on my own."

The next morning, at first light, George Arbuckle showed up at Jacob Poplar's front door.

When Poplar answered, his hair was sticking out in every direction, and his shirt was only partially buttoned.

"What is it, George? Don't tell me we lost more cattle..."

"I'm leaving, Mr. Poplar...I'm real sorry about not givin' you more notice. But I need to go.".

CHAPTER 7

WHEN I DESCENDED THE STAIRS of Mrs. Tilford's Boarding House that Friday morning, I stopped at the familiar figure standing at the desk in Mrs. Tilford's den.

"Mr. Arbuckle, are you here to see me?"

George Arbuckle turned with a puzzled expression. "Um…no, actually. I'm sorry. I didn't remember that you lived here."

I felt sweat along my hairline, and my face heated up like a wood stove. I left the house. "Pardon me." I barely noticed nudging a man as I walked with my head down, trying to hide my embarrassment. I felt like such a fool.

By the time I arrived at the bank, I managed to compose myself, or so I thought. But the moment I entered, Allison said, "What's wrong?"

"What do you mean?"

"Catherine, it's all over your face."

I took a quick intake of breath. I told Allison what happened, and Allison tried to wrap her arms around me. But I was still embarrassed and stepped back. "I'll be okay."

"He probably won't even remember," Allison said, but I didn't believe that for a minute.

"Is everything okay?" In the midst of Allison's consolation, we hadn't heard Lars emerge from his office.

We dropped our eyes.

"We're fine," Allison declared.

Lars studied us, raising his chin and peering at us from his lofty height. "You're sure?"

We both nodded, then when Lars turned and ducked back into his office, we covered our mouths to keep from laughing.

"So do you think he's going to be boarding at the house?" Allison asked.

"I can't imagine why...he works at a ranch. That's why I was so surprised to see him there. Why else would he be there, except to see me?"

"No good reason I can think of," Allison said, and we both laughed again.

That evening, I walked home quickly, adjusting my hair, and checking my appearance in the passing windows.

"Why are you in such a hurry?" Allison chided me.

"I'm not walking any faster than usual," I insisted.

As we passed the Gem Theater, one of the girls leaned over the balcony rail and yelled "We have openings!" The laughter rang out from the house.

We rolled our eyes at each other.

"Those poor girls," said Allison. "It's such a shame they have to live like that."

"Allison...you're way too kind. They're old enough to make their own decisions."

"I know...I just think it's sad."

But I was barely listening, and by the time we got back to the house, I felt a nervous fluttering in my chest.

"I've never seen you walk so fast, Catherine Boland."

"Nonsense."

When we arrived, I made my way directly to my room to straighten my hair, then I descended the stairs, trying to slow my pace, as well as the breath racing through me. But when I entered the dining room, and surveyed the faces of those around the table, I saw no sign of the beaked nose, the ruddy complexion. I settled into my seat, trying to hide my disappointment. And as Mrs. Tilford began to serve the meal, I had to bite through my tongue to keep from asking about George Arbuckle's appearance that morning.

The forks clinked against the flowered china, and everyone talked about their day, and I heard nothing. I didn't taste the roast beef or smell the buttered peas. I couldn't feel the cool breeze that fluttered the drapes. The sounds floated around me as if they were all under water.

"Catherine, you're so quiet this evening," Mrs. Tilford finally commented. And just as I was about to compose an explanation, Mrs. Tilford interrupted with a joyful "Oh." She jumped to her feet. "Here he is...I'd like to introduce you all to our newest tenant."

And there he was. Standing so awkward and unpolished in the doorway, his hair lying flat on one side and sticking up a little on the other. Clearly the last thing in the world he wanted was to be introduced. He apologized for being late, then nodded politely while Mrs. Tilford came around the table and grabbed his upper arm.

"This is Mr. George Arbuckle...he'll be staying here until he finds another job, which I'm sure won't take long at all...did you have any luck today, Mr. Arbuckle?"

"Matter of fact, I did, ma'am."

Mrs. Tilford turned to the rest of us and clapped her hands together in front of her, prayer style. "Can you imagine? One day! What did you find, Mr. Arbuckle?"

"I'll be working at the Three V, near Belle."

"Oh yes...of course I've heard of that...that's one of the best outfits around. Does that mean you'll be leaving us already?"

"I'm sorry, ma'am, but yes, I'll be leaving in the morning."

"But tomorrow is Saturday." The minute the words left my mouth, I felt my face redden, and the eyes around the table swiveled toward me. This was ranch country...of course Saturday meant nothing. Saturday was a work day just like Sunday and Monday and every other day because that's what ranches require...that's what animals require. Nobody said a word, and George's discomfort was compounded. He looked as if he wanted to leave right then.

"I'm so sorry," I muttered. "Of course it's none of my business."

For the rest of the meal, I tried not to look George's way, but I found it impossible to avoid. There was something so painfully humble about the man. He looked as if he was expecting to get caught breaking some rule of etiquette with every move. He watched what others did as they ate, the way they held their forks, the way they used their napkins. He didn't exactly copy their movements, but I could see that he was recording the information.

Although his hands were rough, they moved with a certain grace, as if he might be the kind of man who had a secret talent…a gifted artist, or a fiddler. By the time the meal ended, I was desperate to find out whether George was planning to come to the dance the following evening. It was a ways from Belle Fourche…nearly thirty miles, so it seemed unlikely that he would make the trip back. But a girl could hope. As it turned out, there was no graceful way to address the issue, so I went to bed in despair about whether I would ever see this man again.

When I made a final trip to the water closet before bed, I passed Allison's room.

"Are you okay?" I heard from behind the door.

I cracked the door open a sliver. "How did you know it was me?"

Allison smiled. "Everyone has their own way of walking…are you going to be all right? You looked like you were going to bite through your fork at dinner."

"I'm fine." I thought about saying no more and excusing myself to a good night's sleep. But without thinking about it, I whisked into the room and sat on the bed. "I don't know what it is about this man...I can't take my eyes off him."

Allison chuckled. "You're smitten."

I blushed. "I don't like it."

"Oh come on...it's fun."

I thought for a moment, realizing I had no desire to voice what was in my head. That I was afraid I'd never see George again. And I was also afraid of how important this all seemed. I was surprised to feel a hand on my shoulder. I looked up at Allison, who gave me the warmest, softest smile. "Catherine, fate has a hand in these things, don't you think? You don't have to worry about it."

"Easy for you to say."

Allison laughed. "I do wish it was all as easy as it sounds. Love is way too complicated for that."

"Love?" I frowned. "Allison, we're not talking about love." Now that made her laugh.

RO

Early the next morning, before any of the others were up, George slid his stockinged feet along the floor, carrying his satchel in one hand and his boots in the other until he was outside, on the front porch. He sat, pulled his boots on, and filled his lungs with the fresh morning air.

"Mr. Arbuckle."

The voice behind him made George jump a bit. He turned to find the dark-haired teller from the bank standing in the doorway.

She smiled. "I'm sorry to scare you."

George felt his face get hot. "It's all right."

"You're leaving so early!"

George nodded. "Don't want to be a bother." The blood rushed hard and fast to his head. "Just want to get to work."

"Do you mind if I ask you something, Mr. Arbuckle? I'm Allison, by the way." She shook his hand.

"I s'pose not...I don't know much about anything but cows, though."

Allison giggled, and George felt his hands start to tremble a bit...he hadn't meant it as a joke. And he couldn't imagine what this woman would possibly want to know from him.

"Are you a single man, Mr. Arbuckle? I mean, I know you're not married, but are you...available?"

George didn't know what to say. This woman...he didn't even know her name until just now. But she was beautiful. She couldn't possibly be expressing an interest in him, could she? He wasn't even sure he would want to court a woman this beautiful...the pressure would be more than he could bear, he thought. And now he couldn't even remember what she asked...did she ask whether he was single, or did she ask whether he had a lady friend?

"I am not," he answered., hoping to end the conversation. Hoping to discourage her. And when he sensed some disappointment in her expression, it was almost a relief to him.

"Oh...well, that's good to know then...thank you for being so kind as to answer, Mr. Arbuckle."

George tipped his hat. "My pleasure, ma'am."

As George rode out of Deadwood, he studied the sky, wondering what kind of day to expect. The sun was just beginning to spread its golden glow along the horizon. George soaked in the sounds of early morning. The ring of a hammer echoed from the blacksmith's shop, and two young men shouted insults at each other as they pitched hay into the stalls of the livery stable. Several men lay propped up against various buildings, sleeping off the night's activities. George was amused to see an old cowboy with his head resting peacefully on the shoulder of a young Indian, both sleeping with mouths wide open. He wished he could be there when these two woke up.

Just as George rounded the last building on Main Street, Puck jumped to one side, and when George turned to see what scared him, Preston Sanford sat ten feet away, his horse jerking its head. He was with another man, who was chewing a wad of tobacco. The second man looked familiar, and George assumed he must have been at the hanging. It was a morning of surprises, it seemed.

"Mornin', George," Sanford said.

"How you doin'?" George looked behind him, wondering whether there was someone around who might prevent these guys from doing anything unpleasant.

"I'm good, George. You?"

"Fine...just on my way out of town...off to work."

"Yeah...did you enjoy a little night on the town, George?" The two men positioned their horses in a wedge, so that George couldn't move forward.

"Yeah, I guess you could say that."

Sanford and the other man looked at each other, and Sanford chuckled. "All right, George...you can't bullshit me."

George held his breath. "I'm not sure what you're talking about, Mr. Sanford...no offense."

"You had any breakfast yet, George? Let me buy you some breakfast."

"I'm kinda in a hurry." George looked at the sun, which was now inching its way up over the horizon.

Sanford tilted his head forward, staring at George from the tops of his eyes. "You like Lil's?"

"Never been."

George sat with a plate of steak and eggs, wishing he had an appetite. The food looked good. He popped a piece of steak into his mouth and began to gnaw like a cow chewing her cud.

"So who did you talk to, George?"

George shook his head. He gulped a swig of coffee.

"Come on, George. You left your job...and I know LeFont came to see you. Who did you tell?"

"You got me all wrong," George said. "I never wanted to get involved in the first place.

And I would never do that."

"What do you mean, you never wanted to get involved?"

George shrugged. "Just that."

Sanford studied him closely. "You ever hear that saying about changing a horse mid-stream, George?"

"'Course I have."

"There's a good reason for that, you know...you get comfortable on an animal, you don't want to spook him, right?"

"I never got on this animal to begin with," George said.

"I don't understand how you can say that. What were you doing there that night?"

"They come and got me...they woke me up and said I better come along, and it didn't seem to be no two ways about it." George managed a bite of egg, feeling Sanford's eyes hard on him.

"Why'd you leave your job?" Sanford asked.

"Change of pace." George finally swallowed the bite of egg. He wondered whether either of these guys had a job...how did they have so much time to devote to this hobby of theirs?

Sanford gave him that same look, the lowered chin, eyes in the top of their sockets. Didn't believe a word.

"George, how do you feel about spending the day with us?"

George blinked. "Why? What would we do?"

Sanford winked, and the other man, who had yet to speak, laughed. "You'll see," Sanford said.

George shook his head. "I can't...I have a job waiting for me."

"George." Sanford set his fork down next to his plate. He leaned toward George. "Did you tell this new job you were going to be there today?"

George could not lie. But he didn't answer the question.

"That's what I thought…they can wait another day. I know Dan Hardin. Plus…you're my good luck charm, you know."

George could not imagine a way out of the situation. How did Preston know where he was going to work? One step out of line with these guys, and he'd be sitting in the sheriff's office before the waitress cleared their plates.

"How did you guys find me?"

At last, the other man spoke. "Don't you recognize me?" George shook his head.

"Mrs. Tilford's Boarding House? I'm Bernie, his brother."

An hour later, after riding north, the three men stood at the door of a ranch house that was in much better repair than that of the average Badlands ranch. It was not a precocious house, but a solid house, large and obviously made from good materials. The wood seemed to shine. When Sanford knocked, and the door opened, George understood why. There stood two familiar faces—the governor and the other man that had been with him the night of the hanging. The governor greeted them with a hearty hello. The other man also greeted them and introduced himself. And when Sanford introduced their third, the man from the boarding house, George learned that he was Sanford's brother, Bernie.

After explaining that his friend had been kind enough to provide his home as a meeting place, the governor led the men to the dining room, where the host's wife offered them coffee.

"Thank you for agreeing to meet with us, gentlemen," Sanford said.

"I was happy you contacted me," the governor said. "Because I meant it when I offered to help.

Sanford nodded. "That's why we're here."

"So what exactly can we do for you?"

As Sanford laid out the plans, George wondered again what on earth he was doing there. The most confusing thing about it was that they all seemed to think he wanted to be part of this. That he'd volunteered somehow. And there didn't seem to be any hope of convincing them otherwise. He was surprised to hear how invested the governor was in helping with their cause. He knew the governor's own ranch was much further south, near Miles City. George couldn't stop thinking about the risk this man was taking. How could someone with that kind of job support something so completely lawless?

George thought back to his last days in Wyoming, just before the Johnson County War exploded. He had taken a job on a cattle drive from Texas back to Wyoming. And it had become clear during the trip that one of the hands was stealing. The thefts started out small. One man noticed a missing buck knife. Everyone assumed he'd lost it. But soon another hand couldn't find his pocket watch. It was a watch he'd inherited from his father, and this led the drive boss to call for a surprise search. Because there were so few places to hide anything on a cattle drive, they all expected the element of surprise would reveal the thief. But he found nothing.

Finally, it was money. And then the speculation began. Everyone was a suspect.

Conversations became shorter. Anytime someone went off on their own, another man followed, even if they were doing their business. George lost a five-dollar gold piece, and that was when revenge started to take on a certain appeal.

George remembered how focused he became on finding the responsible party. How payback became an obsession. It was a very unfamiliar feeling for him. But he was surprised how much he liked it. He liked the mystery of the search. But this current situation was different. He didn't have anything at stake here. Nobody had hurt him. Or taken from him.

The wagon boss had initiated two more searches, neither of which revealed a thing. One afternoon, the crew was moving the herd directly into a hard wind. They crested a hill and the herd picked up speed on the trip down the other side, which was steep. It was the perfect scenario for a stampede, and the hands were working hard to keep the herd under control. It was always tricky when the cattle got restless, because the cowboys had to be alert without showing too much urgency. The slightest movement could cause one or two cows to panic, and the next thing they knew, the herd would be moving as one like massive red wave. It could take hours to restore order, and they could lose several head in the process.

A finger of cattle was moving a bit too fast, and George whistled to a hand named Peterson, signaling him to head off the lead. Peterson was a good cowhand, and he did what he should do, giving his horse a nudge, pushing the animal into a trot so he could get into position without spooking the livestock. But just as he was about to reach the lead cow, his horse suddenly lurched and tumbled over itself. The horse had hit a hole, and Peterson went flying over the horse's neck, landing on his head. His body flopped forward like a side of beef, and a loud crack sounded.

George and two other hands were close enough to see what happened, and they rode over as quickly as they could without further spooking the cattle. George instructed two of the cowboys to get the cattle under control, and the others gathered around Peterson. He was lying on his back, holding his head in both hands, moaning softly. An open wound bled from his forehead. But the man's right leg was bent at an unnatural angle just below the knee. The leg was clearly broken, but Peterson didn't even seem to notice. There was no blood at all, even though the leg was bent ninety degrees to the side. George thought maybe the kid's head hurt so bad that he didn't notice his leg. But when he crouched to take a closer look, there was a noticeable gap between the two parts of the leg. Still no blood.

George reached deep in his pocket for his buck knife. While the others tended to Peterson's head wound, George slit Peterson's pants to the knee. There, lying in the hollow of denim, was all of the stolen loot, between two parts of a wooden leg.

Peterson's leg had been cut off just below the knee. And his wooden leg had snapped in half where he'd hollowed it out to hide the stolen goods.

As shocked as George was by this development, he was even less prepared for what happened next. The wagon boss rode over from the rear of the herd. The boss swung down off his horse, took one look at the situation, pulled his gun from its holster, and shot Peterson right in the head. He then turned to the horse, and he shot the horse too. None of the other men spoke, but George couldn't contain himself.

"Why'd you do that?" he asked.

"They had broke legs," the man said. "Now let's get these cattle back under control before we got a stampede on our hands."

George was sixteen at the time.

"You can be assured that we'll keep your name out of this, governor." Sanford looked directly at George. And George wondered again how he'd ever become part of this. Now it seemed his trustworthiness was in question, and the reason was because he left his job rather than give up any names. Nothing made any sense. But George nodded, just for the sake of avoiding further suspicion.

But the governor was studying him, and George felt his face take on color.

"Can I ask you something?" The governor pointed at him, holding his hand right in front of his own face, pointing his finger at George like a tiny pistol.

"Of course, sir."

"No, actually, I don't even have to ask." The governor turned to Sanford. "Why is this man here?"

Sanford's jaw dropped, as he was going to speak. But he thought for a moment. "He's one of us," he finally answered. George noticed a slight tremor in Sanford's voice.

"No he isn't," the governor said, and George panicked. How the hell could he tell? "You've dragged this man into this thing without his cooperation." The governor leaned toward Sanford. He looked up at him, tilting his head to the side. "Why would you do that?" He didn't wait for Sanford to answer.

He walked over and planted himself right in front of George. "You need to speak your mind, son. Let people know what you're thinking." Then he turned around and offered his hand to Sanford, who also stood. "Let me know if you need anything else, Preston."

CHAPTER 8

"DAMMIT."

I saw the surprise come to Allison's eyes.

"I jabbed my finger with the needle." I let the dress I was mending settle on my lap. I couldn't remember being so disappointed. All week, I had been looking forward to the dance as an opportunity to get to know this young man that had such ridiculous power over me. I was even hoping that spending time with him would break the spell somehow. Now that he'd disappeared, he would almost certainly not be there, and I was embarrassed how much this bothered me.

"Catherine, I wonder whether you should even go to the dance. You're just going to be miserable."

"No I won't...I'm not going to let this spoil my evening."

"Well I hope not."

I briefly considered taking offense, but I knew Allison was right. My friend had seldom seen me in a foul mood. "I'm sorry, Allison."

"You don't have to apologize to me...I'm not the one who's going to have to dance with you." And she winked.

Allison and I arrived late. The town hall smelled of sweat and sawdust as couples swirled across the floor. I took one look at the happy crowd, and decided the best way to avoid feeling left out was to dive in. So I grabbed the nearest uncoupled man by the hand and pulled him onto the dance floor. I ignored the surprised look on his face, which quickly transformed into a smile as we eased into the rhythm of the music. Although it was a crisp spring night outside, the building was warm. I could already feel the moisture gathering in the bosom of my dress, and down the small of my back.

The man I danced with was older, not much younger than my father would have been. But he was a fine dancer, and I insisted that he stay for another song, ignoring his plea that his wife was going to get jealous.

"Who's your wife?" I asked.

"Molly O'Brien. My name's Sean."

"Oh, I just met Molly at the bank..." I twisted my neck, found Molly and waved to try and ease her mind. But Molly stood with her arms crossed, frowning.

"I better let you go," I agreed.

But I didn't let this deter me. I searched the crowd, found a young man standing by himself, and pulled him out to the dance floor. Although this partner proved to be very eager, he wasn't as skillful as Sean O'Brien. But his enthusiasm made me laugh.

"You're supposed to let the man lead," Allison squealed as she swished by in another man's arms.

I howled. "I'm sorry, am I leading?" I asked my partner.

"It's okay...you're better than I am."

The mood of the night continued to surround and inspire me. I felt the skitter of the fiddle up my spine, and the words of every song seemed to reach in and bolster my heart like a pool of warm water. I could almost feel it bobbing in my chest. Each time someone laughed, the sound wrapped me up like two strong arms. So by the time the dance was halfway over, I could not have been happier that I'd decided to come. I couldn't imagine the night getting any better. "Are you thirsty?"

I turned to see Allison's sweat-sheened face, cheeks red and stretched into a broad smile.

Her bottom lip almost looked swollen it was so bright red. "Yes...let's get some water," I said.

We shouldered our way through the joyful crowd, politely declining requests for the next dance. We smiled at each other, delighting in the attention. It was when we had almost reached the well that I noticed a tall, distinguished man with grey hair and a felt cowboy hat with a wide blue band. I had seen this man around town before, and always noticed his bearing...the way he carried himself. But it was when I saw the two men with him that I stopped. Walking just behind him was Bernie Sanford, from the boarding house. But more importantly, just behind Bernie, clearly not at all happy about being there, was George. I stopped suddenly, drawing a look from Allison. She turned in the direction I was facing, and when she saw George, she winked.

"Today's your lucky day."

I took a deep breath, adjusted my collar, patted my sternum, and walked right up to George, who hadn't looked up from his boots. I stood two feet from him and said, "You made it!"

George lifted his head, and I realized from the minute his eyes met mine that he had no idea what I was talking about. He didn't remember talking about the dance at all. And I wondered whether I would ever speak to this man without lodging my foot firmly between my teeth.

"Hello," George managed to say.

"You want to dance, George?"

The other two men raised their eyebrows and smiled.

"I'm not much of a dancer," George said.

"Don't worry...she'll lead," Allison said.

"Hello Allison," Bernie said. "Maybe we should join them."

Allison smiled wide and held out her hand, which Bernie grasped.

The four of us ducked inside and tilted our way into the tangle of bodies, merging into the motion. George's cheeks took on a red sheen that looked almost hazardous to his health, but I knew it was just another sign of how adorably bashful this man was.

"I thought you would be at the ranch," I said, holding my mouth close to his ear.

"I was planning on it...I got waylaid." George's face took on a different expression, and I sensed a strong shiver run through him.

"Are you all right?"

"Sure." He forced a big smile. "I'm good." But it was clear that something was on his mind. I curbed my desire to ask. I didn't want to say one more foolish thing.

"So you plan to leave for the ranch tomorrow?"

George turned red again and thinking about how to answer seemed painful for him. Here we go again, I thought. What have I done now?

"I'll probably leave either tomorrow afternoon or Monday morning," he finally answered.

"Well, I hope that proves to be a good arrangement for you."

"It's a good outfit." George nodded with conviction.

"Better than the one you left?"

George's face flushed again. "Just different, I guess...both are good."

I decided to change the subject...I seemed to have a knack for finding uncomfortable topics. On the other hand, I was pleasantly surprised to realize that, despite the awkward conversation, George was a very good dancer. I even gave over the lead to him. He moved with a quiet, effortless strength that seemed completely opposed to his verbal self. We danced for several songs, enjoying the music, and the easy chemistry we had on the dance floor. I finally decided it was time for more conversation.

"Where are you from, George?" I asked. Surely this would be safe.

"I'm originally from Iowa...but we moved to Wyoming when I was a kid. What about you?"

"We moved down here from Canada when I was a teenager…to Belle."

"When did you move to Deadwood?"

"Just a week ago."

George raised his eyebrows. "You seem pretty settled in already."

I blushed and nodded. "I was very fortunate."

"Why'd you leave?"

Now it was my turn to get uncomfortable. I tried to show a brave face. Just answer the question, I thought. "I had a business there…a hat shop."

"Yeah?" George pulled his head back and scrutinized me, and I felt exposed somehow.

As if he could tell I was holding something back. "Yes…and I had to sell it."

George frowned thoughtfully. "Tough?"

I nodded and blinked away the tears that were welling up behind my eyes.

"Hey you two…you're holding up progress." Allison's beaming face appeared just a foot from mine, and the smell of liquor followed like a cloud of smoke. Allison's eyes drooped, and Bernie showed a smile that looked downright stupid.

"We're older than you," George responded, and we all laughed as Allison and Bernie immersed themselves back into the sea of sweating bodies.

"You know him?" George asked.

"Not really...he lives in our house. You must know him, since you came with them."

George shook his head. "I just met him today."

"Was he part of why you got waylaid?"

Now George could barely look at me. He turned his head to look behind him, as if he was searching for someone or something. "You thirsty?"

"Yes, as a matter of fact."

We made our way outside, where the quiet calm of night was slightly jarring after the warm jumble of sound and motion. George led me to the well, and the tin dipper felt almost painfully cold against my lips. The water tasted wonderful.

We stood looking at each other, smiling comfortably, when George's face suddenly changed. His eyes narrowed, and his lips pulled tight. I turned to see what had prompted the change. Across the way, Bernie was leading Allison from the hall. His walk was purposeful and grim, while Allison stumbled behind him, trying to keep up.

"Hey Allison!" I shouted.

Allison stopped, nearly causing Bernie to lose his balance. She looked around as if she was surprised to know there were other people there. When she spotted us, she waved.

"Where are you going?" I asked.

"Oh, just for a walk," Allison said as Bernie gave her arm a subtle jerk. They started walking again, and Allison made an impaired attempt at another wave. I felt a sudden urge to run after her, but I wondered whether I was overreacting. I remembered Mrs. Tilford's warning about Bernie.

"I wouldn't trust that guy." This statement from George nearly prompted me to throw my arms around him.

"Do you think we should do something?" I asked.

George shrugged. "Like what? She's a grown woman, right?"

I watched my friend disappear into the darkness and felt a sinking fear. "I suppose so."

But I felt even worse when I noticed a tall figure standing between me and my departing friend. Lars had just arrived, and he was also watching Allison's trek into the night.

MONDAY MORNING, ALLISON'S HANDS SHOOK as she counted out the money in her drawer.

"Are you okay?" I asked.

Allison nodded, but in the next instant she turned to me and said, "He's going to be so angry."

"You don't know that."

"Come on, Catherine. I don't need that...not from my best friend."

I thought for a moment, then nodded. "You're right."

"Well you didn't have to agree that quickly."

We laughed, but it was a brief moment of levity as the truth smothered it.

"What were you thinking, Allison?" I took Allison's cheeks in my hands and turned her face toward me.

"You know the answer to that, Catherine...I had too much to drink. I wasn't thinking."

"Of course."

"Do you think you can forgive me?"

"Oh stop; you know I'm not going to judge you. I'm your friend. I'm more worried about the rest of them…you know how people latch onto this stuff."

"Oh god. They're going to throw me in the Gem Theater."

We both laughed again, with slightly more lift this time.

"We both know that's not what you're really worried about though…not whether I forgive you, or whether they will." I held Allison's chin firmly, turning her to face me. The tears dribbled from the corners of Allison's eyes.

"I know. I didn't think he'd be there."

I nodded. "I bet he came just to see you."

"Oh, now you're just making it worse." Allison twisted out of my grasp, and I was just about to apologize when the front door jiggled, and I moved to my station while Allison took her handkerchief and tried to wipe the evidence from her face.

"Good morning, ladies." Lars' stooped figure ducked inside, turned to lock the door, and tipped his hat.

We sang our "Good morning, Lars" in unison.

I watched for any change in his usual routine. He whistled as he took off his jacket and hung that and his hat on the coat rack near the front door. He took out his pocket watch and compared it to the grandfather clock in the corner, then tucked it back in his vest pocket, dug into his trousers for his first piece of morning licorice, and started humming as he made his way back toward his office. So far, so good. Allison and I exchanged a look…a conspiratorial hope that maybe things would be just as always.

We opened the bank, and the usual flow of morning customers made their transactions. At midmorning, when there was a natural lull in activity, Lars poked his snowy head from his office and said in the gentlest voice, "Allison, could I see you for a minute?"

We looked at each other, and Allison's eyes opened wider. "Of course, Mr. Larson."

When he closed his door, which Lars never ever did, my breath sped up. The conversation never rose to any audible level, which I took as a good sign, but I could hardly wait to find out what was happening behind that door. One customer came in, and then two others.

And it seemed to be a much longer conversation than I expected. Worse yet, when Allison emerged, she gave no indication...no sign of either relief or worry. She did not pack her things. She went about her business as if nothing was different, and there was no way to ask her what happened with Lars twenty feet away.

By lunchtime, my temple was throbbing with questions.

"So what happened?" I grabbed Allison by the upper arm.

We spread our lunches out on a blanket in the grassy field. Cold fried chicken, apples, and cookies.

"It was the strangest conversation, Catherine."

I scooted closer to Allison. "What did he say?"

"Well...he started out by giving me a speech about how important it is that we remember that we work with the public, and that we have to present a certain image in the community. He didn't say a thing about Saturday night. He just went on and on about how important our image is."

"Mm." I didn't want to interrupt Allison to let her know that it seemed perfectly in keeping with Lars' personality that he would address the issue this way. From the side.

Allison chewed on her chicken for a couple of bites. "Then he asked me whether I'm happy at the bank…and whether I can see myself working there for a long time, or if it's just something I'm doing temporarily."

"What did you say?"

"Well, I told him that I really like working here…that I could see working here for a long time, but that I have other things I'm interested in, too. And he asked me what those things are."

"I didn't know you had other things you want to do…so what are they?"

"Well that's just it…I don't really know. It just seemed like the right thing to say. So I started babbling about wanting to start a candy store, or maybe teach school for a couple of years…"

"I like the candy shop idea…we should do that together!"

Allison smiled, and then she got a serious look on her face and shifted her body so that she was facing me directly. "But that's when Lars stopped me right in the middle of what I was saying, and he said to me, 'Allison, what about starting a family? Is that one of the things you'd like to do?'"

I leaned forward. "He said that?"

"He did! So I said, 'Well, I did think that I'd like to have children someday, but I hadn't been thinking about it that much lately, seeing as how I don't even have a beau.'"

"Of course."

"That's when things got very strange, Catherine."

"They weren't already?"

Allison turned her head and looked across the way with a dreamy expression. "He got up from his chair, and he came around his desk…"

Allison paused, and my breath caught in my throat. I wanted to shake Allison and get her to finish the story, but she seemed absorbed in the memory.

"He stood there in front of me, real close to me, and he didn't say anything for the longest time." Allison turned to me. "I didn't know what to do, or what to think, Catherine. I actually started to get a little bit scared."

"Yeah?"

"Yeah, it started to feel kind of spooky."

"What did he do?"

"Well, as it turns out, I think he was just really nervous. Because when he finally said something, his voice was shaking."

"So what did he say? Good god, Allison, you sure know how to keep someone in suspense."

"He asked me to marry him, Catherine. Right there in his office."

I lowered my chin. "You're kidding."

Allison shook her head, still looking rather stunned.

"What did you say?"

"I didn't know what to say, Catherine...after what happened Saturday night, I was so shocked that he would ask."

"But what did you say?"

"I didn't say anything at all...I didn't even tell him I would think about it or anything. I was too stunned to speak."

AFTER ONLY ONE WEEK at the Three V Ranch, George knew he'd made the right decision. Although he hadn't been any more successful at making friends, this had never been a priority. People baffled him in ways that animals never had. George found comfort in the limits of animals. Cattle acted on instinct, without any motive other than protection or hunger.

With humans, you never knew what kind of unpleasantness from their past might affect their behavior. You never knew who might be trying to make up for wrongs done to them twenty, thirty years ago. Although no one could know for sure, it seemed highly unlikely that any cow had ever refused to go through a gate because they had been rejected by a potential suitor. It was hard to imagine that any cow had ever stopped talking to another cow because she didn't compliment her new winter coat.

George had always been most comfortable when he had a routine. When he knew what was expected and knew where he stood in the scheme of things. So on the first day, when Dan Hardin told him "You're in charge of all of the cattle south of the river," George felt his heart swell a little.

He put all of his energy into getting to know the cattle. The first day, he found two lame cows that he instructed one of his hands to herd back to the barn for medical attention. He found another cow trapped in the bog near a grove of trees, and he asked two other hands to work at getting her free. From the looks of it, she'd only been stuck for a few hours, so they freed her without doing any permanent damage.

George rose before dawn every morning and rode as much of the surrounding area as he could each day, exploring every creek, wet or dry, every stand of trees, every pasture and hill. The quiet of the prairie comforted him and helped him forget the events of recent weeks.

He watched herds of deer gnaw on the thick wheat grass along the banks of the Belle Fourche River. He borrowed Hardin's rifle and shot a coyote from fifty yards. He inhaled the rich aroma of sagebrush and felt the dry heat against his skin like a reminder of all the best things about life in the prairie. And each evening he returned home just before dark, his body tired but his mind alive with thoughts of what he could do to help improve the operation. He made a mental list of suggestions for Mr. Hardin. He knew he should wait a few weeks before he presented his ideas to the boss; he didn't want to appear pushy. But he also knew with certainty that he could be a big asset to this ranch. It was the one thing he knew he did well. And before he retired each night, he drew maps of what he'd seen, and imagined how he might work this land if it was his...how he might redirect the water to different pastures. He dreamed of making it his own.

Late one Saturday evening, George entered the bunkhouse, ignoring the glances of the other hands, and started toward his bunk.

"There was a guy here to see you," one of the hands said.

"There was?" George turned.

The guy just nodded.

"What did he say?"

He shrugged. "He said he'd be back."

"Did you ask his name?"

The hand shook his head. "Tall guy…grey hair. Nice duds."

George's breath caught in his throat. Sanford, he thought. What the hell could he possibly want now?

That night, for the first time that week, George did not sleep well.

RO

I stopped in front of Kellogg's Clothing Store, admiring a long sky-blue dress on display in the window.

"Come on, Catherine." I felt Allison's hand grasp my forearm.

I looked up, surprised by the force of Allison's request. "What's the rush, Allison?"

"It's Bernie."

"Oh." I craned my neck, looking behind us, where Bernie walked with the same older man we'd seen at the dance. "Where has he been lately? I haven't seen him for days."

"I don't know and I don't care." The sharp bite in Allison's reply brought my eyebrows to the middle of my forehead.

"Have you talked to him since…"

"Absolutely not. I despise that man."

I kept my mouth shut, although I was glad Allison had come to this conclusion. "Have you talked to Lars about his proposal?"

Allison shook her head, which brought me to a dead stop. "Allison!"

"What?" Allison also stopped.

"What are you waiting for? You know you're in love with that man."

Allison looked down at her feet. Then she turned and started walking again.

"Allison! Don't you dare walk away from me." I caught up to her. "What is it?"

"Catherine, I need to tell you something...I need to tell someone, and you're the only person I can trust."

"Hey girls!" A voice rang out from above us, and we both looked up to see that one of the girls in the Gem Theater leaned out of an upper floor window, her ample bosom resting on the sill. "I heard you could get a job here."

"Oh shut up!" I shouted, which just brought a peal of laughter from the girls.

The taunter lifted her skirts. "You just need one of these."

"Vile woman," I muttered.

"They've all had hard lives, you know. Not like us."

"I know you're right, but they have no right to throw their misery in our faces."

"Maybe not, but...well, maybe you have a point." Allison slowed to a stroll and looked in every direction. "Catherine, I'm worried." She grabbed my forearm. She covered her mouth and began sobbing.

"Come on…let's get back to the house."

Allison sat on her bed, the most defeated person I'd ever seen. Her eyes were hooded, dark and afraid.

"What is it, Allison?"

"Catherine…" She looked up. "I don't remember what happened that night. I have no memory of it."

"Oh no. Allison…do you think…" I couldn't even bring myself to say it.

"I don't know."

"So is that why you haven't talked to Lars?"

"Of course it is, Catherine. Yes…what if…"

I patted Allison on the hand. "Listen…even if you did, and I doubt you did even in that state…there's only one person who knows for sure, and nobody's going to care what he says. You need to decide what you want to do about Lars and just put that night behind you."

"You really think so?" Allison's big brown eyes pleaded.

"Absolutely. Just move forward."

Allison still seemed deep in thought. Something was left unfinished. I took Allison's hand.

"There's something else I need to tell you."

"What else could there possibly be? Don't tell me you're seeing someone else!"

"No, nothing like that. It was something Bernie told me that night, before my mind went blank. He told me something."

"Yeah?"

Allison nodded. And the pained look in her eyes returned. She turned to me, and her eyes pleaded with me to forgive her before she even spoke.

"What is it?"

"It's about George."

I sat alone in my room, trying to absorb the information I'd just received. I'd been puzzling over George Arbuckle ever since the dance. He told me that night that he wasn't seeing anyone. He told me this voluntarily, without any prompting. And it was clear that we liked each other. That we were interested, and that a certain spark ignited when we talked, and danced. And since then...nothing. And I had been wondering why. Wondering whether I'd done something wrong. Or whether he might have heard about what happened in Belle Fourche, before I moved.

But now I suspected that it was something else.

"He killed a man," Allison told me. She also informed me that George told her he was involved with someone the morning he left the boarding house.

I had a hard time believing any of it. Bernie was a scoundrel, there was no denying that. So his word held very little sway with me. But why was George with those men that night? And why did he seem so disturbed when he got there? Something happened, and it seemed likely that whatever it was affected George deeply. Even if he didn't kill a man, the fact that this man was telling people he did could be enough to throw anyone into a panic. How many others were spreading this rumor? Did George hear murmurs wherever he went? Did people cross the street when he approached? It was all too horrible. I had to find a way to see him. More than that, I had to find a way to gain his trust.

GEORGE WRESTLED A CALF TO THE GROUND while another hand put a knee into the calf's ribs and applied a branding iron to its flank. The smell of burning hair had drifted for three days now, until it was part of the air they breathed. Part of the atmosphere. Along with the grime mixed with sweat, heat from the fire, and the bawls of mothers searching for their calves.

George's body was tired, but his mind was working hard. He hoped they would be calling it a day soon, as he had plans for the evening.

"Arbuckle!"

George turned to see one of the other hands striding toward him. George stood. "What?"

"Somebody wants you back at the house."

"The house?"

The hand nodded.

"What the hell for?"

"How should I know?"

George sighed. This didn't make any sense. It was late in the day...what could possibly be so urgent that they needed him right then? At least they weren't far from the house. He could come back.

When he approached the house, he recognized the horse tied to the hitching post, but he couldn't remember who owned it. His memory was jogged when the door opened, and there stood Preston Sanford. George couldn't suppress a groan.

"How you doin', Arbuckle?"

"Not too bad."

"Come on in." Preston stepped to the side and made room for George to enter. Bernie was sitting on the sofa, smoking a cigarette. "You were hoping you'd never see me again, weren't you?" Preston added.

"That's true."

"You ready for another adventure?"

"Tonight?"

Preston nodded.

"No sir...I'm not interested."

Preston chuckled. "Not interested. That's good."

Mrs. Hardin appeared from the kitchen. "Anything you boys need? Coffee?"

"No, we're fine," Preston answered. "We won't be long, Mrs. Hardin."

Once she retreated, George decided it was time to get to the bottom of this situation. He had been thinking a lot about what the governor told him, about speaking his mind. "Why are you guys so damn interested in having me around? There must have been twenty guys there that night...guys that wanted to be there...why me?"

Preston smiled. "You're kidding, right?"

George frowned. "Hell no, I'm not kidding. I been telling you all along. I don't know how I even got involved in this...I don't believe in what you're doing. Even the governor saw that. How come you don't see it?"

"George, don't you realize you have a gift?"

George gaped. Preston's smug grin bore down on him like a bright light. "What happened out there was not what you think."

Preston's smile took on a darker shade. "Yeah?"

"It wasn't a miracle...nothing like that."

Preston looked toward the kitchen, and then toward every other part of the house. "Look, Arbuckle. I don't care whether you believe it or not. You're in this thing. You bring something to this whole operation. You back out now and we'll throw you to the dogs."

George studied the expression on Preston's face and saw a frightening coolness that seemed to freeze any possibility of rational thought. He felt once again that he was in a position where he had only one choice unless he wanted to die. "What if I say no?"

"I just explained that."

"Not really...you said you'd throw me to the dogs...what does that mean?"

"I don't really have to spell it out for you, do I, George?"

George thought about it. "No, I guess not."

RO

I rolled onto my side and stared out the window at a full moon as shiny and white as a new pearl button. I couldn't remember the last time I'd had such a hard time falling asleep.

Allison's claim about George was disturbing for two reasons. First, it brought my judgment of character into question. But I also felt an overwhelming desire to help George if he was in trouble. It made no sense, of course. How could I possibly help? And why would I even want to? Especially if he was in legal trouble. Especially if he was lying to me about being single. What was wrong with me? And why was I awake and thinking about all of this when I had to get up and go to work the next morning?

It was in the midst of these thoughts that I heard an unusual noise, like an animal scraping its claws against the house. A raccoon, probably. But I got up to investigate. At least it gave me some way to fill a few sleepless minutes.

I wrapped myself in a night dress and crossed the room, peering out into the darkness.

And when I saw the figure of a man, less than ten feet away, I almost let out a scream. The only reason I didn't was because I was suddenly unable to breathe, much less speak. Standing right there, looking directly into my eyes, was the man I'd just been thinking about. Once I gained my composure, I quickly raised the window. "George, what on earth are you doing here?"

"Catherine, I'm sorry if I scared you...but I need some help. I couldn't think of where else to go."

"Do I look scared? Get in here."

"Are you sure?" George didn't move. "You're not supposed to have fellas in your room, are you?"

"George...get in here."

George approached tentatively, then swung a leg up over the sill. Just as he was lifting himself up, a knock sounded on my door.

"Catherine, is everything okay in there?"

"Yes, Mrs. Tilford, I'm fine."

"I thought I heard voices."

"It's just me...talking to myself...I'm having a hard time sleeping."

"Would you like me to get you something? Some warm milk? Or a little whiskey?"

"Oh, you're so kind, Mrs. Tilford, but really, I'll be fine. I just need to lie down."

"All right...but you please let me know if you need anything."

"I will."

As the footsteps retreated, I turned to help George, but he was gone. I leaned as far out into the night as I could and looked both ways. George was there, to my right, pressed so hard against the house that he almost blended in with the paint. I motioned for him, pumping my arm. But George was paralyzed.

"George!" I said in a loud whisper. "Get...over...here."

I helped George climb into the room, tugging at his elbow. He was trembling all over. His face looked drained of all blood. Although it was a chilly night, his skin was slick with sweat.

"What's happened to you?"

"I'm in big trouble, Catherine."

"What is it, George?" I could barely contain my joy that he had come to me. When he was in the middle of a crisis, it was me he came to see. "Come and sit down, over here." I led him to the rocking chair in the corner, where he sat with a tired slump. "Now...tell me what happened, George."

George covered his eyes with one hand. He breathed quickly, as if he was about to pass out. "I didn't even want to get involved."

"With what, George? What are you talking about?"

He lowered his hand, and his eyes appeared to focus on something besides the present, something in a different time and place. "I should have just said no when they came that first night."

"Just tell me, George."

And suddenly he was there...in that room with me. His expression shifted...transforming from lost and disconnected to fearful. "You're going to hate me, Catherine."

My heart broke. I reached out and touched his forearm. "George, how could you say that?"

"I just know...I know what you believe."

"How?"

George looked at me, and I was surprised to see tears in his eyes. "Because you told me."

I sat quietly and watched him compose himself. He pushed the backs of his rough hands against his eyes, rubbing away the tears. And he pulled a breath deep into his lungs then let it out slowly.

"Is it the vigilantes?" I finally asked.

I could feel him gauging my expression before he answered. I kept my gaze steady. And at last, he nodded.

"I believe you, George. I believe that you didn't want to get involved."

I saw the relief in his eyes. And I saw something else there, too...a hunger...a need to tell it all. And I was surprised and overwhelmed to experience a sudden desire to reach out and pull this man to me. An ache. I had to breathe in through my nose to keep from wrapping him up in my arms.

"Tell me what happened, George."

Over the next half hour, George told me everything. I had to remind him to whisper when he got excited about certain parts of the story. He started with being awakened in the middle of the night, and about his inability to comprehend what he was getting himself into. He told me about his job as an unarmed lookout, which made me laugh, and about the men riding right by him without making any effort to shoot. And of course, he told me about the hanging, and his voice caught in his throat as he told me the details of this man's death. His eyes started to water as if he had never cried before in his life. George made no attempt to hide these tears, simply wiping his face clean from time to time.

Again, I had to restrain myself from comforting him in some way. I wanted to kiss his face. I smelled hay and dirt on him, and I wanted to caress his arms with my face, taking in those deep aromas.

But through it all, a question nagged at me, and I hoped the answer would come if I just let him talk. I listened as he told me about the sheriff coming to his old place and accusing him of killing the rustler. And about how Chester told the sheriff about his involvement, which made George realize that he had to leave that job. But when he got to the part where two men intercepted him on his way to his job at the Three V, I couldn't hold back any longer.

"George...why on earth would they come for you like that? There must be dozens of guys around here who believe in what they're doing."

George nodded vigorously. "I asked them that same thing. Several times. I still can't figure out why they were so damn anxious for my help." And he told me about the praying, and how Sanford believed he was some kind of miracle worker.

And then George went silent. His beaky nose turned down, and his eyes closed for a moment. He seemed to be blinking away some deep emotion, his eyelids popping open and closed with remarkable speed. Finally, he spoke, and his voice, still whispering, was choked, low and warbling. "I've never felt so trapped."

I now knew two things. I knew that whatever hunch I may have had before about being in love with this man was now confirmed. I didn't know whether I'd ever met anyone who seemed, at first appearance, to be so completely uncomfortable with words. And yet the way he described the events of the past few days was vivid, filled with images and emotion. Once he started talking, it was as if he'd just been waiting for a chance. Waiting for someone who would listen.

The second thing I knew was that I had to help him.

"George..." I gripped his forearm, wanting to touch him more but knowing it was out of the question. "You know what you need to do."

"I do?"

I nodded and gave him my most assuring smile. "You need to go back out there to that job...you wanted that job, George. I could see it from the way you talked about that ranch."

George thought for a moment, then nodded. "You're right. I like this place...it's a good outfit."

"You can't let these guys scare you out of living your life, George. You can't give up the things you love because of them."

"But what do I do when they come after me again? They aren't going to like the way I left tonight."

"How did you get away from them?"

"I just told them I needed to get some of my gear, and I rode like hell away from the place before they figured out I was gone."

I smiled. "It's going to be hard, George. There's no way around that. But you just have to tell them no. You have to refuse to take part in their little schemes."

He looked at me, and his eyes showed a fear that I had seldom seen. "They could kill me, you know."

I wanted to say no...that they wouldn't do such a thing. But of course he was right. And I knew it wouldn't be right or fair to say such an untrue thing. Instead, I did what I had wanted to do from the time I saw his face in her window. I eased out of her chair, and sat on the arm of the rocking chair, and wrapped him up in my arms.

"Catherine?"

A light tock tock tock sounded against my door again. "Yes, Mrs. Tilford."

"Are you sure you're all right in there?"

WHEN GEORGE ENTERED THE BUNKHOUSE exhausted after the three-hour ride back to the ranch, he was surprised to see a familiar face lying asleep with his mouth open. In his bunk.

"Chester!" George shoved a heel into Chester's shoulder. Chester lifted his head, his eyes barely open. "What are you doing in my bunk?"

Chester blinked and chewed the air, trying to whet his mouth. "They told me you were gone."

"Get out."

Chester frowned, but sat up slowly, rubbing his eyes. "Where am I supposed to go?"

"What the hell are you doing here anyway, Chester?"

"I'm gonna be working here."

George felt his fist clenching at his side and tried to breathe it loose. "Well, get out of my bunk."

Chester turned his head, surveying the room and the lack of empty bunks. "I guess I could use my bedroll."

"That's right...use your bedroll."

George lay down and hated how much different it suddenly felt to be there.

And he couldn't believe how much he'd told this woman he barely knew. Where had those words come from? And why her? He wasn't even afraid that he'd told her too much.

RO

The next morning, I moved through my preparations for the day with a combination of cheer and worry. I still couldn't get over the fact that the man who seemed to hold this power over me had shown up at my window. Bu I was anxious about what happened after he left. I knew this world of men too well to believe that he could just return to the ranch without consequences.

"Catherine, what is going on with you today?" Allison wrapped her hand around my upper arm. "You're bouncing around like a frog leg in a skillet."

"Am I?"

"You are. And I've never heard you talk to yourself before...something's going on."

I took a deep breath. "I have a lot on my mind...I didn't even realize I was talking to myself."

Allison waved me away. "What could Catherine Boland possibly have to worry about?"

"What's that supposed to mean?"

Allison shook her head. "Come on...we need to get going if we're going to get to work on time."

"Now wait one minute here, Allison...you're not going to get away with that." We whisked out the front door, with Allison holding her dress aloft with one hand, sashaying ahead of me.

"Do not walk away from me, young lady!" I tried to trot after her, but I wasn't as nimble as my friend. "Tell me what makes you think I have less to worry about than you do."

"That's not what I said." Allison turned suddenly, and I nearly ran into her.

"But that's what you meant...what are you talking about, Allison?" I grabbed her arm. "Listen, I'm worried that you're hinting at something...not something about me, but something about you."

Allison spun again, swinging her dress as if she could sweep the subject away with the fabric. Her heels pocked against the wood sidewalk.

I redoubled my efforts to keep up with her and was making steady progress until a face appeared. A face coming right at me. The face was smiling, but the face changed when it recognized me. The face became hard and cold. And I stopped walking.

"What are you doing here?" I asked, but the face just kept going, not hearing me because I didn't say it out loud. I only thought it, wishing that Lonnie Piper didn't still affect me this way.

RO

Thirty miles away, George dragged himself out of bed after two hours of sleep. Once he tugged his clothes on, he staggered to the ranch house and knocked on the door. Dan Hardin answered with a piece of toast in one hand. George could smell the strawberry jam.

"How you doin', George?"

"Not so good, Mr. Hardin. I got a problem here."

"You don't look so good...come on in. Any problem of yours is a problem of mine." Hardin took a bite of his toast, chewing earnestly while he led George to the kitchen. "You want a piece of toast?"

"It's all right...I had my breakfast already," George lied.

"So what's the problem, George? Let's get this taken care of." Hardin brushed the crumbs from his hands and licked the corners of his mouth.

"It's your new man, Dan. Chester."

And as George explained what happened at the previous place, without referring to the lynching, he watched the expression on his boss's face turn from concern to something harder to define.

"How did he end up coming here?" Hardin asked.

"That's what I'd like to know." George pulled at his sleeve, trying to scratch an itch underneath. "I'm guessing they asked him to leave."

Hardin nodded thoughtfully. "I'll talk to him."

George stood. "I appreciate that. I don't want to make trouble or anything, you know. But..."

"You don't trust this guy."

"No sir, I'm sorry to say it, but that's right."

RO

I sat in my room, in the middle of my bed. I had not moved for a half hour, it seemed. "You knew this day was coming," I kept repeating to myself. "You knew it was coming." And yet it didn't make it one bit easier. Saying this didn't make me feel one bit better, either. I'd been unable to think all day. As the hours ticked away at the bank, I'd gone through the motions like someone who'd been lost in the mountains for a week. I bumped into things, mumbled to myself, forgot to eat.

"What is wrong with you?" Allison stood in my doorway, her elbow propped up against the jamb. She was wearing her night-gown.

"Are you going to bed already?" I asked.

"Catherine, it's ten o'clock. Why weren't you at supper?"

"Allison!" A voice from downstairs echoed through the halls.

"Yes, Mrs. Tilford." Allison's face expressed her annoyance.

"I need to talk to you if you have a moment."

"I'll be right down." Allison held her finger up. "Don't go to bed yet. I'll be right back."

I returned to my former state, staring blankly. My mind could only see one thing. Lonnie's face coming toward me. I had forgotten everything else that ever happened, was happening now, or would happen. I could only see those eyes, bearing down on me, through me, without any sense of recognition. It was as if he saw me as a clear pane of glass. Again, I lost track of time, but the next thing I was aware of was Allison sitting on the bed next to me. She was crying.

"Allison?"

"What?"

"What's the matter?"

"Good god, Catherine. Are you that lost in your own head? I just told you."

I laid a hand on Allison's forearm. "I'm sorry. I didn't hear a word you said. Tell me again, please."

"Mrs. Tilford told me to move out."

"You're kidding!"

Allison shook her head, then raised her eyes with a look of concern. "And...she wants to talk to you too."

RO

For the first time in several days, George Arbuckle rode alone out in the open, pushing a small herd of cattle toward the home ranch of the Three V. This was what he loved, the enormous quiet, the lack of distraction except for an occasional wandering cow. Without thinking, George spent a good part of the day taking long, deep breaths, in through his nose. The smells of sage and moist earth and ripening grass filled his whole body until he sat up straighter in the saddle, buoyed by nature. By the soul of this wide open country.

As he wrapped up his day, corralling the cattle then combing down his horse and setting a bucket of oats under her nose, a voice muttered his name just a few feet behind him.

He turned to find Chester standing behind him. "Holy Christ, you scared the hell out of me." He then realized that Chester was pointing a gun directly at his chest. "Whoa now...what's going on here, Chester?"

Chester's eyes were red. "You know god damn good and well what's going on, George. Is this what it's come to then? You've turned coat on me? You've gone yellow?"

"Well now, let's just take a minute here and talk about what you mean, Chester."

"You've always treated me like a god damn kid, George, and I'm good and tired of it. You know exactly what I'm talking about."

"If you mean the little talk I had with Mr. Hardin, then yeah, I guess that was a little underhanded, Chester...but you gotta think about this."

"I don't gotta do nothing, George."

"No...you're right. There's nothing you have to do."

"That's right." Chester shuffled his feet a little, and the gun seemed to tilt down toward the ground. Chester looked unsure about what to do next, now that there wasn't anything to disagree about.

"So tell me what you want, Chester. What's it gonna take to make things right here?"

Chester breathed in through his nose and started to stalk back and forth. He kept the gun aimed at George as he paced.

"Chester, why did you leave the Hash Knife?"

Chester strode right up to George, just inches from his face. "That ain't none of your business, George."

The sight of the gun, the smell of the metal and gunpowder just inches from his nose, sucked the air right out of George. His lungs were petrified by the odor. "All right," he whispered.

"Listen, the thing you don't understand, George, is that most people don't know what to do in a pickle like this. Most people aren't like you, George."

"I'm not sure where you got the idea that I know what to do, Chester. But it ain't true. I get just as scared and confused as the next guy."

Chester emitted a loud snort. "No you don't...see there, that's just what I mean...you talking to me like that, like I'm a man who don't know the difference between one truth and another. You see why I get so mad? Do you, George?"

George nodded, mainly because he didn't think he had much choice with a gun halfway up his nose.

"Good. At least you see that much. Now we're getting somewhere." Chester started pacing around George, making a circle around the barn, kicking up straw and the smell of dry manure. The more he paced, the faster he went, and George began to worry that he was working up to something. As if he needed to pace himself into a sense of reason.

"Listen, Chester...I had a long day, and I'm sure you have too. I'm about ready for some grub and a good night's sleep. How about you?"

"No, George." Now Chester was right in front of him again. George smelled his breath, the waft of onions and tobacco.

"Okay." George surrendered his palms to the gun. "Whatever you say, Chester."

In all the time he'd been working and living in the same bunkhouse with Chester, he'd never seen this kind of anger. Chester seemed on the verge of breaking in half inside. So it was almost not a surprise when, a moment later, George heard a loud pop and felt a sharp pain in the side of his head. His vision went completely white for a moment, and then confusion, and the next thing he knew, he was waking up. He was still in the barn, lying on his side in the straw. His head pounded, as if whatever hit him was repeating the act over and over again. George lifted his head, although it hurt like hell, ready to scan the barn for any sign of Chester. What he didn't expect was to see him lying next to him. But there he was, also on his side, a puddle of blood under his head. His eyes stared straight at George with the same vacant expression George had seen on Bones' face. And again, the single hole, right in the middle of his forehead.

RØ

I settled onto the green paisley sofa that dominated Mr. Tilford's sitting room and told myself that I was not in a position to speak my mind about Mrs. Tilford's decision about Allison. This was none of my business. On the other hand, why else would I be here if not to discuss what was happening to my friend? And of course, speaking my mind has never been something I avoid.

"Mrs. Tilford, I know you have a reputation to uphold, but I have to say that I think you may be doing Allison a disservice by asking her to leave. You know what kind..."

"Catherine, please..." Mrs. Tilford's voice was firm.

"I'm sorry. It's not my place."

"I need to ask you to leave, too, Catherine." Mrs. Tilford lowered her chin and gazed at me from beneath a furrowed brow.

"What?"

"Catherine, I know you had a man in your room the other night. I saw Mr. Arbuckle leaving. I can't have this kind of thing going on in my house. You and Allison have given me no other choice."

My breath caught in my throat. "I'm so sorry, Mrs. Tilford. It's true that Mr. Arbuckle was in my room, but he was in serious trouble...there was nothing untoward about it...he was not here for that purpose at all."

"That doesn't matter, Catherine, and you know it. A rule is a rule."

"Yes of course." But even as I said this, I couldn't help but think that Mrs. Tilford was being incredibly unreasonable. "I'll be out by tomorrow evening."

Mrs. Tilford flipped her fingers toward me. "You don't need to leave that soon...you can stay until the end of the week."

"No, no...I'll be out tomorrow evening."

CHAPTER 13

GEORGE STOOD OVER CHESTER'S BODY. Dan Hardin hovered behind his shoulder, clicking his tongue. Five other hands gathered around them, silently studying the dead man.

"You sure you're okay, George?" Hardin asked. George nodded, and even that hurt his head.

"That stupid son-of-a-bitch," Hardin said.

George noted the echoes of Preston Sanford, and a quiet shudder swept through him. His head pounded.

"Who do you think might have done this?" Hardin asked.

George shrugged.

Hardin shook his head, staring down at Chester. "Well, you were right to be worried, I guess."

George sighed. "I'm sorry to bring this on your place, Mr. Hardin."

"Hell, George...it wasn't you."

Two other hands lifted Chester by his legs and arms and carried him outside the barn.

George and Hardin followed. The men draped Chester's body over his horse, then looked at Hardin.

"Take him on into Deadwood. Tell the sheriff what happened. And I think Chester's got some family there. A sister, maybe?" Hardin looked at George.

George shrugged.

"You don't know if he had family?"

George shook his head.

"How long did you work with him?"

Again, George shrugged, and felt it in his head. "Maybe a couple years."

Hardin chuckled, his chiseled face folding up inside itself. "I like that about you, George. You don't think about anything but work."

George felt an awkward grin curl his lip.

"Well…" Hardin gazed out across the ranch, taking a deep breath. "I s'pose we ought to get back to the house for supper."

George nodded, but the thought of food made him dizzy. Still, he trailed along behind Hardin and the three other hands, stumbling a couple of times when his head went light.

Just before they arrived at the house, Hardin dropped back and walked next to George. "I been thinking about something, George."

"Yeah?"

"You got yourself a girl, George?"

"A girl?" Now George's head really hurt. "Well…no, I don't…why?"

A big hand suddenly landed on George's shoulder. "I need someone to start running the outfit over on the Little Missouri, over by Alzada. But I have a rule about the men who run my cattle."

He stopped, looking George straight in the eye. After a few strides, George realized Hardin was waiting for him to say something.

"What is it?"

"They gotta have a wife."

George frowned. Now all he wanted to do was sit down. "So...you're telling me that if I get married, I could run that place?"

Hardin nodded. "Think about it. Now let's go eat."

But George didn't hear him. He was lying on the ground, out cold.

CHAPTER 14

I WOKE UP EARLY THE NEXT MORNING with Allison curled up next to me, both arms and legs locked around me. I gave her a gentle nudge.

"Allison...wake up." There was no response. "Allison."

A stirring finally started beneath the covers. A quiet moan. Allison's auburn hair emerged. Then her pale face.

"I'm sorry, Catherine. I couldn't be alone last night."

"It's okay."

Allison propped herself up on one elbow. "What are we going to do, Catherine?"

I was ashamed at how annoying I found Allison's helplessness. I couldn't help but feel as though our problems had become quite separate. But I decided maybe I was just tired. "Let's just see what happens, Allison. I'm sure things will work out."

Allison dropped her head on my shoulder, and I patted her head. But I really wanted to get up and get my day started.

"If nothing else, we can stay at a hotel for a night or two," Allison said.

"Do you know of any other boarding houses?" I asked.

Allison lifted her head. "Catherine, nobody else is going to let us stay at their place after this. The word's going to get out."

"Nonsense!" I threw back the quilt, climbed from the bed, and wrapped myself in my dressing gown.

"What are you so upset about?" Allison crawled slowly from the bed, rumpling her hair with one hand.

"Allison, I think maybe we should talk about this later, when we've had some time to wake up."

Allison frowned, then shrugged. "All right."

RO

When George woke up for the second time that day, he was in the back of a wagon, wrapped in a blanket, rocking slowly with the movement of the vehicle. There were two men on the buckboard. He couldn't tell who they were from the back.

"Where are we going?"

"Hardin told us to take you to town. You been shot."

It was then that George noticed another figure lying next to him. This man was completely wrapped up in a canvas tarp, even his head. "Is that Chester?"

The man in front nodded.

George groaned, lying back down. He was freezing. "Wait, did you say I've been shot?" He pulled himself back up to his elbow.

"That's what Hardin said...he didn't notice until you passed out. Looks like a bullet grazed your head. You're lucky to be alive, Arbuckle."

George pondered this fact, feeling the pain in his head. For the first time since he'd been injured, he decided to explore the wound. The pain seemed to be coming from somewhere just above his ear. He reached up and when his hand touched the spot, he just about cried out it hurt so much. "Damn," he muttered. "Shouldn't this thing be covered up?"

"Boss said it stopped bleeding, so it should be okay," the hand answered.

George sighed and lay back down, wishing he at least had something to wrap his head with. Between the pain and the cold, it felt as if the air was burrowing right into his skull. He looked around the wagon bed and found a chunk of old dirty cloth. Probably not the best idea, he thought, but he went ahead and wrapped it around his head anyway. And then he fell into an immediate, deep sleep.

RO

I waited until I heard Allison leave the house before I made my way downstairs. I was relieved to see Mrs. Tilford's door firmly closed. I emerged from the house to a crisp spring day and hugged my coat tightly around my body. I was looking forward to working today, to being in an environment where I knew what to expect. Several people spoke to me on my way down the street, and I was happy to respond with a heartfelt hello. But when I saw a wagon pass by with what appeared to be two men lying dead in the back, I stopped.

"What happened?" I asked the driver.

"Rustlers," he said. "They got another one."

"What about the second man?"

"Oh, he'll be okay. He just got grazed."

The injured man lifted his head, and a filthy piece of cloth fell from his face, and I gasped. "George!"

"Catherine." George's reply was weak. "Hey, stop the wagon for a minute!"

The driver tugged at the reins, and the horses jerked their heads as they pulled to a stop. I approached the wagon, where George struggled to sit up. The gash split along his scalp as if it had opened up one whole side of his head. "Oh my god, what happened to you?"

"It's nothing," George said. "Just grazed. But that's not important. I wanted to ask you something."

"Yeah?"

"Yeah...well..." George glanced at the two men on the buckboard, who had both turned completely around. "Do you guys mind taking a walk?"

"What for?"

"Just for a couple minutes."

The two men climbed from the wagon, grumbling. I pulled my watch from my purse, and realized I was going to be late for work. I tried not to think about it. George struggled to pull himself to a sitting position. He looked me in the eye for a moment, but dropped his head before saying, "Will you marry me?"

"What?"

He lifted his head. "I'm askin' you to marry me."

"George, that's the most ridiculous thing I've ever heard. We hardly know each other."

George nodded. "Yes...you're right. Okay." And he laid back down.

I stood by the wagon, wondering what I'd just done. George seemed to have passed out already, and now he was not only seriously injured, but probably heartbroken too. And why? Because he asked me to marry him. The whole thing was absurd.

"George!" I leaned over the side of the wagon. "Are you awake?"

"Yeah, I'm awake."

"Do you know where you're going? Is there somewhere I can come and visit you after work?"

"I'll probably be back at the ranch by then."

"Okay, well...please let me know the next time you're in town. Okay?"

"What for?"

"Because we need to talk more about this. We've never even courted, George. I can't agree to marry you just like that. But I'd like to get to know you better."

George lifted his head. "You would?"

"Yes. I would."

A very slight smile came to George's face before he lost the strength to hold his head up any longer. He laid back down and was snoring softly in seconds. I reached into the wagon and squeezed his hand before I went along my way. But first I asked the driver, "Where are you taking him?" And when he told me, I asked whether they expected George to be there overnight.

"No idea, ma'am."

I couldn't concentrate on anything at work that day, but it was different from the day before. While Lonnie had scrounged around in my head like a hungry mouse the day before, all I could think about today was when I'd get a chance to check whether George was all right.

I had to ask several customers to repeat their questions, and I gave one customer five dollars too much. Thankfully, she noticed the mistake and returned the money. There was a cool distance between Allison and me, which didn't make the day go any faster.

By the time the grandfather clock struck five, I couldn't stand in one place. "Good night, everyone," I called out before leaving the building.

"Wait!" Allison said.

I took a deep breath and turned.

"Aren't we going to find a place to stay?"

"I'll meet you back at Mrs. Tilford's in a couple of hours...I have something else I need to do first."

I could see the hurt in Allison's eyes, but I didn't want to take the time to explain. I stepped out into the cool spring air and started heading east. But only five minutes into my journey, a voice from behind made me jump.

"Hello Catherine." I recognized the low rumble at once, and I instinctively picked up my pace. "What's the rush?"

I could feel the presence hovering just behind me. "Go away," I commanded.

"Well, I would go away if that's really what you wanted, Catherine, but I know you better than that."

I whirled, and came face to face with those cold, steely eyes. "No, you only think you know me."

Lonnie started chuckling, quietly, almost under his breath. "There's no use trying to pretend, Catherine. We've been through this before."

I drew myself up, feeling the rage well up along with the tears behind my eyes. "This is not pretending, Lonnie Spicer. This is the real me. You've just never paid attention."

"Is everything all right here, Miss Boland?" Another voice came from behind.

"Who's this child?" Lonnie's eyes got even colder. "Are you a delivery boy?"

"Leave him alone, Lonnie. Everything's fine, Mr. Smalls." I touched Mr. Smalls' shoulder. "I can handle this."

Despite the fact that Lonnie glared at him as if he was about to bite, Mr. Smalls held his bearing. He stood straight, his expression calm, even smiling slightly.

"Run along, little dogie," Lonnie said.

"Would you like me to walk you home, Miss Boland?" Mr. Smalls asked.

My initial instinct was to say no, but I gave the matter further thought. "Actually, that would be greatly appreciated, Mr. Smalls."

A smile curled Lonnie's mouth, and it made me freeze. I remembered this smile and what it meant, and knew that we needed to move along.

"It's this way." I turned, and when Mr. Smalls offered his arm, I wedged a hand into the crook of his elbow and tried to remember to keep breathing.

We walked for several strides, and when I heard nothing, I imagined that Lonnie was at least following us. But I heard no footsteps, nor the familiar growl. After a few more strides, I began to breathe a little more freely.

"Thank you so much for that, Mr. Smalls. You really didn't have to do that."

"I don't mean any disrespect, Miss Boland, but that's not how I see it. You were obviously afraid...it was my duty to step in."

"You're a good man then. And I thank you again. But you really don't have to walk me all the way."

"It would be my honor, Miss Boland. But I do have to ask why we're going in this direction."

"Oh, I had to leave Mrs. Tilford's."

Mr. Smalls stopped. "I'm so sorry to hear that."

WHEN GEORGE CAME TO HIS SENSES for the third time in twenty-four hours, he wondered whether he was stuck in a dream that wouldn't stop. One that repeated the same scene over and over again. But this one had a variation. He woke up to an unfamiliar face. A young man with big lampchops framing a small, serious face.

"Hello, Mr. Arbuckle."

"Who are you?"

"My name is Donald Smalls. How are you feeling?"

"Are you a doctor?"

Mr. Smalls smiled. "No, I'm afraid I don't know anything about medicine. I'm just a friend of Catherine's."

George tried to sit up, but the pain in the side of his head threw him right back against the pillow. "Is she here?"

"She'll be right back." Donald Smalls placed a hand against George's shoulder. "Are you feeling better?"

"I'm good." George didn't want to tell this man the truth, that his head felt as if it had been split like a watermelon.

"Well they said you're going to be fine, so that's good. But you were very lucky."

"Yeah, I s'pose I was....an inch to the left, that bullet would have killed me."

Donald nodded. "That's right."

"Do you know if they're going to let me go home soon?"

To George's annoyance, Donald Smalls found this question amusing. "Oh no, Mr. Arbuckle. I don't think that would be a very good idea."

"Well now...I certainly don't mean any disrespect, Mr. Smalls, but I'd just as soon hear it from someone who's trained in the field."

Donald bowed. "Of course. It's just that I've been speaking with the doctor. He said you've lost an awful lot of blood. You're going to need a couple of days to recover."

"No...I need to get back to the ranch...there's too much to do for me to be lying around..."

The young man smiled. "Whatever you say, George."

And now she was there in the room. George tried once again to lift himself from the pillow, but the pain just about knocked him unconscious again. He laid back down. "Hello Catherine."

"How are you feeling?" She laid her hand against his cheek, which took his breath away.

"I feel great," he answered.

Donald Smalls chuckled again, and George wished he would leave the room.

"You don't have to be a hero, George Arbuckle." Catherine leaned over and fixed a firm gaze on him. "That was a close call."

George nodded, just barely.

"Do you think you can eat something?" She laid a hand against his forehead.

"I'm not real hungry," George said.

"Well you should eat something." Catherine held a small piece of bread up to George's mouth. He opened and allowed her to drop the dough on his tongue. But the act of chewing was like a hammer against the side of his head. So he began working the bread around in his mouth, soaking it in his saliva until it was soft enough to swallow. When she tried to give him another bite, he shook his head.

"George..."

"Do you think you'll need me anymore, Miss Boland?" Smalls asked.

"I'm sorry, Mr. Smalls. How thoughtless. I'll be fine. But I appreciate your help."

Catherine turned and shook Donald Smalls' hand with both of hers. George was embarrassed to realize that this simple gesture brought a feeling of intense jealousy to his heart. On the other hand, he was happy Smalls was leaving. He waved when Donald told him to get better. And it was then that a question came to George.

"Is that why you don't want to get married?"

"Is what why I don't want to get married?" Catherine looked sincerely confused.

"Mr. Smalls."

Catherine lowered her chin. "Mr. Smalls? It just so happens that Mr. Smalls was kind enough to accompany me here when

I...well, it doesn't matter. The point is, he lives at the boarding house, and he is a very nice young man. A religious man."

George nodded, feeling childish. "Shouldn't you be at work?"

Catherine smiled. "It's almost seven o'clock in the evening, George, which just goes to show why you should not go anywhere."

"How did you know where I was?"

Catherine studied him. "Do you remember seeing me on the street earlier today?"

"That was today?"

"Okay...just wanted to make sure. Your friend told me where they were taking you."

"Catherine?"

Catherine held another piece of bread up to his mouth. "Yes, George."

He took the bread from her hand and held it between his fingers. "Tell me what you want to know."

Catherine's cheeks glowed red. A big smile stretched across her face. "We have plenty of time for that, Mr. Arbuckle. I don't want to hurt your head any worse than it already is."

George smiled. How was it that this woman seemed to know just the right thing to say? He popped the bread in his mouth and rolled it around on his tongue, trying to work up enough saliva to soften it.

For the next half hour, Catherine broke off pieces of bread for George, feeding them to him one at a time, then holding a glass of water to his mouth. They didn't speak much. She asked if he needed his pillow adjusted, and whether one piece of bread was too big. George couldn't remember a time when he felt so comfortable in someone else's company. A part of him didn't want to say anything and run the risk of disrupting the mood.

Once George had finished eating, Catherine settled into a chair next to his bed and pulled some knitting from her bag. The clicking of the needles had a soothing effect on George, and he found himself fighting the urge to fall asleep again. "Aren't you going to eat something?" he asked, his voice weak.

Catherine smiled. She patted her stomach. "I have plenty of reserve."

"Is the doctor coming back?"

Catherine shook her head. "I don't think so."

"Isn't this his house?"

"No...actually, we're in a hotel, George. I had them move you here after the doctor was finished examining you. I hope that's okay."

George nodded. "There's some money in the bottom of my boot. Take what it cost for the room."

Catherine nodded. "I'll get it later."

But George knew she wouldn't. "Won't they be expecting you at the boarding house?"

She shook her head, offering no explanation, but she suddenly sat up. "Oh no!"

"What?"

"I forgot to meet Allison. Oh, she's going to be so angry."

"Well go ahead...I'll be fine."

She shook her head. "No, it's too late. She won't be there. I don't know where she is."

"She's not at the house?"

Catherine reached out and patted his hand. "Don't worry about Allison, or me, George. Just rest."

CHAPTER 16

THE NEXT MORNING, I ENTERED the bank with a hand on my back, stiff from sleeping in a chair. It was hard to decide which was more worrisome...leaving George alone in the hotel room or facing Allison.

"Good morning," I called out.

Allison stood behind the counter, and she didn't respond. But Lars shouted hello from his office.

"I'm so sorry I forgot to meet you last night, Allison. I know you're mad. But George got shot yesterday, and someone had to take care of him."

Allison looked up from what she was doing. "He got shot?"

My heart swelled at her response. I rounded the counter and wrapped my arms around Allison. "I really am sorry."

"I was really angry."

"I'm sure you were."

"But George got shot?"

I nodded.

"Who got shot?" Lars emerged from his office.

"Catherine's beau," Allison said.

"He's not my beau."

Allison rolled her eyes. "Anyway...what happened?"

As I related the story, Lars and Allison listened with intent expressions. But halfway through, I realized I might be telling too much. I didn't want to say something to implicate George.

"I heard about that guy getting killed," Lars said. "But I didn't know George was the other one. Is there anything we can do?"

"That's very kind. But I don't think so."

As soon as Lars ducked back into his office, Allison sidled up next to me. "I hate to bring this up now, but I don't know what I'm going to do."

"You mean about a place to live?"

Allison bit that fat lower lip, and she shook her head.

"Oh no...Allison, you're not serious."

Allison nodded.

I sighed. "Are you sure?"

Allison dropped her head, and the tears came. I wrapped an arm around her.

RO

After lying in bed for a few hours once Catherine left for work, George got restless. His head still hurt like hell, but it wasn't quite as bad as it had been the night before.

He rolled out of bed and found the chamber pot underneath. Leaning over made him dizzy, but he was able to relieve himself and tug on his clothes. George thought briefly about getting back to the ranch until he realized there was a bit of a problem. He didn't have his horse.

So he crawled back into bed. He picked up a book that Catherine had left for him but fell back to sleep after two paragraphs.

The next time George awoke, it was because of a feeling. A feeling that someone else was in the room. He lifted his head to see a man sitting ten feet from the bed. "Hello," he said. "Are you the doctor?"

The man showed a slow smile. "Yes," he said. "I'm a doctor of sorts."

"What does that mean?"

The man leaned forward, folding his hands between his knees. "Let's talk about you instead. How are you feeling?"

"Fine."

"Yeah?"

"Yeah, I feel fine."

"That looks like a pretty nasty wound."

"I was lucky."

The man nodded thoughtfully and leaned back in the chair. And the longer the man looked at him, the more uncomfortable George became. The man had a calm anger in his eyes, as if he was the kind of man who could hurt people without much thought or contemplation. Or guilt.

"So...what can I do for you?" George finally asked.

"Well, you can start by telling me who you are."

George couldn't help but chuckle.

"What's funny about that?" The man stood.

"Well, I guess since you showed up here, I figured you already knew that."

The man nodded. He stood up and walked toward the bed. George hadn't noticed how big he was when he was sitting. The man's shoulders were massive, wide and high and almost throbbing.

"So if you don't even know who I am, why are you here?" George asked.

The man leaned over him. "I followed someone."

Catherine, George thought. Shit. Who was this guy? Some old beau of hers, most likely. "Well, I'm sorry, but unless you give me more to go on, I'm not inclined to tell you much. And I'd just as soon you leave. I need some rest, according to the doctor."

"Yeah?"

George nodded, trying to come across as assertive and weak at the same time, as if doing anything to him would be much too easy. This man seemed to be the type who would want a challenge. More of a fight.

"What if I told you I ain't gonna leave until I get a little more information."

George sucked in a breath. "Well, I'd say you're welcome to stay. Just don't expect me to say much."

The man stood up straight and seemed to contemplate for a moment. He walked back to the chair, sat down, and looked out the window. "Did you hear about this guy got killed the other day? Out at the Three V?"

George studied him. "'Course I did...everyone's heard about that."

"I been thinking about these vigilantes, wondering if they know how much danger they've put themselves in." He looked at George. "And their families, too. You know, that's the thing most men don't think about when they get this wild notion about being a hero. They don't think about how it's going to affect everyone else if they get hurt or kilt."

George nodded. "I think you're right about that. Some guys get caught up in how mad they are...all they can think about is getting even."

The man nodded and seemed sincere about pondering the matter. He was an odd duck, George decided. One of these guys who's always thinking too much. Getting caught up in his head.

"This is a pretty small town out here," the man said. "We probably know some of the guys in that crowd, without even realizing it."

George hummed. "That's probably true."

"Anyway, the reason I brought that up is because I just want you to know that this is not the kind of man I am. A vengeful man."

"Oh?"

He shook his head. "Nope. I don't believe in gettin' even."

George somehow didn't believe him. But more importantly, he had no idea what this had to do with him. "Well, that's a good quality, I think."

"Do you?"

George nodded.

The man smiled, standing up again. "Well, I don't know if it is or not. The only reason I don't believe in it is because of what I was saying before...about putting your family in danger and all. I got a wife and kids...a bunch of sisters, too. They'd be pretty shook up if something happened to me."

"Sure they would."

"So what about you? You married?"

George shook his head, against his better judgement.

The man nodded, thoughtful again. "There's not enough women for every man out here. That's part of why there's so much killin' and fighting, you know. The Theater there can only do so much good."

George chuckled.

"It's true, isn't it?" the man asked. "We need women, no two ways about it."

"I s'pose."

"Yeah, no two ways about it."

The whole conversation was starting to exhaust George. Where was this guy going with all this? What the hell did he want?

"So you're married, huh?" George asked.

The man nodded and sat up straighter in the chair. "Yeah, my wife...she's a saint, I'm telling you, the stuff she puts up with." He fixed a steady gaze on George. "I'm not an easy man to live with."

George dropped his eyes, uncomfortable with where this conversation was going. More uncomfortable.

"You know...I don't mean to be rude, but I'm getting pretty tired," George said. "If I just flat out fall asleep, don't take it personal."

The man nodded. "I can see how you might get tuckered out pretty easy with that gash in your head." He stood, rubbing the front of his shirt smooth. "I'll leave you now."

George hoped his relief wasn't too obvious.

"I do have one last question for you though." The man approached George's bed again, and George's breath caught in his throat. He looked George directly in the eye. "Do you think everyone has memories they can't live with?"

George cleared his throat. "I s'pose most people do...not everyone, though. No."

The man nodded one last time. He plucked his cowboy hat from the coat rack by the door and tugged it on his head. "I'm sorry to interrupt your day."

"It's okay."

"Good luck with getting healed up."

"Thanks."

When the man was out the door, George felt a relief wash over him. He was just about to drift back to sleep when there was a tap on the door, and he had the overwhelming dread that the man had come back to finish whatever it was he started.

"Who is it?" he called out.

"It's Doctor Mellory."

"Oh come in."

After the doctor had examined George's wound, and applied a bandage, he said, "I see you had a visitor."

"Yeah, how did you know?"

"Oh, I saw Mr. Spicer leaving when I came up the stairs."

"You know him?" George propped himself up on an elbow and was happy to realize that it didn't hurt nearly as bad.

"Oh sure. I've known Lonnie Spicer for years."

"Who is he?"

The doctor looked at him with surprise. "You sound like you don't know him."

"I don't...he just showed up."

The doctor frowned and looked at George with obvious doubt.

"I know it seems odd....I thought so too," George said.

The doctor nodded. "Well, Mr. Spicer is a locator...he lives in Belle."

"I wonder what he's doing here in Deadwood then," George said.

"Could be looking for a section for a new homesteader. At any rate, let me get to your health here."

George nodded. "Am I going to be able to get back to work?"

"You should be fine to get back to the ranch tomorrow. That wound is healing nicely."

"Thanks, Doc. Say, can you let them know? I need a way to get back out there."

RO

Hurrying down Main Street, it bothered me to realize how many people I was hoping I wouldn't see. Between Lonnie Spicer, Bernie Sanford, and Mrs. Tilford, it seemed I'd developed more enemies in a week's time than I'd ever had. But the main question in my head was whether George would still be at the hotel.

By the time I reached the door, I could feel the beat of my heart. I swung the door open, only to find George standing over the chamber pot with his night shirt pulled up above his waist. I slammed the door.

"Oh god, I've done it again." I raced down the stairs, trying to decide whether I should just run away and not come back. I stopped just outside the hotel, sat down on a bench, and tried to collect myself. Five minutes later, I tapped on the door.

"Come in."

Even with the invitation, I opened the door slowly, peering inside before I let myself in. "I'm so sorry."

"Don't worry about it...we all have our way of dealing with our needs." George winked.

I laughed. "Well, I'm usually very conscious about my manners. I can't believe I didn't knock."

"It's okay....really."

"How are you feeling?"

George was propped up in a sitting position, and he flexed his arms. "Much better. I think I'm ready to get back out there as soon as I can find someone to take me."

"That's great, George." I clasped my hands together. "I see the doctor was here...did he say the same thing?"

"He did. He said it's healing up good."

"Good!"

"I need to ask you about somethin' else."

I settled into the chair, so thrilled to see him feeling stronger. "Okay."

"Do you know a fella named Spicer?"

I gasped. "No!"

"You don't?"

"Yes!"

George laughed. "Well which is it?"

"I do know him, but please tell me he didn't come here."

"Well, I guess I could tell you that, but it'd be a damn lie."

"Oh god...no." I put a hand to my forehead.

"Maybe I shouldn't have brought it up."

I stood. "No, of course you should. He came here?" George nodded.

"Did he say what he wanted?"

"No, the guy was talking in circles. I don't have a clue why he came here. He wouldn't even tell me his name. The only reason I know it was because the doctor knew him."

I sank onto the bed.

"Is he an old beau of yours?" George asked.

I took a deep breath. "Yes." I looked at George, expecting an expression of disapproval or irritation. Something unpleasant. Instead, his eyes showed concern.

"George, you remember the night you came to my window?"

"How could I forget? It was only a few days ago."

"Well...I thought it was brave of you to tell me what you told me that night. It would have scared a lot of people away, and you trusted me for some reason."

George looked at his hands.

"Now I'm going to try and gather up that same courage."

He lifted his eyes. "Okay."

"But this is not an easy story to tell."

"You can tell me anything, Catherine." He held his hand up like an oath. "I mean that."

"Okay." I took a deep breath, closed my eyes, and started. "I met Lonnie Spicer when he came into my hat shop one day."

While George sat quietly, his bright blue eyes alight with curiosity, I walked through the years of heartache I'd endured with Mr. Lonnie Spicer. I focused on the highlights, of course, as one does when trying to give a story its best spin. And of course, by highlights I mean the most horrendous things Lonnie did. I made it clear that Lonnie never laid a hand on me, in the violent sense at least. He never hit me. Which was part of what convinced me that the torment might well be all in my head. And he fed this myth whenever I questioned why he didn't show up for a date, or why he suddenly left without explanation. He fed it with suggestions that I was letting my insecurities show, taking things so personally. That if I honestly believed he didn't love me, I was overlooking the facts, missing the big picture. He would point out examples of men who were much worse than he was, and he was good at it.

"Why did you stay with him?" George finally asked when I was near the end.

"I honestly thought I loved him, George."

"He said he's married. With three kids."

I nodded. "That was a fact that he managed to keep from me for almost a year. I still don't know how he managed that."

"The man is a bastard," George decided.

I chuckled. "I believe I've used that very word myself."

We let the silence settle before George reached out and laid a hand on my shoulder. I leaned into it, and I felt everything about him wanting to nestle up against me. He wrapped his arm around my waist and pulled me toward him. I scooted onto the mattress, until I was in the same seated position, hip to hip, and I draped my arms around his neck. They were weak, loose. Until he pulled me closer, and my hold on him tightened. And then we were both holding onto each other as if we might get lost in the world if we let go.

George turned toward me, and I did the same. My head went light as my mouth touched his, and parted slightly, my tongue sliding along his upper lip. He cradled my head in his hand, and his hair tickled my fingers as the intensity of the kiss increased. I felt his breath against my chin. My hand moved along his shoulders, back and forth, then down his back, where I began to massage the muscles along his spine. I felt dizzy. He pulled back.

"Are you okay?" I touched his cheek.

George nodded. "I'll be fine." And then he couldn't wait to kiss me again. He pulled my face to his, and our tongues danced. My hand slipped inside George's shirt, and the feel of my flesh against his chest made him gasp. He had to pull away again.

I chuckled. "I'm sorry. I can't seem to control myself."

"I'm not complainin'."

"Just having trouble breathing?"

George nodded. "A little."

"There's no hurry." I touched his cheek. The touch brought a smile to his face that looked like it might stay there.

"So what does this mean, Catherine?"

I continued stroking his cheek. "We'll have to see, George."

"You still don't want to marry me?"

"I never said I didn't want to. I just don't want to decide yet."

"Well this seems like an odd thing to do with someone you're not sure you want to marry."

I pulled my head back. My hand dropped to my side. "Excuse me?" I could tell George regretted the statement. "Do I need to remind you about Georgie Porgy?"

"I'm sorry...that was uncalled for."

"It most certainly was."

"It's just that I've never..." George was clearly struggling to find the words he wanted, and I wondered whether he'd ever talked this much to a woman in his life. Especially at close range.

I took his face in both of my hands. "I've never felt this before either, George."

"You haven't?"

I shook my head. "Absolutely not."

"What about that Spicer guy?"

"That was a mistake."

"It probably didn't feel like a mistake then, though. Right?"

I tilted my head back, thinking. "You know, that's probably true, George. But...well, you know how sometimes you feel something in your stomach? Like a little thorn, or a burning? Like the world's trying to tell you something."

George nodded. "I have felt that. So on top of everything else, he lied to you. About being married."

I nodded.

George sighed. "I'm sorry you had to go through that. Nobody deserves that."

I rested my head on George's chest. I slipped my hand back inside his shirt and began to caress his chest. "That's such a nice thing to say."

George let his head lean back, resting against the wall. He didn't seem to notice the pain it must have caused. "I don't know about that. It's just the truth."

"Even better."

George turned his head and looked at the clock. "Don't you need to be at the boarding house for supper? Mrs. Tilford will have your hide!"

I sighed. "I left the boarding house."

George turned his head, looking down at me. "You did?"

I nodded.

"When?"

"Yesterday."

"Wait a second...you didn't leave there so you could be here with me, did you?"

"Oh George, don't get too puffed up about yourself now...just because I'd do anything for you doesn't mean everything I do is for you."

George laughed.

"She asked Allison to move out because...well, just because."

"God, people worry so much about what everyone thinks."

I nodded. "They really do."

"So you left because of that?"

"Well, sort of. It doesn't matter...it seemed like the right time anyway. So no regrets."

"But where are you living?"

"Right here at the moment."

George looked around the room. "Where's your gear?"

"Mrs. Tilford is letting me store it there until I find something else."

"Did you spend the whole night in that chair?"

I nodded. "It wasn't so bad."

Apparently George could hear the lie in my voice. "Don't lie to me...that must have been horrible uncomfortable. We'll switch tonight."

I looked up at him. "Well maybe we don't have to switch."

"Huh?"

I touched his cheek again, and it felt as if a thin stream of hot water ran straight from my fingers to my heart. It swelled up with heat and something I figured must be love. I buried my face in

George's neck, pulling his smell deep inside. I couldn't help but compare...thinking back to how hard it was to lie next to Lonnie Spicer in our last days together...how everything about him became unpleasant to me. George smelled sweet, like clean, honest sweat and fresh bread. He tilted his chin forward, and we kissed again.

CHAPTER 17

WHEN GEORGE WOKE UP the next morning, he was disappointed to find that Catherine had already left. He thought back to the night before, right after they'd finished, how they lay there looking each other straight in the eyes, and George had felt no desire to turn away, or blow out the lantern, or leave. They even woke up and made love again in the middle of the night. And now he wished she was still there. And he knew that if he didn't do whatever it took to get this woman to marry him, he would be a damn fool.

George made his way downstairs and ordered some eggs. He was surprised how much better his head felt, and luxuriated in the aroma from last night's activity. But as soon as he had finished eating, he got restless, wondering when someone would show up to take him back to the ranch. He asked the desk clerk whether he knew of anyone heading toward Belle Fourche, and the clerk told him he'd keep an ear to the ground.

But the morning dragged on, and George became so bored with waiting that he decided to go for a walk. He told the clerk he'd be back within an hour and walked out into a crisp wind.

Dust drifted above Deadwood in great clouds, giving the day a dusk-like appearance. George walked down Main Street, puzzling over the strange looks he was getting until he remembered the huge bandage on his head.

It was a mostly quiet day, a Wednesday, with mothers dragging pre-school children through their daily errands, a few cowboys propped against the Gem Theater, sleeping off the whiskey, and a few carpetbaggers trying to peddle worthless merchandise.

George walked aimlessly, feeling some stiffness in his legs. He couldn't remember the last time he'd lain in bed for two days. It was probably when he had the mumps as a kid. He thought back to his mother trying to force some chicken broth down his swollen throat. It was only a few months later that she herself was dead, from a bad piece of beef.

Halfway down the street, George realized he was nearing the bank, and his heart started to bob up into his throat. Would he be interrupting her if he stopped in? He decided against it and kept walking.

"George!" He turned, and there she was, standing in the doorway, waving to him. He thought about how quickly she must have moved to get there. The smile on her face was huge, unencumbered by anything resembling doubt or guilt or discomfort. "Where are you going?"

He reversed direction and stood in front of her, wanting to embrace her, right there on the street, right in front of the whole sky. Instead he dug his hands deep into his pockets, to prevent them from doing something socially unacceptable.

"I just decided to take a walk," he said. "I'm getting a little cabin fever cooped up there."

"You didn't find a ride yet?"

"Nah, it's okay. Someone'll turn up."

"Maybe they forgot about you." Catherine winked. "Why don't you come inside, and I'll introduce you to Lars."

George beamed. "All right."

Inside, Allison had her back turned when George entered, so he said hello to her. She turned and gave a slight smile, then went back to stacking receipts. Catherine led George to Lars' office and knocked on the door jamb. George had noticed Lars before in his trips to the bank, and at the dance, and had always been fascinated by him. For all of his size, and the striking appearance of his yellow hair, Lars had always seemed unaware of how intimidating he was.

"Lars, I'd like you to meet George Arbuckle. He's..." Catherine became suddenly flustered, and ended up patting George on his upper arm. "Well, he works at the Three V."

Lars stood, unfolding like a straight razor. He was a good foot taller than George, and George had an irrational flashback to being a child.

"I recognize you, George. You are one of our customers, aren't you?" Lars' hand swallowed George's.

"I am," George answered. "Good memory."

"Well it pays to remember the people who keep us in business." Lars stepped back and propped his fists on his hips. "Looks like you've been in a bit of a battle there." He pointed at his own head.

George looked at his boots. "Yeah, it was nothing."

"Oh, it was not nothing, George." George was surprised to feel Catherine grab him affectionately by the arm. "You two actually have something in common. Lars has also been shot."

"I heard you'd been shot," Lars said.

"Just grazed, actually. But I remember when you got shot...isn't that when Catherine saved your life?"

"Oh, hardly." Catherine slapped his bicep.

"Was this the rustlers?" Lars asked.

George shrugged. "They're not sure...it could have been."

Lars shook his head. "Well, I hope you heal up quickly."

"Thank you."

They shook hands again, and Catherine led George back out to the lobby. "I should probably get back to work," she lamented.

George nodded. "Yeah, I'm guessing that guy will take a strap to you soon if you don't."

Catherine laughed. "You saw right through his act."

George stood dumb. He couldn't believe how much a simple smile from this woman warmed him up inside. He didn't want to leave. So they stood awkwardly for another moment.

"Okay, well...I better see about getting a ride back out to those cows. They're going to be worried about me."

Catherine's laugh rang through the bank again, just as the door opened.

George turned and nearly ran into Preston Sanford. He again found himself staring up at someone taller.

Preston gave a quick nod to George, as if he was someone he knew only as an acquaintance. He stepped past George and Catherine to Allison's window.

"I best get back to the hotel," George said quietly.

Catherine pulled him outside the door. "I hope you'll still be there when I get back from work."

George could hardly stand to acknowledge this sentiment, but the smile on his face showed how much he liked hearing it.

"You better hurry so he doesn't follow you." Catherine tilted her head toward the bank.

George nodded, wanting to kiss her goodbye. But they exchanged affectionate waves and he scurried back to the hotel, checking over his shoulder every few strides. When he entered, the clerk motioned him over.

"Someone came by lookin' for you, Mr. Arbuckle. Said he was here to give you a ride."

"Did he say where he'd be?"

"He's coming back. He said an hour, but that was about a half hour ago."

"Thanks."

George went to the room, thinking he needed to pack up his gear. But when he got there, he realized he didn't have anything with him except the clothes he wore. So he cleaned up as well as he could in the wash basin, went out to the outhouse to empty the chamber pot, and straightened up the room. Then he went down to the lobby to wait.

George was immersed in a story in the newspaper when he heard his name. He folded the newspaper to one side and looked up to see Sheriff Pierre LeFont.

"I hear you had a little accident."

He nodded.

"I need to ask you some questions," LeFont said, surveying the lobby. "You mind if we go up to the room?"

George shrugged. "Fine by me."

Because George had so little memory of what happened, the questioning was brief, which seemed to annoy LeFont. But George had no idea what to tell him. He didn't know what happened, hadn't seen anyone.

"Well, let me ask you one last thing." LeFont paced the room, chewing on the inside of his lip. "Why would Chester be spreading your name around as the one who killed that rustler?"

George shifted in his chair. "I can't tell you a thing about what was going on in that man's head, Sheriff. I didn't really know him that well."

"Well you know, I took you at your word on this once before, George. And then just a day later, you left the Hash Knife after Mr. Poplar stuck his neck out for you."

George nodded.

"So you gotta admit that brings up some questions in a guy's mind."

"I can see how it would. But the reason I left was because of Chester, not because of Mr. Poplar."

"You left because of Chester?"

"Yes sir." George held the sheriff's gaze, hoping to inform him with a look that this was as much information as he was willing to give.

"And what did he do to you, Mr. Arbuckle?"

"Well, I'd just as soon not get into that."

LeFont sighed. "I thought you might say that." He frowned. "Listen...I'm having a hard time figuring this out. You seem like a nice enough fella, and I know you're a hard worker. That's all I hear from everyone I've talked to. But every time something happens around here, you seem to be around. That makes me wonder, you know?"

"I'm having a hard time figuring that one out myself, Sheriff. It's a real inconvenient coincidence, the way I see it."

The way LeFont looked at him made George wish he had a better explanation. It even made him wonder whether he should be making something up...some plausible explanation for how this kept happening. But he knew that lying now would only mean having to come up with more in the future. He knew he wasn't clever enough to sustain that kind of deceit.

LeFont started for the door. "Okay, George. I'm afraid we'll be seeing more of each other before this is over. I just hope it doesn't end with me putting cuffs on you or cutting you down from some oak tree somewhere."

George stood. "I'd just as soon it had a different ending myself, Mr. LeFont. Sorry to trouble you."

LeFont chuckled. "Well, you know...it is my job."

George nodded.

RO

As I prepared to leave work, I approached Allison. "Allison, do you have somewhere to be after work?"

She shook her head.

"Do you want to have supper with me? My treat."

Allison didn't respond. She looked away, then pretended to be absorbed in a document, mouthing figures silently.

"Allison, what's wrong? Let's talk about it."

Allison stopped what she was doing, lifted her eyes, and said nothing. Then she turned her attention back to her document.

I lowered my chin and said in a loud whisper, "Allison, don't do this...I'm your friend, remember? You don't have to go through this alone."

But she ignored me, focusing on the paper in front of her as if it was the most important thing she'd ever read.

"Allison, I'm sorry if I did something, but I'm not going to just walk away from you now...I'm not that kind of friend, and you know that."

She looked up at me, and this time she clenched her jaw into a stubborn barrier that looked to be impenetrable. I considered giving up but decided to give it one last try. I walked over to Allison, tentatively wrapped an arm around her shoulder, and said, "You know you're my best friend, don't you?"

Allison shook off my arm with such force that it made me jump back.

"Fine! You want to be alone with your problems, that's where you'll find yourself!" I whirled and started toward the door before I felt something on my shoulder.

"Can I have a word with you, Catherine?" Lars tilted his head down, looking at me from the tops of his eyes.

"Of course."

I watched Allison make a hasty departure as we made our way to Lars' office. So I thought it was odd that Lars closed the door. He folded his hands together and set them on his desk as we sat across from each other.

"Catherine, I think you know that I value a good working relationship with my employees." He raised his brow.

"Yes, I do, Mr. Larson. I noticed it from the first day."

Lars gave a single nod. "And that also means between my employees."

I nodded.

"So I get concerned when things get tense around here. I don't like it."

"I understand that, Lars. But I don't think..."

"Catherine...." Lars held a hand out, palm toward me. "I do want to hear what you have to say, but let me finish."

"Of course."

"Even though Allison is about the same age as you, she is much younger, if you know what I mean."

"I think so."

"So even though she has more seniority here, I think it is actually you who hold more responsibility for the dynamics between the two of you."

"That hardly seems fair, Mr. Larson. You heard how she..." The palm again. I stopped myself. "I'm sorry."

"It's okay. We can discuss this, but I want you to hear me out. Catherine, I don't know who else to talk to about this, but I'm very worried about Allison."

And the shift in my mood was immediate, seeing the fear in Lars' eyes. "Why? What has she told you, Lars?"

"That's just it, Catherine. She hasn't told me a thing. But I see more than she realizes, you know."

"I know you do, Lars. I know how much you care about her."

Lars leaned across the desk, the pink rims on his eyes looking suddenly pinker. Wet. "And you do, too, Catherine. You love her as much as I do."

I reached out and grabbed Lars' hand. "I do. You're right."

Lars took a deep breath, and leaned back again, pulling his hand away. His cheeks were crimson. "So...um...I'm sorry. I'm really not sure why I said all that, but was there anything you wanted to discuss?"

The irritation started to gurgle again, heating my face. Why did men always back away when things started to get emotional? It was maddening. "Is there something you'd like me to do, Lars? I don't even know where Allison is staying, but I would be happy to try and talk to her again."

Lars shook his head. "I don't know where she's staying either, so...no...I don't think there's anything you can do. Again, I'm sorry."

When I finally left the bank, I argued with myself about whether it was worth searching for Allison. Checking all the hotels in town would take up most of the evening, and there was no guarantee she was even staying in a hotel or using her own name. But the truth was that I wanted to get back to our hotel in case George was still there. I finally decided to ask Mrs. Tilford whether Allison had told her where she was staying.

I entered the boarding house just as they were sitting down to supper. A couple of tenants said their hellos, including Mr. Smalls. But most of them showed some discomfort at my presence, so I hurried over to Mrs. Tilford, bent down, and asked my question.

Mrs. Tilford simply shook her head, not speaking, and I swallowed hard and departed as quickly as I had come.

RO

George checked his watch, realizing that his chances of getting back to the ranch that day were slim. He had sent a letter along with the mail wagon to let them know he was ready to get back, but they would have just gotten it that afternoon. George was also surprised that Catherine hadn't returned from work yet, and he started to worry about whether Lonnie Spicer might have gotten his hands on her. George stood and started up toward his room when a voice called his name from behind. Without even turning, he recognized the voice of Preston Sanford.

"I hear you need a ride," Preston said.

"Nope...not me."

Preston raised his brow. "That's funny, because that guy there just told me you did." He tilted his head toward the clerk.

"Hm." George shrugged.

"Seems like one of you must be lying."

"Yeah, I guess it does seem that way," George agreed.

"So you don't need a ride?"

"Nope...thanks for the offer though."

"What happened to your head?"

"I cut myself shaving."

Preston chuckled, but his eyes were starting to get a little glassy, the lids slightly lowered. "You know, George...you're in a bad spot right now. You know that, don't you?"

George frowned. "How do you mean?"

Preston tugged at his dungarees, pulling them higher. "You got both sides mad at you...both sides wanting to teach you a lesson."

George nodded thoughtfully. "I'll give that some thought, Mr. Sanford."

Preston breathed in deep through his nose. "Sooner or later, a man's got to choose, George. Whether it's God or the devil, or right from wrong, or good versus evil, a man's got to figure out which side of the aisle he's sittin' on."

George nodded. He noticed that the clerk had been watching this exchange with some interest. And now he wondered why.

"How did you know where to find me, Preston?"

Preston bent low, his eyes taking on a particularly nasty glow. "You're supposed to be dead, George Arbuckle."

RØ

I hurried toward the hotel, embarrassed and humiliated by my appearance at the boarding house. Just before I got to the hotel, George emerged from the building. He stood on the porch and nervously surveyed the street.

"George!"

When he saw me, he shuffled down the stairs as fast as his injury would allow. "You're here! We need to stay somewhere else."

"Why?"

"I'll explain, but for right now, we just need to go somewhere...do you know anything about the other hotels?"

I shook my head.

"I stayed at The Deadwood Inn a couple of years ago, and it wasn't too bad."

"All right."

I went up to the room and gathered my things while George waited outside. I checked out, and we made our way down the street toward the inn.

"George, what happened?"

"What do you mean?"

"Why are you so nervous?"

"It's nothing, Catherine."

I stopped walking. I reached out and grabbed George's sleeve and pulled him toward me, twirling him around. Several passersby paused before continuing their journey.

I spoke quietly, through my teeth. "George, let me make one thing clear to you right now. I am in this with you all the way, but only if you make me one promise."

"What's that?"

"You need to tell me the truth, at all times. Do you understand that?"

George nodded.

"I don't think you do."

"Okay, tell me why you don't think I do."

"Think about it. I have no way of knowing whether you've made all of this stuff up about how you got involved in this. You could have been lying all along. But I don't think you were. You know why?"

"Why?"

I turned away. "I don't know why either." And then I looked at him. "I just believed you."

George stood quiet, and I could feel him getting anxious again, just from this brief interruption. I turned back toward him, and gently pulled his head toward me, positioning my mouth just an inch from his ear.

"You need to keep telling me the truth so I can hold on to that trust, George. That's our only hope."

"Okay, Catherine."

I pulled back. "So was it Lonnie? Did he come by again?"

George shook his head. He told me about his day, with visits from both the sheriff and from Preston Sanford, as well as his suspicions that the desk clerk might be involved.

I started walking again, and George struggled to keep up.

"George, we have got to figure out a way to get you out of this. There must be a way."

"If you help me figure that out, I promise I'll marry you, Catherine."

I laughed. "I thought you already promised that."

"I'll marry you twice then."

"You need to be careful, George. You don't want to add bigamy to your growing list of crimes."

"Good point...I guess I'll have to come up with another promise."

"You work on that while I get checked in."

"Here, let me give you some money."

I tried to protest, but he pressed a gold coin into my palm, then surprised me with a kiss on the cheek. As I went inside, I my face was burning hot.

CHAPTER 18

A POUNDING ON THE DOOR brought George from a deep sleep to a full shout, sitting up in bed. Catherine propped herself up next to him.

"What is it?" she asked.

"Who is it?" George shouted.

"Miss Boland?" a voice offered tentatively.

Catherine frowned at George. "Yes?"

"I'm so sorry to disturb you...this is the desk clerk. I have an urgent message for you."

"Coming!" Catherine threw off the blankets and wrapped herself in her dressing gown.

She opened the door just enough to accept a note, then closed it with one hand while she held the note to her face with the other. Her free hand went to her mouth, which she covered to try and muffle a sob.

"What is it?" George asked.

But she didn't speak, walking back to the bed with a stunned expression before she sank down next to him.

George watched Catherine as she questioned Pierre LeFont. He wanted to stand next to her and wrap an arm around her as she absorbed the horrible news.

"She was trying to perform a medical procedure," LeFont said for the third time.

George knew what he meant, but it was clear that Catherine was trying to think of everything but the obvious.

"What does that mean?" she asked again.

"Miss Ingram was pregnant," LeFont finally explained.

Catherine nodded, pressing her fingers to her forehead, and it was clear the message had finally gotten through. "Thank you, Sheriff. Thank you for finding me."

"Think nothing of it, Miss Boland."

LeFont tipped his hat to George, offering a look of sympathy. George gave him a nod.

The sheriff left the lobby, retreating out into the still Dakota night. "Shall we go back to bed?" George asked.

"What time is it?" Catherine asked.

George looked for a clock. "It's only three o'clock."

Catherine covered her face, and her shoulders shook. George wrapped an arm around her. "I just feel like there's something I should do," she said. "I feel like I should do something."

"But there really isn't a thing you can do," George assured her, patting her shoulder.

Catherine shook her head. "You're right." But he could see that this did nothing to relieve the pain. He could see she was hurting.

Catherine took George's face in her hands and kissed him on the forehead. "When will I see you again?" she asked.

"No idea. I'm sorry."

"I know."

"Are you gonna be okay?"

Catherine nodded. "What choice do I have?" But she was crying again. She was clearly not okay. Catherine sat down on the bed. "Just so you know, I have an answer for you."

George sat up. "You do?"

She nodded, with a sly smile. And George leaned toward her and took her in his arms.

BOOK TWO

ARBUCKLE

IN A PURE WHITE FIELD, TWO FIGURES APPEARED, like two tiny smears of chocolate on a vast cake of sugar coated frosting. The snow glittered in the early morning sunlight. The field sloped upward and away from the two figures to two small hills, behind which a herd of red Hereford cattle marched through the knee-deep powder to bury their white faces in clumps of pale green hay. A sled moved slowly through the herd, with two ranch hands in the back burying pitchforks into a mound of hay and tossing the small bundles to the snowy ground. A team of cream-colored horses struggled to haul the bucking sled through the deep snow, making trails where there were none.

Further down the incline, the Little Missouri River was frozen solid in its narrow banks, covered with snow, like a white snake winding through parallel trails of bare black trees.

Following the river another two hundred yards, a small cluster of buildings sat nestled in a shelter belt, surrounded by a few cottonwood trees. This was the Montana branch of the Three V Ranch, where George Arbuckle was now the foreman. Where he and Catherine had now lived for three years.

Back down the hill, a closer look at the two smears of chocolate revealed that the smaller of the two was making the same motion over and over again, unfolding and then whipping forward with the force of released tension. Closer still, and the larger figure turned out to be a horse, standing patiently to one side, tossing its head, pawing the snow for grass. Thirty feet from the horse, George Arbuckle swung his axe, breaking through ice to a hidden pond. Although it was twenty degrees below zero, the chopping motion warmed his body. But his face hurt, and each breath burned his lungs like an icy flame and echoed in his ears in the silence. Moisture gathered on his upper lip.

George retrieved his shovel, cleared more snow, then went back to chopping. A half an hour later, he studied the size of the hole, stuck his thumb and forefinger in his mouth, and emitted a shrill whistle. He waded back to Puck, mounted, and pushed up the knoll, moving to the outside of the herd to help the two other hands move the cattle toward the pond.

The cattle were confused, hesitant to leave their food, but the cowboys whooped and pushed their horses close enough to almost bump into the cows. George was always amused at how quickly cattle forgot the routine, even after going through the same thing day after day for weeks.

"Watch that one over there." George pointed to a cow who was straying away from the herd, and one of the hands plowed after her.

A cloud of cow breath hovered above the blanket of red coats, but it seemed as if it was even too cold for the cattle to talk, as few expressed their complaints out loud. But they did stop from time to time to stare at the sled, where the two hands were still pitching hay onto the snowy blanket. And they looked at George or one of the other hands, their expressions questioning.

Why waste all that good food?

The cowhands punched their heels into the horse's flanks, flapping their hands against their thighs, but the shouts were scarce. The act of yelling hurt their frozen throats, their lungs.

Once the first few cattle figured out where they were going, the momentum shifted. The cattle trundled down the hill like a red wave, and the cowboys were able to relax and watch. The weight of the herd broke through the ice, creating a bigger hole, and George was grateful for a shallow pond.

"All right, boys...let's go get some breakfast," he shouted, feeling the air like a hot poker down his throat.

RO

Four hands plus George and I sat up to a round oak table, where I had placed plates piled with scrambled eggs, biscuits, and white gravy.

"How cold is it out there?" I asked.

"Cold enough to freeze your tongue in your mouth," one of the hands said. The others laughed.

"I think it's about fifteen below," George said, and I smiled.

"My exacting husband," I offered.

As the hands dug into their breakfast, I turned around in my chair and spooned from a small bowl of overcooked bananas, dipping the spoon into the open mouth of George, Jr., our one-year-old baby. With the help of the other hands, George had built the two-room cabin where we lived so we could move out to the Little Missouri branch of the Three V. We were now across the border in Montana, but just barely. South Dakota was ten miles directly east of our house, and Wyoming was about the same distance to the south. We couldn't have been much more crowded into the corner of our state.

"Today we need to get out there and look for missing cattle," George announced. A couple of small groans sounded.

"I know...it's going to be cold. It's going to be a long day," George added.

He dictated which hands he wanted to go out together, in pairs, and which pastures they should search. The men nodded as they chewed, asked few questions, and finished their breakfast in a silent recognition that they would need every ounce of energy to get through the day of brittle cold. They were a good crew—young but hard-working, and mostly well-behaved as long as they were on the ranch. Their trips to town were another story. But that day, I was more focused on my husband. He seemed to be distracted, and I knew why.

Fifteen minutes later, the men departed, and George pulled his boots on, preparing to join them.

"George, is something bothering you?"

George looked up, surprised. "No, I'm fine. Why?"

I continued clearing dishes, but I kept my eye on him. "You seem distracted."

"Well, Catherine, this a bad storm, you know...a lot to think about."

I nodded. "Yeah, I know. But you've been through this before...something's different."

George shook his head. "I don't think so." He pulled his coat on. Tugged on his hat.

I approached, drying a plate with a dishtowel. "George, did you read the paper we got last night?"

George sighed. "Of course I did...you know I always do."

"Does that have anything to do with your mood?"

George stopped what he was doing. "Catherine, please...I need to get going."

"George, please don't go through this alone again. Talk to me this time."

"Okay. I promise."

My shoulders sagged, but I also knew that he couldn't take the time to have this conversation. And he said as much.

"We'll talk more about it tonight."

"Fine." And I went back to my dishes.

I heard a heavy sigh as he left, and a cold blast blew through the room as he swung the door shut.

The article reported that Preston Sanford had been spotted in the Black Hills. It was now three years since Preston Sanford disappeared, after George reported him to Sheriff LeFont. But before he vanished, Sanford had made it clear to anyone within earshot that he would kill George Arbuckle at the first opportunity. George and I had discussed that this was the risk we were taking by turning Preston in. We knew even when we made the decision that it was only a temporary solution. We knew that even if Preston didn't come after him, George would always be in danger. Although the vigilante activity had died since Sanford's disappearance, we knew that it could heat up again at a moment's notice if Sanford came back. We didn't even have to talk about it. But it scared me to death, sometimes waking me up at night when I heard a noise outside.

I finished the dishes, taking a deep breath. The last three years had been the best of my life. Being married, becoming a mother, and the two of us in charge of his little corner of the Three V. All of this had exceeded our expectations. And we had hoped it would continue this way, without interruption. We felt like we were on our way to our dream of owning our own little place.

Once I had finished cleaning up from breakfast, I put little George down for a nap, and set up the cream separator. The wind sounded as if it was going to come right through the walls, and there were even a few places where it was coming through. I had done my best to patch these cracks, but every few days another would appear, like house flies.

Once I finished separating the cream, I set about churning some butter. I had just finished pouring the cream into the churn when little George began to fuss, so I got up and plucked him from his crib.

"What's the matter, little man? Did you think you were all alone?" I tucked a knuckle into his mouth.

George pushed his fists into his eyes, then opened them up and continued rubbing with the backs of his hands. I bounced him on my hip for a while as I finished setting up the churn. Then I set him up on the floor with his favorite toys...building blocks that were a gift from a neighbor.

I set up my chair at the best angle and began pumping the handle on the butter churn. I sang as I churned, the early strains of "I Dream of Jeannie" drifting through the drafty house.

George started crying, and I looked over to see that he was just upset about his blocks tipping over. "It's okay, baby...just stack them up again," I called to him.

George cried for a bit longer, then seemed to decide I was right, picking up a block, chewing on it for a few seconds, then carefully placing it on top of another. He formed a V with his fingers and picked up another block, studied it, and bent low, carefully positioning it on top of the second.

I smiled and went back to my song. I could feel the cream beginning to thicken. When I got to the chorus, I closed my eyes and felt the music flow through me. I was so absorbed in the moment that when a hand came to rest on my shoulder, my first thought was that George had come back to talk...that he had second thoughts about leaving in the middle of our conversation.

But I quickly realized that something was wrong. There was something rough and angry about the way the hand touched me. And then another hand covered my mouth, and I tried to scream, but the hand pressed hard against my face—so hard that it felt as if my teeth were digging into the inside of my mouth. I smelled angry sweat, and horrible breath passed along my neck and up my nose.

I heard Junior scream and tried to tell him it was going to be okay, but all I could do was mumble into the rough, stinking hand. An arm surrounded my torso, and I felt myself being lifted off the chair. I started kicking, and the grip around my mouth became tighter. I tasted blood. I kept fighting, but this man's strength felt like a force greater than anything I'd ever imagined, fueled by something more than his physical being. It felt as if the anger inside him jerked me in the direction of the back of the house. He walked in a slow, steady rhythm, holding me so tightly around the chest that I was afraid he was breaking my ribs. The taste of blood made me nauseous, and as it began to flow more quickly, I coughed. I couldn't breathe. My efforts to fight melted away the more his force overtook my entire body.

He pushed me onto the bed, falling on me from behind, still holding my mouth, and I felt a hand slide up under my dress. I screamed louder, and thought I heard the scream ringing in my ears, but realized it was little George. I felt that rough, stinking angry hand push up between my legs, and inside me, which felt as if a fire had ignited inside me, and it was then that I bit him, clamping down as hard as I could on the meat of his palm.

That was the last thing I remember.

RO

George could barely feel his face as he rode toward the barn. They had found several cattle trapped in a coulee, where the cattle had run into a fence and been buried by a drift. It took three of them all day to extract these cows, which were miraculously still alive, and George couldn't remember being so stiff and sore. He combed and fed and watered Puck, then walked stiffly toward the house. Dusk was dropping slowly across the horizon, bringing a blue tint to the snow.

When George entered, there was a strange feeling about everything inside the house. It was freezing. He didn't smell any food cooking. And it was almost completely dark. The lantern had gone out, and as he made his way toward the bed, he saw only a slight glow from the fireplace.

He called Catherine's name, and heard a knocking sound in the corner near the bed. He called her name again, with more urgency, and the first thing he saw when his eyes adjusted was little George at the foot of the bed, pounding a block against the floor. And there, lying on the bed...Catherine, a dark stain coloring the quilt around her head. George rushed to the bed, throwing himself next to her. The motion woke her, and her eyes slowly opened.

"George?"

George cradled her head in his hand. "Catherine, what happened?"

"Someone was here. Somebody..."

"Shhhh..." George put a finger to her mouth. "Okay. Maybe it would be better if you didn't talk." George got up and lit the lantern and carried it over so he could get a better look at her. And an anger started burning in his throat.

He held the lantern close and studied her head. He found a small cut just above her brow, but other than that, there didn't seem to be any other open wounds. But there was a large bruise that covered one side of her face. Her dress was bunched up over her waist, and her underclothes gathered around her ankles.

"Who did this?" George said through clenched teeth.

"I don't know, George. I never saw his face."

George's first thought, his instinctive reaction, was that whoever attacked his wife would have left tracks. He rushed outside, not even bothering to don a coat, and he rounded the house. But of course, there were tracks everywhere, going in every direction. There was no way of telling the intruders from his, or any of the countless other trails. The house was surrounded by trails leading out and coming in, like spokes in a wheel. George roared into the cold air, then rushed back inside when he felt the cold like a wet blanket inside his clothes.

In the bedroom, Catherine was sitting up. She had straightened her clothes.

"Lie down, sweetheart," George said.

"I need to get supper ready...the boys will be here any minute."

"I'll take care of supper. You need to rest...you took a hard blow to the head."

"I'm okay." Catherine stood, with her hand resting on the mattress.

"Catherine, lie down!" The words exploded from George's mouth, and they sent Catherine reeling back onto the bed. Little George started crying.

Catherine looked up at him with horror. "George, do *not* yell at me."

"I'm sorry...don't we need to get a doctor?"

She shook her head. "No...I'm fine, George. I'm not hurt that bad."

"But you were out cold...how long were you lying there?"

Catherine looked at him, and George knew it was no use trying to convince her. She had made up her mind.

George went to the other side of the room, his mind bounding from one thought to another. Was it possible that Preston Sanford had already made his way to their home, and put his plan for revenge into motion? Or was this some random act, someone who just came out of nowhere, in the middle of the worst blizzard in five years?

George donned his coat and went out to the meat locker, where he found some steaks.

Back inside, Catherine was at the stove. She had cleaned the blood from her head and fixed her hair.

"What are these hands going to think when they see you like that?" George asked.

Catherine turned. "Do you want me to hide until it's better? Do you realize how long it's going to take for this to heal?"

George unwrapped the steaks, then realized they were still frozen. "These steaks aren't going to be thawed in time...what else can we make?"

"There's some leftover chicken out there...bring that in and I'll make something with that and these potatoes."

George rewrapped the steaks and took them out to the meat locker, where he found the chicken. He brought it back inside. Two of the hands followed him in. Catherine greeted them, keeping her back to them as they made their way to the table.

"Supper's going to be a little late, boys, so make yourselves comfortable," George said.

The men talked about the long day, laughing with the relief of having it over and done with. The other hands drifted in, and George repeated the announcement about a late supper as they passed by the stove. Catherine fried the potatoes and mixed them with some vegetables and chicken. She made gravy and mixed it all together while George boiled some peas and mashed them up for little George. Loud laughter and jibes continued to echo from the dining table, until Catherine brought the chicken dish over to the men.

The silence that followed was abrupt and absolute. But only for a moment. It was then filled by the sounds of discomfort—coughing, the click of silverware, loud yawns, and one man blowing his nose. Anything but conversation.

George sat up to the table and thought about whether there was any way of addressing the matter. He thought about asking whether any of them had seen anyone, but the possibility that the attacker might be among them eliminated that idea. He thought about telling them the truth, then studying them all for any signs of guilt. But he didn't think Catherine would appreciate that.

"Mrs. Arbuckle had an unfortunate spill going out to gather the eggs this morning," he finally announced.

He could feel the heat of Catherine's glare as the men offered their concern and condolences.

"So are we just going to pretend that nothing happened?" Catherine asked.

George peeled off his dungarees and his shirt. He adjusted his union suit and tucked his legs under the covers. The quilt was still discolored, despite their efforts to clean out the blood. Little George cooed from his crib, sucking on a knotted dishrag.

"What do you suggest?" George asked. "You want to put an article in the paper?"

"Yes. Maybe it would keep him from doing it to someone else."

"I'm not having it advertised that my wife got attacked by some stranger." George rolled onto his side, away from Catherine.

"George Arbuckle, you better not turn your back on me. Are you saying that you're ashamed of me?"

George turned his head, looking at her from the sides of his eyes. "Of course not, Catherine. Why would I be?"

"That's what I'd like to know. Why would you be embarrassed about having this in the newspaper?"

George rolled over and rose to one elbow. "Catherine, you know how people talk."

She nodded. "Yes, I do know. And I'm counting on that. The more people talk, the more chance of somebody hearing something. The better chance of making this guy so uncomfortable that he leaves the area or says something to the wrong person."

"And if he doesn't?"

"If he doesn't, then at least we tried."

"No."

"George, what are you saying?"

George sat up straight. "Do you really want everyone to know that this happened?"

"Yes....yes, I do. I did nothing to cause this. Is that what you're worried about?"

George closed his eyes.

"It is, isn't it? People are going to say what they say, George. That's not our problem."

"Yeah, well...I guess I don't see it that way."

George didn't see the slap coming, and he certainly didn't expect it, so when Catherine's palm met his cheek, he let out a yelp. And little George started to scream the instant the slap echoed through the bedroom.

"Good god, Catherine. What was that for?"

But she was out of the bed, and she huddled crying on the other side of the room. George sighed, wondering what could possibly be wrong with him to hurt the woman he loved right after she'd gone through something so horrible. He rolled off the bed, took a deep breath, and picked up his crying son.

CHAPTER 20

GEORGE BENT DOWN FROM HIS HORSE to open the mailbox, and once he dug inside and retrieved the mail, he realized the day had arrived. The headline of the *Ekalaka Eagle* stared him dead in the face.

LOCAL WOMAN ATTACKED IN HER HOME

George tied Puck up to the rail, went inside, and held the paper out to Catherine, who was feeding little George from a bottle. She reached for the paper, and quickly read the article. Then she set the paper to one side and went back to cooing into little George's ear.

"At least they got the facts right," she finally said.

"Yeah, that's a nice change," George echoed. "Did you sleep any better last night?"

Catherine shook her head.

"I didn't think so...you seemed restless."

"So were you."

George sighed, retreating to the kitchen.

"Can you bring me more milk?" Catherine called.

"Hungry kid, huh?"

"He is."

"Should I warm it up first?"

"Yes, please."

George placed a pan on the woodstove and filled it with a small glass of milk. He retrieved the bottle from Catherine while it was heating, and little George immediately started wailing.

"One second, little boy," Catherine assured him. "You're so impatient! Just like your mother."

George filled the bottle with warm milk and returned it to his wife.

"How was it out there?" she asked.

"Muddy. Most of the snow is melted."

"The stock will like that."

"As long as they don't get bogged down in it."

"Well I'm sure you'll rescue them if they do."

George paused. Was there a hint of accusation in her tone? Lately it had become almost impossible for him to distinguish between perception and reality. He tried to talk himself out of responding, but it felt as if he was rolling downhill, and that there was no way of reversing direction, despite knowing exactly what he was about to crash into.

"What did you mean by that?"

Catherine looked up, frowning. "What?"

"What you just said, about rescuing the cattle. What did you mean?"

Catherine rolled her eyes. "George, please..."

"No, Catherine...I don't think it was an accident."

"Really." She stated this, without a hint of question in her voice. "You honestly think I sit here all day and try and think of things I can say to you that will remind you of what happened?"

"No, that's not what I said."

"No, it's not, but that's what you seem to believe. Every day it's something else."

"Well I don't think you plan it, but I do think that these things come out for a reason. They don't come out of nowhere."

On the one hand, George wished he could just stop it all right there, and not say another word. But he knew...knew....that the hill was just getting steeper, that they were now rolling too fast. That the incline had to be followed right down to the inevitable crash.

But Catherine just looked at him and shook her head. She started to say more, but stopped herself, and waved a hand at him with a dismissive motion.

"What?" George asked.

"I don't think that's the right question, George. It should be 'why'? Why are you doing this? Why are you using this to push me away?"

"I'm not." George could feel how unconvincing this statement was even as he said it. Catherine just shook her head, emitting a dismissive puff of air through her nose.

RO

"You guys warm enough back there?" George turned from the front bench of the wagon, yelling to their neighbors Gary and Jenny Glasser.

"We're fine," Jenny answered.

"Nice and bundled up," Gary added.

I shivered next to my husband, hoping that his suddenly cheerful outlook on life was a good sign. Ever since I had been raped, George had been unbearable, acting as if he himself was the victim. I always knew that George had his limitations. But this was the first time in our marriage that I started wondering whether I'd made a mistake.

I tugged at the canvas, trying to adjust it to cover my legs.

"Do you know who is going to play Santa this year?" I asked.

"I haven't heard," George said. "But I'm getting to the point where I could almost audition for the part." He patted his stomach.

Gary and Jenny laughed, and I smiled. Gary and Jenny had been the first to contact me after the news broke. And so far, the only ones. But I had been amazed how much it touched me to have one house along the Little Missouri River extend a comforting hand.

George steered the team off the main road, toward the cluster of wagons and horses gathered around the Albion Town Hall.

The four of us stepped down from the wagon, into a few inches of fresh snow, which was still falling in a slow, lazy slant.

I was nervous. This was the first time we had attended a public gathering since the article came out. As much as I felt as if it didn't matter who approved, I also knew that people could be unpredictable. And cruel. I had tried to talk to George about it, and of course he pointed out that he warned me.

I held little George in a tight bundle of blankets in one arm as we approached the hall. In the other arm, I held a still-warm mincemeat pie. George helped me down from the wagon, taking the pie, and the five of us made our way toward the hall.

The moment we entered, the entire hall went silent. It was the worst thing I could have possibly imagined. But I walked right in, and Gary and Jenny followed behind. George eventually caught up to us, but his head was bowed, his stride more of a shuffle. I held my head steady and high, but I felt the sting of tears dancing along the inside of my eyelids. I held them inside, without a blink, and walked directly to the kitchen, where I set down the pie and greeted the people I knew. Most of them responded, but the greetings were muted.

Only one person approached with the obvious purpose of doing so, and I nearly burst into tears when Lars Larson took my hand in both of his and held it tightly.

"I'm so happy to see you," Lars said. He didn't even have to say what else he meant, because I saw it in his eyes. The expression of sorrow. We had shared this feeling ever since the day Allison was found alone in her hotel room, and I felt it more than ever on this night.

"How are you, Lars?"

"I'm good. Still trying to find three people that can do as much work as you did."

I slapped his upper arm. "Oh, you always exaggerate."

"I really don't." He still held my hand and reached up with his other to offer little George a finger. "My goodness, look how big you're getting!"

"But what are you doing way out here?" I asked.

Before Lars could answer, a voice said, "Hello Lars."

I turned to see George standing just behind my shoulder.

"George, how are you doing?" Lars showed a genuine affection in his greeting.

"I'm all right...working hard to keep my cows alive."

"That's a full-time job." Lars bowed his head. "I know Mr. Hardin speaks very highly of how well things have been going since you took over out here."

George nodded, and his eyes lit up. "That's good to hear," he said.

For the three years I had been married to George, I had always taken pride in his abilities as a rancher...everyone who knew him was aware of his work ethic, and his feel for livestock.

But on this night, I was irritated. Because I knew that it was where he escaped when he didn't want to deal with what was happening in his own home. There was always something that needed to be done on the ranch. Always something important.

"Well I best get back to my little lady before she thinks I've deserted her." Lars gripped my hand again.

"Little lady?" My voice rose. "Now I know what brought you out here. Who is it?"

"You'll see," Lars said, winking.

My heart was still buoyed by this exchange when my husband turned away. This small gesture pierced my heart, and I felt like throwing a fork at him. I looked around and realized that Gary and Jenny were also out of my sight, and for a brief moment, I felt utterly alone.

So I quickly turned my attention to George, Jr., who was wiggling to get down from my grasp. He pointed at the floor. "You want down?" I eased him to the floor, and tried to hold his hand, but he broke away and started wobbling across the kitchen. I kept an eye on him, knowing he'd probably topple.

I was both pleased and annoyed that little George seemed to have a destination. He was weaving his way through the various legs and skirts straight toward his father. I followed and offered to help him when he fell. I reached out a hand, but he shook his head. On his feet again, George Jr. tottered onward, palms forward, toes out, knees rising marionette style. And once he reached his father, George bent down and picked him up. George was talking to one of our nearest neighbors, a man I didn't know all that well. I slid up next to George and was shocked when the man turned on his heel and walked away.

"What was that?" I asked.

George simply looked at me.

I was relieved when someone announced that they were just about to start the Christmas program. Everyone shuffled toward the stage, where chairs were lined up in neat rows. We found seats near the middle, and it soon became apparent that nobody wanted to sit near us. Just as I was starting to think about how ridiculous people were acting, someone eased into the seat next to me. I turned, pleased to come face to face with a head of snow white hair.

"Lars! Long time no see," I said.

Lars laughed and leaned back a little. "This is Addie, Catherine. Addie, my best employee ever, Catherine Boland. Oh, I'm sorry...Arbuckle."

"So nice to meet you, Catherine." Addie shook my hand. "Lars talks about you all the time. He has been wondering whether he'll ever find another teller as good as you were."

I was trying to listen to what this poor girl was saying, but I could hardly think, looking at Addie. The resemblance to Allison was astonishing. "Thank you," I finally muttered. "I'm so happy to meet you. And this is George, and George Jr."

The greetings were exchanged just about the time the teacher at the one room school got up to ask us all to quiet down. For the next hour, I sat and tried to enjoy the program, laughing at how cute the kids were as they acted out the nativity scene, and singing along with the rest of the crowd when Zelda Barnes played Christmas carols. But I couldn't shake the growing feeling that the way my people were treating me went against everything we were watching and singing about. As much as the spirit of Christmas seemed to be alive and well in our little town hall, it extended only to those that the collective conscience considered deserving.

I found comfort in the presence of Lars next to me, and in the obvious enjoyment he was getting from his friend. They appeared to be very much in love, but I still felt a little uneasy about this woman's resemblance to Allison. I was surprised I'd never seen her before, all of which made me eager to find out more about her.

When the big finale arrived, and everyone sang "Silent Night" in full but somber voice, I teared up. And for the first time since the rape, I did feel a sense of heavenly peace.

After the program, everyone gathered to eat, and I stuck close to Lars until we found a table. I didn't even pay attention to whether George was following but was pleased when he plunked his plate down next to me.

"So where do you live, Addie?" I asked.

"Oh, I live in Deadwood, but my parents are out here, so we're here for the holidays. The Heaths?"

"Of course." I nodded. "I know them a little. I didn't know about you, though. I mean, I didn't know they had a daughter."

Addie became clearly uncomfortable. But did that stop me? No, I just plowed ahead, oblivious.

"Do you have a job in Deadwood?"

"No she doesn't," Lars jumped in. "She's...she's only been there a short time."

"Oh, well...I'm sure you'll find something soon," I said.

Both Lars and Addie nodded, but I felt as if I had lost them already. I wondered why Lars didn't hire her. Putting my foot in my mouth again. I looked at George, who was completely consumed by his food. No help there.

"Catherine..." Lars lowered his voice. "Is there anything I can do?"

My heart warmed. Finally. Someone made reference to what happened. And not in a negative way. "Thank you, Lars. I'm actually doing all right."

"Well let me know if there's anything we can do."

"I will...thank you again."

Addie went to get some more food, and I leaned closer to Lars. "Where did you meet her?"

Lars' ruddy face turned such a bright red that I immediately, again, realized... "Promise you won't tell anyone."

"Of course, Lars."

He raised a brow. "She worked at the Gem."

"Oh god...I'm sorry." I felt my cheeks flush. "I'm so nosey."

"It's okay....I don't mind you knowing. But..."

"Of course, Lars...no, of course." Now it all made sense. "I'm sure she's happy to be free from there."

Lars nodded. "She is."

And now I wondered...how different was my own reaction to this information from the reactions I was getting? Who was the hypocrite here?

"Lars...why haven't you hired her at the bank? She seems bright."

Lars lifted his brow. "Are you serious?"

"Of course...why not?"

"Catherine, honestly..."

"They'd get over it," I said. "Besides, what could happen? There's only two banks in town. Not everyone is going to switch."

"Oh, you're much too generous about how people can be."

"Maybe not." I raised my brow.

"I wish I could be as brave as you are," Lars said.

"No you don't." This statement from behind stunned me. I didn't think my husband was even listening to the conversation.

I was holding my fork in one hand, preparing to shovel another helping of potato into little George's mouth, and the thoughts that went through my head prompted me to stand up, carefully place the fork on the table, and announce, "I'll be back."

George Jr. immediately started crying, and I just about turned around. But I decided George could take care of the situation just this once. He'd earned it.

I avoided my husband for the rest of the evening, not trusting myself to remain civil. And it felt awful. I hated this distance, especially when I was feeling like an outcast already. I clung to my son and stayed close to Lars and Addie when they weren't occupied. Finally, I found Gary and Jenny and sat with them, not sure what to expect.

"Are you folks having a good time?" I asked.

"Wonderful," Gary answered, smiling broadly.

"We really are," Jenny added.

"Oh good," I said. "The food is really good this year."

Gary cradled his stomach. "I'm stuffed."

Jenny patted her own and nodded her agreement. "I had two pieces of your pie," she confessed.

"Oh, now that's loyalty!" I clapped my hands together.

Jenny patted my arm. Gary seemed distracted, looking the other way. I was embarrassed at how this tiny show of support affected me. I thought about the old saying of knowing who your true friends are. And I wondered whether I needed to think about reaching out to people.

Maybe the reason so few people were behind me was because I'd been a little too busy thinking about my own life.

"Well, I'm about ready for some dancing," Gary announced. "Catherine, would you do me the honor." He stood and extended a hand.

I felt a sob bubble up in my throat, but I swallowed it and extended my hand. "I'd be delighted."

CHAPTER 21

GEORGE WOKE UP EARLY AGAIN. He sat on the edge of the bed, scratching his neck, his head, his abdomen. Catherine rolled over, her eyes blinking wide.

"What time is it?" she asked.

"Go back to sleep."

She rolled away.

George got up and tugged on some clothes. He poked at the cinders in the fireplace and stacked some kindling, then added a log. He struck a match and ignited the fire, holding his hands toward the flame.

He heard the shuffling of feet behind him and knew that Catherine had not been able to get back to sleep either. It was 3:30.

"Do you want me to make some coffee?" he asked.

She started coughing. And then he realized she was vomiting. George frowned. His muscles tightened.

"I don't think I'd like coffee, thanks," Catherine finally answered.

"Are you okay?" he asked.

Catherine appeared in the bedroom door. She looked at George with a pleading expression. He stood and came to her and wrapped his arms around her and pulled her to him.

"George Arbuckle, you are the most stubborn man I've ever met."

"I know."

"What are we going to do?"

"What do you mean?"

Catherine leaned back and looked up at him. "What if this is..."

"It don't matter." George went to the stove, where he dumped some coffee grounds into a pot, filled it with water, and went about lighting the woodstove.

"You can say that now, George...here, alone in our little house with no one around. But what about later? When the truth becomes clear. And maybe people start talking again. What about then?"

George poked at the fire. She was right, of course. And the whole subject reached in and scratched at one of those wordless parts of him, where he couldn't imagine what to say. "Well, what do you want me to say? I ain't about to see you go through what your friend did."

He looked at her, expecting quick anger. But she just gazed at him with an expression that he couldn't quite read. She wasn't angry, but she wasn't about to rush over and give him a hug either.

"Do you realize, George, that this is the first time you've even come close to mentioning Allison's name since she died?"

"Yeah, well...it's not the most pleasant topic."

"Is that what she's been reduced to? An unpleasant topic?"

George sighed. This was just the kind of discussion he hated. He knew he'd said something wrong, although he wasn't quite sure what was wrong about it. But sometimes he could just feel it even as the words left his mouth. And now they were going to talk about why it was wrong, and even after they talked about it, he still wouldn't understand. But he'd know even more than before just how wrong he was. It was a never-ending education that always seemed to lead to him feeling like a failure as a husband.

"You know that's not what I meant. I just meant the way..."

"You need to be careful about how you say things, George. You can't expect people to do your thinking for you."

"I don't expect that, and you know it, Catherine."

"Well, when you say you didn't mean it that way, that's what you're implying."

"Okay...yes, whatever you say. I should think more before I speak."

"George, don't just agree with me to keep me from talking. You know how much I hate that."

"Oh no, I would never do that. Because I can't wait to hear the next chapter of what George can't do right."

"Well now you're just being childish." Catherine turned away and went to the waste can, where she promptly vomited again.

George sighed. "Are you okay?"

Catherine stood up, wiped her mouth with the back of her hand, and planted her fists firmly on her hips. "No, George Arbuckle, I am not okay. I am pregnant, probably with the child of a man who raped me, and my husband can't talk to me without acting like a complete ass!" And she stalked off to the bedroom, where he heard her flop onto the bed.

RO

I walked along the streets of Belle Fourche, toward the market. I was just beginning to feel the full effects of my condition. The morning sickness had ended, but the bloat, the swollen ankles, the heaviness in my midsection, all made movement awkward. I seemed to feel it more than I had with little George.

I thought about the life forming inside me. Although it was impossible to know who the father was, I just had a feeling. In that instinctive way that I'd heard other women talk about, I suspected the worst. And it made me sick again.

As I dug into my bag for the list of things I needed, a familiar voice spoke my name. I looked up. "Mr. Smalls! How are you?"

Donald Smalls did not smile. He stood straight, with his hands tucked behind his back. "I'm doing well, Catherine."

"I'm so happy to hear that. What are you doing in Belle Fourche?"

"I recently moved here. I have taken on a congregation in the area."

"That's very exciting, Mr. Smalls. Or should I call you Pastor Smalls?"

"Not only can you call me that, but you might consider giving us a visit. You could probably benefit from what we have to offer, from what I've heard, Catherine."

I felt my face completely transform. "Good day, Mr. Smalls. I wish you the best."

Although I walked away with as much confidence as I could muster, the tears leaked from the sides of my eyes. I couldn't believe I was crying again. I couldn't remember a time when I'd shed so many tears. I entered the market and tried to wipe my cheeks as discretely as possible. The clerk offered a cheery greeting, which I returned with as much enthusiasm as I could muster.

"What can I help you with today, ma'am?"

I started to run through my list, pointing out items, checking for quality, figuring the cost in my head. I became absorbed in the task, in the feel and smells. The heft of the bag of sugar, and the aroma of coffee. I had forgotten how pregnancy enhanced the sense of smell, how every odor seemed to be stronger, sometimes overwhelming. I unscrewed a bottle of vinegar and just about passed out when I put my nose to the opening. But it also got me thinking about all the things I wanted to can, and I couldn't wait for spring.

Once they gathered everything I needed, I had the items boxed up and deposited on the sidewalk, where George would pick me up once he was finished with his own errands.

Just as I settled on the bench outside the market, I heard yelling from down the street and leaned out to get a better look. About twenty yards down the way, Donald Smalls had set up a wooden box, and was standing on it, shouting his lungs out and holding a bible aloft. I thought I had put the previous incident behind me, but the sight of him brought my anger to the surface.

I rummaged through the groceries, looking for something to snack on while I waited, trying to ignore the preaching. But each time a word like 'sinners' or 'fornicators' or 'adulterers' echoed across the short distance between us, my shoulders rose a little higher. I felt the tension in my neck. I nibbled on a peppermint stick, making a conscious effort to block out the noise.

The turning point came when Donald Smalls shouted out in a clear and deliberate voice, "...and as that great prayer tells us, 'lead us not into temptation.' We must not give in to the temptations that the devil deposits in our path. And by the same token, we must not present those temptations to others..."

I turned, and saw that Donald was looking directly at me. I stood, marched over to the small crowd that had gathered, and planted myself a few feet from his perch.

"Brothers and Sisters, it is never too late to find the peace and comfort that Jesus made available to us by dying for our sins. Even those who have fallen the furthest, those who have followed the path of evil, can find forgiveness in the eyes of the Lord if they only ask..."

I found it interesting that he could look at me directly from a distance, but now that I stood in front of him, Smalls was unable to even acknowledge me. He spoke above my head.

"So can you tell us, Mr. Smalls, what it is that we need to do to gain God's favor?"

"Why certainly, young lady..." Smalls still made no effort to meet my eye as he jumped at the opportunity to continue his sermon. "...in the bible it tells us that if we surrender our hearts to the Lord, he will lead us through all things...he will forgive us all things..."

"And how do we surrender our hearts to Him, Mr. Smalls...how do we go about doing that?"

"All you have to do is bow down and allow me to anoint you with the oils of purity..."

"So in other words, I have to surrender to you, Mr. Smalls...not to the Lord."

"Well, in a sense, miss...but I am only an instrument of his love...you are not surrendering to me..."

"But I am bowing down before you, am I not?"

"Well..." Smalls cleared his throat.

"And how much does this cost me, Mr. Smalls?"

"The Lord will forgive you even the most reprehensible of sins if you simply ask."

"How much do I give up of my pride, my sense of dignity, of honor, Mr. Smalls, in order to be worthy of being anointed by someone like you?"

"Catherine!"

I heard the familiar voice from behind. George was sitting in our wagon, his expression pained.

"How much?" I asked again.

"You can't afford it, Mrs. Arbuckle," Smalls said.

I burst forward, plowing directly into Donald Smalls' knees. Smalls fell over backward, his feet flying into the air and he landed with a thump.

"Catherine!" Now George was shouting. "Come here!"

RO

George flicked the reins of the wagon with extra vigor, causing the team to toss their heads and voice their protests. "What in the world has gotten into you?" George asked.

Catherine was still stewing, her jaw set. She held George Jr. in her lap, bouncing him nervously on her knees. "Do you honestly have to ask that question, George?"

"I wouldn'ta brought it up if I knew the answer."

"George, do you have any idea what's going on here?"

George sighed. "I don't know what you mean."

"Think about it, George. These people...people we thought were our friends....are turning their backs on us."

"Yeah...I do know that."

"And you just expect me to take it, is that it?"

"Well it was a choice you made." George could barely open his mouth, his teeth were clenched so tightly.

"This is what it's going to come down to, isn't it, George? You're going to punish me for that forever, aren't you?"

George wondered what he should do. He could not deny that he wished Catherine had never decided to go public with what happened. Especially considering it had done nothing for the case. The sheriff hadn't even bothered to investigate. The attacker hadn't been found. There didn't appear to be any advantages to the decision at all. So how could he justify all that had come with it? He hadn't even told Catherine about all the comments he'd heard since the article came out. Or about how people looked at him. George couldn't help it...he was angry that this was happening to them.

"George, are you going to talk to me?"

"I don't know what to say, Catherine."

"So you *are* punishing me."

"No...that's not what I mean."

"But you're still angry...you think I brought this on."

George clamped down. Nothing he said could possibly help. For either of them.

I EASED ANOTHER LOG into the fireplace, then repositioned the screen blocking the fire from little hands and feet. George Jr. crawled after me as I went back to the stove, where a lamb stew bubbled in the pot. I picked up a wooden spoon and stirred, holding the spoon to my nose, then my mouth. I sipped, then heard a sound just outside the door.

I rushed to the other side of the room, where I picked up a rifle leaning against the wall, held it to my shoulder, and charged toward the door. I stood at the side window and peered outside, the rifle at the ready. Little George tried to keep up with me as I checked each window.

"You've got to stop this," I said to myself. "This isn't normal." I sat down at the dining room table and tilted my head against the barrel of the gun. "Nobody's out there," I muttered.

A half hour later, I was doing the same thing again. George Jr. had stopped trying to follow and was ripping up an old Sears catalog. I leaned the gun against the wall again and tried to focus on my chores. I still had a lot to do before the boys came back from the field.

But my mind wouldn't stop. I sat down and closed my eyes for a few minutes, resting my hands on my now-swollen belly. I was six months along, and already looked much more pregnant than that.

I tried to remember the last time I'd had a chance to talk to someone besides George or the other hired hands. Was it the day Jenny Glasser stopped by? That must have been it. That was almost two weeks ago. "No wonder I'm losing my mind," I mumbled.

I thought about the conversation that had become part of my life now. The evenings with my table surrounded by young boys. Most of our hands were either teenagers or barely in their twenties. The few exceptions, a couple of men in their thirties, were typical cowhands, men who were much more comfortable in the company of cattle or barrooms than in a family home. So the conversation around the table was usually just what you'd expect from young men stuck with each other's company day and night.

But I had come to crave the evening conversation. I immersed myself in the discussions about which cows were suffering from some kind of disease, and where they needed to put in more fence. I remembered every detail and made myself part of the conversations. I missed the atmosphere at the bank, where Lars and Allison both enjoyed talking about a variety of things, from music to politics. And because this was the closest I could come to that, I embraced it.

Allison had been on my mind a lot since I'd seen Lars and Allison's double. I missed my friend. I missed many things about that time in my life. But the best way to avoid thinking about that was to focus on the life I had now.

"Okay...you need to get supper ready," I scolded myself. "Get yourself together."

I checked the bread dough I had rolled out earlier in the day and it had risen perfectly. I folded it into a pan and tucked it into the woodstove, then stoked the fire again. I checked the stew and moved it to the edge of the stove to keep it warm.

I was just getting ready to put some carrots on the stove when a huge crash sounded from somewhere in the house. I grabbed the gun, and rushed toward the sound, rifle at the ready. I rounded the corner to the bedroom, aiming the rifle in front of me. George Jr. sat in the middle of the floor, surrounded by the broken pieces of my mother's serving dish.

I fell to my knees. I set the gun aside carefully. George was not crying. He seemed fine. No blood. But when I started sobbing, he joined me.

RO

George and the other hands rode toward the barn as a group after a long day of digging post holes. Spring was leaking out into the land in various shades of green. The Little Missouri River seemed to rise a little more each day from the runoff, and the ponds bubbled with frogs.

The calluses on George's left hand had broken a few days before, and he checked the wound, which was damn sore. It looked angry, worse than yesterday, and George was concerned it was getting infected. He would ask Catherine to put some antiseptic on it.

"Any of you boys going into town this weekend?" Several of them answered in the affirmative. "I might ask you guys to pick up a couple of things, if you don't mind."

One of the more eager hands offered to get whatever he needed, and George thanked him. Among the more pleasant benefits of his new position was the fact that, for the first time that he could remember, the men George worked with really seemed to enjoy his company. He knew without a doubt that one of the main reasons for this was his wife. She took each of these kids under her wing like they were her younger brothers, and George was sometimes amazed at how she could get them talking. It was, of course, the main reason he'd fallen in love with her to begin with.

The boys started talking about the dance coming up that Saturday night in Alzada, wondering which of the local girls would be there. It was the same conversation they had every single day, and George drifted off into his own thoughts, planning what they would do next week.

The cattle needed to be moved down from winter pasture, but they still had to finish this fence before that happened. It was later than he'd hoped to move them, but the winter had lasted much longer than usual.

But he had confidence in his crew. They could get it all done. It was a satisfying thought.

They fed and watered their horses, and George went ahead to check the mail while the crew went back to the bunkhouse to clean up for supper. There were a few pieces of mail, including a copy of the *Ekalaka Eagle*, and a letter to Catherine, and George tucked these under his arm while he checked his palm again.

Inside, George smelled the rich aroma of stew, and fresh baked bread. Catherine was just setting the table, her hair jutting out in great pink feathers. George gave her a peck on the cheek and asked how her day went.

"Fine," she said. "George broke my mother's plate, but other than that, it was fine."

"Hm." George sat down at the table and began reading the paper. There was a short article about the continued search for Preston Sanford, who was still at large. They were speculating that he'd headed south toward Texas, which George prayed was true.

The other hands entered in twos and threes, settling around the table. Catherine filled their glasses with milk, and brought out the pot of stew, setting it in the middle of the table. The men ladled stew into their bowls, and handed the fresh bread around the table, tearing off chunks.

"So who has a date to the dance Saturday?" Catherine asked, and the men all chuckled, their faces flushed. "Come on now...surely you've got some cute little lady meeting you there, don't you, Clay?"

Everyone looked to the young man next to George, a handsome kid with black hair that always looked as if it had been polished.

"Naw, Mrs. Arbuckle, I don't have a girl."

"Pshaw...I don't believe you for a second, Clay."

"He really doesn't," another added. "Not since he got drunk and threw up on that Daisy girl."

George couldn't contain his laughter, but Catherine tutted them.

"You boys...that's just not nice. I bet every single one of you has had something like that happen."

"Not like that!" another claimed.

"Well, Clay, you just have to brush yourself off and try again," Catherine said.

"Yes, ma'am." Clay could hardly look up from his plate, and George decided it was time to change the subject.

"I saw in the paper today that Bernie Sanford got married."

The mention of this name brought up more reaction than George expected. He didn't think most of these kids would even know who Bernie was. But many of them expressed a strong opinion, all negative. George asked how they knew him.

"Everyone knows Bernie Sanford," one hand said.

George couldn't miss the expression on his wife's face.

"The man is evil," she finally chimed in. "I feel sorry for that girl."

"Who is it?" one of the men asked.

When George told them the name, the reaction was just as strong. "Those two deserve each other," one man said.

The discussion moved on to other topics, but George was dismayed to realize that the mention of Bernie's name had put his wife in a sour mood. And she wondered why he never brought up Allison's name, he thought. It seemed that any reminder of that time in her life was more than Catherine could bear. And each time it happened, the foul mood would simply have to run its course. George hadn't figured out any way to bring her out of it.

So George did what he could to stay out of her way for the rest of the evening. He knew better than to try helping with the dishes or offering to make her some tea. He tucked his face in his paper, and played with little George, who was particularly fascinated by one of his mother's shoes. He kept bringing the shoe to George and holding it up to him.

George would take the shoe and study it as if he had no idea what it was or what to do with it, and little George would start jabbering in half-formed words. George would pretend that the explanation made complete sense to him, and that he finally understood. "Ah!" he'd say. "Thank you, George."

His son would laugh like he'd never heard anything so funny, then he'd totter off for a while until he came back to repeat the routine.

After Catherine put George Jr. to bed, George started to doze behind his paper, and he forced himself to his feet. On his way to the bedroom, he noticed the pile of mail.

"Oh, I forgot to tell you there's a letter for you," he called to Catherine.

"There is?" She appeared, wiping her hands on a dishtowel.

George held the envelope out, then headed off to bed. Just moments after he had undressed and buried himself in the covers, his wife entered the bedroom. She sat on the bed, and George felt her hand on his back. He rolled over, and she held the letter out to him. George sat up.

"Who's it from?"

"Just read it."

George smoothed the paper against his knee and tilted his chin forward.

Dear Mrs. Arbuckle-

I'm writing to tell you that your not alone. What happened to you happened to me to. I would rather not tell you who I am, but I think I know who did this. If you want to write to me, you can send a letter to Post Office Box 59 at Belle Fourche. I just thought you might want to know that someone else has went through this.

A friend

George looked at Catherine. She was smiling. "So that's good?"

"Yes. It is."

"Not for her," George said.

"No, not for her."

I HAD TO BE HELPED DOWN from the wagon as I was seven months into my pregnancy. George held one of my hands and wrapped his other arm around my waist. I felt as if I had a barrel strapped to my abdomen.

George led me up the sidewalk toward the Miles City Land Office.

"How you folks doing today?" a young man approached us with a broad smile and a ready handshake.

"We're doing just fine, thanks," George answered. "And we don't need your help, either."

"Well now, how do you know that, sir?"

"Because I know what you are, and we already have our plots picked out."

"All right, sir...have it your way. But I've got some fine pieces of land to offer."

"I'm sure you do," George muttered.

"George, why do you have to be so rude to the young man?" I asked. "He's just trying to do his job."

"Those guys are parasites," George muttered. "No self-respecting man would take a job like that."

Although the Homestead Act had been passed ten years earlier, it was only recently that most of the local settlers had started submitting their claims on 160 acres of land. The main reason for this was that with the range still being open, there hadn't been much benefit to owning a piece of land. What mattered more was whether you owned stock. It had also become clear to anyone who lived in the area that 160 acres was hardly enough to matter. Although it sounded like a lot of land to anyone coming from the East, 160 acres wasn't nearly enough to support a family in a country with so little water.

But now that fences were going up, people were finding ways to gather up chunks of land by filing claims for each member of their family and buying up the neighboring plots.

For months now, I had been suggesting to George that we get to Miles City and file a claim, but he always had something more important to do. The day before, I noticed a man traveling along the road with a wagonload of lumber, obviously off to build a house on his own claim, and I finally insisted that we not wait a day longer.

We entered the office and filled out the forms for two sections right along the Little Missouri River, one of which held the house where we lived. We shook hands with the clerk and got up to leave.

The minute we stepped out into the afternoon sun, I swore softly.

"What?" George asked.

I tilted my head. Lonnie Spicer was standing just a few feet away.

"Well well," Lonnie said. "How you doing, Catherine?"

I felt George's hand on my elbow.

"Excuse us," George said, leading me past Lonnie.

"Boy oh boy, if I didn't know any better, I'd say you're acting like a jealous husband, buddy."

"What do I have to be jealous about...she's with me."

"George," I warned.

"Just because you're with her doesn't mean that's your bun in the oven, though, does it?" Lonnie started laughing.

George turned, and I grabbed him by the arm. "George, no!"

But he was out of my grasp in a moment, and before I had a chance to turn my ponderous body, I heard a thump. Then another. And by the time I turned, George was lying on the ground, just as Lonnie brought his fist down with another punch, right into George's midsection.

"Lonnie, no!!" I tried to run toward the men, but even two steps in my condition brought a pain to my abdomen that pulled me up short. I realized that there was nothing I could do even if I got there. Instead I screamed for help.

By the time two young men broke up the fight, George had gotten the worst of it. While the two men held Lonnie away, I sank to my knees and studied George. A cut sliced across his forehead, and a gap appeared where he'd lost a tooth. His eyes looked scared.

"Are you okay?" I asked.

"No, not really," he muttered. "I think I lost."

I sighed. "Yeah, you did."

"I'm sorry, sweetheart."

"Well, the good news is it wasn't a contest. So you know, you really did win after all."

"Oh good."

"You found yourself quite a man there," Lonnie called out.

I checked myself from responding. I didn't even turn around. I could hear that a struggle was still going on behind us. I said a silent thank you that we'd left little George with Jenny Glasser for the day.

"Do you think you can sit up?" I took out my handkerchief and wiped blood from George's face.

The crowd began to disperse.

"I think so," George said. "God, I'm sorry...I should have just let that son-of-a-bitch talk."

"Yes you should have."

I wrapped an arm around George's shoulders, helping him rise to a seated position. "Is that okay? Are you dizzy?"

"Nah, I'm fine. Hell, it's just a few bruises." George began wiping his own face. "Goddammit, I think he broke my nose."

"You're going to look more rugged than ever."

"You think I'll look tougher?"

"Definitely."

We watched as the men dragged Lonnie Spicer down the street. He was smiling, which made me sick to my stomach.

"What did you ever see in that guy?" George asked.

I just sighed. I studied the cut above George's eyebrow. "This is kind of deep, honey. I wonder if we should find someone to sew it up."

George put a finger to the cut, flinched a little when he touched it, and said, "Naw...it don't hurt that much."

"Oh, you're such a horrible liar, George Arbuckle."

"Would you rather I was good at it?"

I smiled. "Come to think of it..."

I helped George stand, and held him around the waist. He mirrored the gesture, and we walked in a staggering embrace.

"We're a sad pair," I said.

"We really are. Should we stay at the Olive?"

"Oh George, we can't afford that."

"Well I think we should...we just became landowners, plus I just got beat up. I deserve a reward for sticking up for you."

I smiled to myself. It was rare for George to even think of spending more money than was necessary. He was a true Scotsman. "All right...why not?"

We checked into the Olive Hotel, and George cleaned himself up. The cut on his forehead looked much better once we cleaned off the blood, and other than a knob on his cheek, he didn't look too bad.

"You're sure you're feeling okay?"

George nodded. "Just a bit of bruised pride."

I turned myself sideways and wrapped my arms around George. My tummy snuggled up against his hip. "I was angry when you went after him, but that was very brave."

George snorted, grinning. "Not really."

I kissed him. "I'm not really hungry yet, George."

"No?"

I kissed him again, on the mouth.

George cleared his throat. "Honey, come on now...you don't want to..."

"Don't tell me what I want."

"But won't it hurt you, with...the baby?"

I took George's head in both hands and pulled his mouth to mine. I kissed him hard. He responded for a moment, but then pulled away. "Catherine, what's gotten into you?"

"George, come on...just relax. When are we going to have a night without the baby around again?"

I was sure that George was going to pull away again. He had that scared rabbit look. But I kept kissing him, holding him tight. I took his hand and led him to the bed. George looked at the door, as if he was worried we were going to get caught.

"George, come on now...we're married, remember?"

He laughed nervously. "Of course..."

"What are you nervous about?"

"I'm not nervous." But he was trembling. Sweat gathered along his scalp. He looked pale.

"George, do you realize how long it's been?"

George didn't respond.

"You don't want to, do you?"

"It's not that, honey...I'm just...well..."

"George!" I took his face in my hands. "Answer this question....do you realize the last time we did that?"

George looked at his feet.

"Is it because of what happened? Because you know, it's hard to think otherwise."

George sighed. "I don't know, Catherine." He tried to turn away, but I kept my hold on his face.

"George, don't run away. If we don't figure this out, it could go on like this forever. Is that what you want?"

George's blue eyes, those eyes I had fallen in love with, those steady, bright blue eyes, showed a fear that made me want to cry. I could see that he not only couldn't make love to me, but he couldn't talk about it.

I took a deep breath. "Let's go eat."

RO

The next morning, George woke up with a groan. He felt a deep pain in his crotch that almost threw him to his knees when he stood.

"What's wrong?" Catherine was sitting at the mirror, combing out her hair.

"Nothing...it's nothing." But George could barely walk.

Catherine swooped over to his side. "George, what is it? And don't say 'nothing'...I can see it in your face."

George sank back onto the bed. It felt as if his genitals had been jammed up inside him. "That son-of-a-bitch kneed me yesterday," he finally admitted.

Catherine sat next to him on the bed. She laid a hand on his knee. "Down there?"

He nodded.

"So that's why...last night?"

George looked at her.

"George Arbuckle, why on earth didn't you just tell me that, instead of letting me ask all those questions."

George didn't answer. He didn't answer because he knew that wasn't the only reason he couldn't make love to his wife. But he didn't know what it was. He didn't know what was wrong with him.

"George, I think we should have you looked at."

"No no no...I'm fine. It's just...you know, I just need to walk it off." George stood, and again the pain shot straight through his abdomen. He clenched his teeth. "I'll be fine by the time we get home."

"Oh come on, George...you can't travel like this...it will be like getting kicked over and over again."

"No really, Catherine...it's not the kind of thing that they can do anything about anyway...I just have to give it time. And riding wouldn't be any worse than sitting around. Besides, we can't leave the Glassers wondering what's happened to us."

Catherine shook her head. "I swear I've never met a more stubborn man, George. Honestly."

"Well we make a good pair then." George limped toward the basin, where he dipped his hands in the water and doused his face.

"I'd take that personally if it was true," Catherine said with a smirk. George chuckled.

Once he was up and around, George felt better. In the dining room, they ate some biscuits, then gathered their things and prepared for their departure to the ranch. George kept an eye out for Lonnie Spicer everywhere they went. He couldn't remember the last time he'd wanted to kill someone. He couldn't remember ever wanting to kill someone.

When they got to the wagon, George went to help Catherine up to the running board, but she pushed his hand away. "I don't want you to hurt yourself."

"Maybe you should help *me* into the wagon."

"This is what we're going to be like in twenty years," Catherine said.

"Hell, this is what we're like now," George replied as he rounded the wagon.

"Hello Catherine, George."

George turned to find Lonnie Spicer standing on the boardwalk, his hands in his pockets. George started to climb up into the wagon, making no effort to respond.

"I wanted to apologize to you both."

George frowned.

"Don't listen to him," Catherine said.

"Seriously, George...I was way out of line." Lonnie came around to George's side of the wagon and offered his hand. George was surprised to find that he felt like accepting the handshake. Wasn't it just a minute ago that he felt like killing this guy? Wasn't it just yesterday that this guy had knocked him around? But there was something about the look in Lonnie's eyes that made George believe his apology.

"George, ignore him. He doesn't mean a word he says." Catherine kept her eyes focused straight ahead.

George decided it couldn't hurt to shake the man's hand. So he reached out and gripped Lonnie's hand and shook.

"I also have something for you, Catherine," Lonnie said. He rounded the wagon, and George tensed up, preparing to throw himself across the wagon if Lonnie tried anything.

But Lonnie reached deep into his pocket and pulled out a slip of paper. He handed it to Catherine, who hesitated, but finally reached out and took it and studied it.

"That's been too long coming," Lonnie said.

George was surprised to see that his wife was speechless. Her mouth had opened slightly, as if she had something she wanted to say, but couldn't find the words.

"You folks have a good trip back...looks like it'll be a nice day for it." Lonnie shaded his eyes and looked off toward the east, where it did indeed look clear. The sun was soft, not too warm.

George still didn't feel right about saying anything to Lonnie, so he clicked his tongue and flipped the reins, putting the team in motion. The wagon clanked its way down the main street of Miles City. George could feel the pain in his groin, but it wasn't as bad as he expected.

"So what is that?" he asked Catherine.

"It's a check, George...he just paid me back that money."

"He did?"

Catherine turned to him, her face still blank. "Do you think we should keep it?"

"Catherine, isn't that the money you got from selling the hat shop?"

She looked at the check for a moment, then nodded slowly. "It is."

"Then of course you should keep it. That's your money."

Catherine nodded, but her face still showed very little expression. "I can't believe he did that."

I HURRIED BACK FROM THE MAILBOX as fast as my swollen belly would allow, holding the paper and a few other items in one hand, and a particular envelope in the other. I entered the house, answered George Jr.'s nonsense question with a pat on the head and a kiss on his cheek, and tossed the bulk of the mail on the dining room table. Then I settled into my favorite chair, and slipped a fingernail under the flap of the envelope. I slipped the letter from inside and unfolded it.

Mrs. Arbuckle,

Thanks a lot for writing back to me. Your right that it's been real hard going through this without anyone to talk to. I guess it won't give too much away to say that I'm also a married woman, and my husband doesn't let me talk about it.

It happened to me about six months ago. He come in the house and I swear, I didn't hear a peep. I suddenly feel this hand around my mouth, then an arm around my waste, and I was on the bed before I knew what was what! He tried to keep me from seeing his face, keeping me on my stomach the whole time. But I caught enough of a look that I'm almost positive I know who done it.

I would like to tell you his name, but I think if it ever got back to him that I did, he would kill me. That's what kind of man he is. But let's keep on writing, and maybe I'll get comforterble enough to say.

Your new friend

P.S. I heard a rumor that there's another woman to.

I folded the letter and slipped it back into the envelope. I closed my eyes and rested my head against the back of my chair. Another one. I wondered how many more that nobody knew about.

"Mama."

I opened my eyes to see George holding out a sock. I reached out and took the sock, but dropped it immediately, realizing that George had been chewing on it. It was soaked.

"Thank you, honey. Let's go get another sock for you, okay?" I stood and took little George by the hand, leading him to the bedroom.

An hour later, I took out the letter and read it again. And again. And then I leaned back in my chair again. And I realized two things. First, I realized how disappointed I was not to know this man's name. I had hoped that finding out who he was would give me a purpose. It would give me a chance to do something about the situation.

And second, I wished I knew who this woman was, so I could climb into our wagon and ride over and talk to her. I wanted to talk to her for hours. It made me miss Allison. I checked the rest of the mail, and found three more letters, which made me feel a little better. For the past couple of weeks, I'd started writing to women in the area asking how many of them would be interested in starting a woman's club. I suggested we meet once a month just to talk and get to know each other, and possibly arrange some community activities. So far, the response had been better than I expected. I had only received one letter saying she wasn't interested. I opened these three letters, all of which expressed an interest, and I added them to the list.

Then I looked at the clock. An hour and a half until the boys were there for supper, and I had barely started preparing.

RO

George studied the dead cow, trying to determine what might have killed her. He walked in a slow circle around the carcass. The cow hadn't been dead long. The flies had barely started gathering. There were no signs of injury or attack. No wounds. George pulled on his gloves and pried the cow's mouth open, looking for blisters or sores. He was relieved to see nothing like that. So it wasn't Hoof-in-Mouth, which was highly contagious. The cow also showed no signs of severe weight loss or diarrhea, which ruled out coccidiosis. George took off one glove and felt the cow's hip. He moved his hand along her back to the shoulder, and that was where he felt an unusual warmth.

"Black Leg," he muttered. "That's good." And as far as losing one of his best cows went, it was good. Because Black Leg wasn't contagious.

George walked over to her calf and wrapped an arm around its ribcage. He lifted, and the calf bawled, and made a feeble newborn effort to kick free. George slung the calf over his horse, then slipped his foot in the stirrup and climbed into the saddle. He settled the calf into a comfortable spot between him and the saddle horn. The calf continued to complain.

"Don't worry...we'll get you back to the barn and get you something to eat." George stroked the calf's neck as she shook her head. "I know...I'm not quite the same as your mama."

George rode in with the satisfying fatigue of another productive day. These were the days that made him most happy. The ranch looked good. The grass was higher than the previous few years, and shiny green. The creeks had risen nearly to the banks with clear water. In the distance, the yellow sandstone of the Finger Buttes reflected the fading light. George had only seen gold dust a few times in his life, but when the light hit the sandstone at this angle, it always made him picture someone taking a handful of that dust and scattering it across the buttes. They almost sparkled.

The calf's coat was warm against George's belly, and smelled of clean soil. All in all, life was good on the Little Missouri. As long as he was out in the pastures.

George approached the house cradling the calf in his arms, fighting a feeling that had become increasingly bothersome. Somewhere between weariness and dread.

"Hello!" he shouted as he entered.

"Back here!" Catherine's voice echoed from the bedroom.

George set the calf down in the main room. "We got us a new baby," he shouted.

"Not yet," Catherine answered.

George smiled to himself. "Well, I'm glad to hear that, but I was talking about this little fella."

Catherine emerged from the bedroom. "Oh, did he lose his mother?"

George nodded. "Black Leg, I think."

"Oh, at least it's not something that will spread."

George nodded. "How you feeling?"

"I feel like there's something growing inside me that's fighting to get out."

George smiled. "Sounds like I better write a letter to the preacher man...you might need to be saved."

"Saved from something, that's for sure." Catherine bent down and took the calf's head in her hands. "You poor thing...orphaned before you even had a chance to get a proper feeding."

"Where's that bottle?" George asked.

"In the pantry...I'll warm up some milk."

"I can do it...you need to worry about supper."

"Oh, it's just about ready. You go ahead and get cleaned up...I can take care of her."

"Okay." For a moment, George thought about kissing her on the cheek, but he couldn't remember the last time he'd done that...he worried that it might throw their whole routine off kilter somehow...they'd found a silent comfort, it seemed, in avoiding the need for touch. Or maybe it was just him. He was afraid to think about it too much. He rolled up his sleeves and dunked his forearms in the wash basin, scrubbing away the smell of cattle with lye soap.

"I got another letter from that woman today," Catherine announced from the kitchen.

"What woman?"

"The one who got raped."

George flinched. God, he hated that word. It sent a shiver through him every time he heard it. Even before all this, he reacted to that word this way. But he could hear something in his wife's voice...a lilt...excitement, or maybe hope. He scrubbed his face and neck. "What did she have to say?" he asked.

"Well, she's pretty scared to tell me much...she thinks she knows who it is, but she won't tell me yet. But she described what he did...it's the same man."

George grabbed a towel and dried off his face and hands. "How do you know?"

Catherine appeared in the doorway. "George, I just told you...she described what he did...it was exactly the same...he snuck up on her, put a hand on her mouth and carried her to the bedroom..."

"All right all right, I get the picture. So now what?"

But he could see that he'd annoyed her. He cut her off, and she hated that. She gave him a cool stare, then whirled back toward the stove.

"I'll just write to her again and see where it goes from there," she answered.

George draped the towel on its rack. The calf followed him to the stove, and Catherine handed him the bottle. He crouched down and wrapped his arm around the calf's ribs. He forced a few drops of milk from the nipple and held it to the calf's mouth. "And what do you hope to accomplish with that?"

George regretted saying this the minute he saw the change in his wife's face. The hurt in her eyes just about knocked him over.

"Sweetheart, I'm sorry," he said. "I don't know what to do about all this...I don't know what to say, or do..."

"Well it's clear what you want to do, George, is to forget that it ever happened."

"Yes!" he said, his voice louder than he intended. "Yes, you goddam right that's what I want. I want it to go away."

"And just how do you propose we do that, George? How are we going to make it go away?"

"Here come the boys," George muttered. In the crook of his arm, the calf suckled away, oblivious to the tension in the room. "We'll talk more about this later."

"I'd be very surprised if we did," Catherine said. "It would be the first time."

George bit his tongue, partly because he knew she was right. And he decided he needed to really make an effort this time.

The dishes were done. The baby was down for the night. The calf was outside, in the small pen near the house. And George felt the same overwhelming sense of fatigue that always seemed to hit at 8:00 every night. Normally, he welcomed this feeling. It was the natural result of a good day's work, a well-earned rest. But he knew this night was different. He tried to fight it.

He could feel the anticipation from the other side of the room, the expectation that the promise would be fulfilled. But George could already feel his eyelids drooping. He knew he better try. He owed her that much.

"So where were we?" he asked, sitting down on the bed.

Catherine groaned as she labored to pull off her clothes and tug her nightshirt over her swollen belly. "George, I know you better than that. You're going to fall asleep any minute."

George sighed and fell back against his pillow. "I'm sorry, Catherine."

"Listen, George...I don't think you realize how alone I am."

"What do you mean?"

"Just that, George. This...this...thing that you won't talk about. It has separated me from everyone."

"How can you say that, Catherine? You've got little George there, and me, and the boys. You have a lot of friends out here. More than we had in Deadwood."

George felt Catherine's weight as it settled onto their bed. He could feel her looking at him, and he opened his eyes. What he expected to see was more of the same hurt he'd seen earlier. He expected to see his wife looking at him as though she couldn't believe how thoughtless he could be. How little idea he had of what was important to her.

But the expression on her face was different this time. This time he was met with a look of profound sadness. He felt as if she had come to a deep recognition of some horrible truth. Something to do with him, or them, or perhaps of life itself. Whatever it was, George could tell from her look that something had been lost. And as much as he wanted to understand, and maybe even talk about it, his body was so overcome with exhaustion that he could only look at his wife and say he was sorry one more time before sleep overtook him.

CHAPTER 25

I LOOKED DOWN AT THE NEW BABY suckling away at my breast, and a heaviness settled into my heart that frightened me. I had studied this boy's face for the three days since he was born-- every feature: the broad little nose, the ears flat against his head, the receded chin, and the wide, round eyes. And there was nothing of George in this baby. There was no way around it. I knew this baby was not his, and it made me sick to my stomach every time I thought about it.

George came into the bedroom. "You need anything?"

I shook my head. "Did George get some breakfast?"

"Yeah, I fed him some eggs."

"You going out?"

George nodded. "Got to see if I can figure out what's wrong with that lame horse. I'll try not to be too long."

I nodded.

"You sure you don't want something...a cup of coffee?"

"That would be nice, actually."

"All right."

After George set a cup of coffee on the table next to me, he left, and I sat quietly for a few minutes, sipping coffee, watching the baby drink itself into a milky slumber. I wondered whether George had taken the time to study this baby and determine the same thing I had. So far, he seemed perfectly happy. But I suspected he was doing the same thing with this that he'd done with the whole situation. Pretending as if everything was fine. Going on as if nothing ever happened.

As soon as I put Jack down, I checked on Little George, who had made his way out into the yard, where he was building a pile of dirt. Then I came back inside and pulled out a sheaf of paper, a bottle of ink, and a pen.

I carefully spread out the first sheet of paper, unscrewed the lid on the ink, and dipped the pen. Then I started writing. More letters to the women in the area. My list was now up to twelve, and we would soon be having our first meeting of the Albion Women's Club.

After an hour, I had a stack of sealed envelopes six inches high, and I went to check on little George. He was still out in the yard, and had somehow managed to turn the dirt hill to mud. He was covered in it. I scooped him up, and George launched into a loud protest. His limbs jerked in every direction as I hauled him to the house.

"It was just about time for a bath for you anyway, young man." I stripped him down and put a kettle of water on the stove. Thankfully, there were still some embers from the morning coffee, and I stoked them with a poker and added two small logs. George raced around the house naked, and before I could catch him he had spread mud to various pieces of furniture.

"George, come back here."

George laughed and ran away, his hands bobbing in the air like apples at the end of a branch.

"George," I scolded, and the tone of my voice seemed to scare him for a moment as he turned back toward me. But he tripped, and his naked little body lurched forward. I screamed just as his head collided with the chest I used for linens. George rolled onto his back on the floor, and blood spurted from a cut just above his eye. He howled, and his body twisted.

I knelt next to him, holding his head firmly and taking a close look at the cut. It was deep, down to the bone, too deep to simply cover with a bandage. "Okay, calm down, honey...just stay calm...keep breathing." I wasn't sure whether I was talking to him or to myself. I gathered him in my arms and carried him to the kitchen, where the kettle was just starting to sizzle. From the bedroom, I heard Jack fussing.

I grabbed a dishtowel and pressed it to the cut. But George threw his head around like a horse trying to avoid a bit. I held him tight against my body with one arm and pulled the lid off the kettle with the other. I dipped the dishtowel into the water, then dropped to my knees and laid George flat on the floor. I held his body as still as I could with one hand and pressed the dishtowel against the cut with the other. George screamed.

"I know it hurts, honey, but we have to chase the germs away."

Now Jack was crying full voice from the bedroom. I held the towel to George's head for as long as I could bear to listen to

Jack, then I sat George up, wrapped an arm around his head so I could hold the towel to the cut, and carried him to the bedroom, where I sat George on the bed and scooped Jack into the crook of my elbow. I rocked him for a minute, until he was temporarily soothed, then I laid him back in his basket, leaned over him and cooed. He sighed, and stopped crying, but I knew it wouldn't be long before he was howling again.

"Let's get you fixed up, George."

George was still crying, but he wasn't squirming as much. I pulled my sewing basket from under the chest of drawers, dug inside for a needle and the first spool of thread I saw, which was blue. I carried George to the kitchen. I opened the door to the woodstove and held the needle as close as I could to the smoldering log. I wedged the needle between a crease on the top of the stove, so it was sticking straight up in the air. Then I carried George outside to the icehouse, where I broke off a chunk and held it against the cut. George cried again and tried to wiggle out of my grasp.

"I know, honey...I know it hurts...just a little longer."

I carried him back in the house, where Jack was now crying full throat again. I plucked the needle from the top of the stove, and as I started for the bedroom, George made another twisting lunge, and slipped from my grasp. He landed with a thunk. I held my urge to scream in check, instead pulling George back into my arms. I studied the cut, which didn't seem affected by the fall. But George was now screaming and flailing again. One arm swung and plunked me in the nose, and it felt as if a pencil had been jammed up my nostril.

I tamped down another scream, pulling the emotion short, pushing it deep into my gut. I focused, holding George as still as I could.

"Honey, calm down...you need to calm down." I wrapped him in my arms, pressing his head against my shoulder. "Sh sh sh sh sh sh." I grabbed the ice, wrapped it in a dishtowel, and held it against the cut.

"Can you hold this against your head?" I asked him. "Can you hold this?" I sat down on the bed, and George nodded.

"Okay," I said. "I'm going to be right here...you just need to hold it for a second." I placed his hand over the towel. "Hold it tight, honey."

George nodded again while I threaded the needle. I tried to block out Jack's crying, plucking the needle from between my teeth and poking the thread with determination.

After tying a knot in the thread, I moved up next to George, settling against him as close as possible. I swung my right leg over him and pinned his arms beneath my knees. I took the needle from my mouth and studied the cut. George was crying quietly now, seemingly surrendering to his fate.

The cut started just above the curve of George's eye socket, and I was grateful that he hadn't fallen an inch closer to the chest and gouged out an eye. It then slanted at an angle toward the corner of his forehead, burrowing all the way to the bone. I knew

I couldn't stop the flow of blood while sewing him up. I decided to start at the bottom, and I clenched my teeth.

"This is going to hurt, honey, but it will be over before you know it. Just hold as still as you can."

But of course, the minute the needle entered his skin, he squealed, and his body contorted, wriggling beneath me. I held his head firmly against the bed and forced the needle through one side of the cut, then the other. Jack wailed from his basket, and I felt tears running down my face. But I held my jaw firm and threaded the needle back and forth, pulling the cut tight against itself. George's crying faded toward the end, and by the time I knotted the thread and bit it clean through, he was reduced to a weary whimper.

I tilted off him, lying down next to him. And I pulled him tight against my body. "See now, that wasn't so bad," I tried to assure him, although I was about to burst into tears.

He didn't respond, but he wrapped his little arm around my shoulder and buried his face in my neck.

"That wasn't so bad at all. You were such a brave boy. So very brave."

I needed to feed Jack, but I noticed that George was shivering. "Good god, you're still naked." I got up and pulled out some clothes, dressed George, then pulled Jack from his basket and lay down next to George again. I pulled out a breast and gave it to Jack and held both of my boys close. And I felt the warmth of their little bodies against me as my milk flowed freely.

RO

When George entered the house, there was an eerie quiet, and he felt a stab of fear. "What happened now?"

He noticed that there was no food on the stove, no bread in the oven. The only signs of any activity from the day was a stack of sealed envelopes on the dining room table, and smears of mud everywhere, on the floor, on various parts of the walls and furniture. A sense of panic started to build. "Catherine?" he cried out.

"Oh my god," he heard from the bedroom. Catherine emerged, frantically adjusting her dress.

"What's going on?" George asked.

"Oh my god, I fell right to sleep and I must have just slept for two hours. I'm so sorry."

George craned his neck, peering back into the bedroom. "Where are the boys?"

"They were also asleep. We had a little accident," she said. "And...well, it doesn't matter. I need to get supper ready."

"An accident?" George made his way back to the bedroom. Jack was in his basket, still sound asleep. But George was sitting up on the bed, rubbing his head. "What happened, buddy?"

George Jr. pointed at his forehead, where a blue caterpillar crossed this skull.

"Catherine?"

"Yes, George."

George made his way back to the kitchen. "What the hell happened?"

"Oh, he was running around the house and he fell against the chest. It's not nearly as bad as it looks."

George hmmed. "You sewed someone up before?"

Catherine looked up. "Of course I have."

George shrugged. "Just wondered. Don't get yourself all riled up. You want me to help with supper?"

"I got it...could you check on the boys?"

"Well I just did, and they seem fine. Jack is still asleep."

"Just make sure. I'm worried about George with that cut."

George nodded, making his way back to the bedroom. George Jr. was lying on his back, staring at the ceiling as if he had been instructed to do so for his recovery.

George sat on the bed. "You doin' okay there, buddy?"

Little George nodded.

George leaned down to get a closer look at the cut. He was impressed with the mending. The sutures were tight, but not so tight that they bunched up the skin. "You took quite a blow there, son...you sure you feel all right now?"

George Jr. nodded again. "I'm hungry."

"Well that's good, 'cause we'll be having some supper in just a bit here."

George got up and bent over the basket, where Jack was wide awake, also staring straight up into the air. "Hey there, little fella." George hooked his finger in the cup of Jack's palm and wiggled. "You had yourself a good long nap there. I hope that doesn't mean you're gonna keep us up all night."

George mapped the boy's features one more time. He had known the minute he saw him. It was more than obvious. And George was surprised to realize that he felt no anger about it at all. He had taken one look at that boy and thought to himself that the boy had nothing to do with what happened. That he deserved nothing but the same treatment his brother had gotten. When it came right down to it, George didn't think he had any other choice. Punishing the boy would be nothing but plain cruelty.

"The boys are here!" Catherine announced from the kitchen.

George picked up Jack, holding him tight against his shoulder. "We're coming! Let's go, Junior...time for some grub."

GEORGE ADJUSTED HIS POSITION on the hard wooden bench. After sitting at the cattle auction for four hours, he was feeling the effects. But he wasn't tired. He never got tired at auctions. He loved everything about them. Assessing the stock, watching the people, listening to the auctioneer...even the smells invigorated George. It was like a theater featuring everything he loved about ranching.

But there were just a few more markers left, so the show was nearly over. George had bought one small batch of heifers, and he was pleased with the purchase. He had struggled about whether he and Catherine should spend the money she got from Lonnie on stock, but she insisted. "It was my money," she had said. "And now it's our money."

"Hello George."

The voice from behind was familiar, but George couldn't think who it was until he turned around.

"Hey Bernie. How you doin'?" George suspected right away that there was something wrong about this. He hadn't seen Bernie Sanford for a couple of years, and they certainly had no reason to talk to each other.

"I'm pretty good...how 'bout you? How's everything out there on the Little Missouri?"

"We're getting along just fine."

"I hear you had yourself another little one, huh?"

George nodded. "Sure did. Another boy."

"Well congratulations."

"Appreciate that. I heard you got yourself up and married too. You got any younguns yet?"

"Yep...a little girl."

"Good, good." George nodded. "Well, I was just getting ready to take off, but it's good seein' you."

"Before you go, George..." George had started to stand up, and Bernie gripped his upper arm. "I got a message for you."

Here we go, George thought. He sank back to the bench next to Bernie, feeling it in his hindquarters.

"Our friend wants to meet with you."

"Our friend?"

Bernie's voice lowered. "C'mon, George...you know who I mean. He wants to meet with you later tonight."

"You're kidding, right?"

"Not one bit."

"Bernie, you honestly think I'm that stupid? You don't think I've heard what he said about me?"

"Of course you have...everyone has." Bernie winked. "He wants to apologize."

George scoffed. "Sorry...no."

"George...you think you can run from him forever? Would you rather meet with him in a safe, public place, or would you rather he pops up out of nowhere while you're riding back to Montana?"

George hadn't considered this. "Where does he want to meet?"

"At the Eureka...he'll buy you some supper. Around six?" George didn't respond. But he knew he had no choice.

"We'll see you then, George." Bernie patted him on the shoulder. "You're looking great."

As George approached the Eureka, he wondered how Preston planned to get away with appearing in public, when he had a price on his head the size of Montana.

But this question was answered when George entered, and Bernie spotted him from the bar. He tipped his head toward the back of the building, and George followed him to a private room. He stopped at the doorway, wondering again about the wisdom of going along. He saw the familiar head of grey hair, and two other men sitting at the table on either side.

"Come on in, George..." Preston stood, coming around to greet him at the door. He shook George's hand, and took his elbow in his other hand, leading him to a chair.

George's stomach was tight, folded into a little bundle. He sat, nodding to the other two men as Preston introduced them. He didn't hear their names.

"So how you doin', George? How's the new little one?" The smile on Preston's face baffled George. Preston looked as if he was talking to his favorite relative.

"Can't complain," he answered. "And you?" He wondered what to even ask. 'What was it like being on the run?' would probably be awkward.

"I'm good, George...real good."

George had to admit that Preston didn't look the worse for wear. Whatever he'd been doing for the past five years hadn't aged him a day.

"We've been real busy." Preston leaned toward George with a conspiratorial expression. A waiter entered the room, and Preston announced that they would all have steaks and whiskey. George shivered. He did not like to take a drink, but he had a feeling that leaving his glass untouched wasn't going to be acceptable in this company.

Once the waiter was gone, Preston picked up where he left off. "Me and these clowns have been chasing down outlaws like nobody's business."

George nodded, trying to appear impressed.

"That's why I wanted to talk to you, George."

"It is?"

"Yeah...hell yeah." Preston reached across and laid a hand on George's forearm. "Listen, first of all...let me just tell you...the past is the past, George. I know I said some things. I can see you're a little nervous. But you don't have to worry...I put that all behind me. I'd a done the same thing I was in your boots."

"Yeah?"

"Really...what else could you do? You're trying to get your feet on the ground, getting married and all...you didn't want to keep running around with this crowd, right?"

George could only nod.

"But I bet you wondered when ol' Bernie here told you I wanted to see you, huh?" Preston adjusted his posture, clearly pretending to become George. "Is that sumbitch Preston going to make good on his promise here and get his revenge?"

The other men laughed as if this was the funniest thing they'd ever heard, and George played along, the laughter coming from the top of his throat. He was still scared to death.

And then Preston made the shift. He dispensed with the lighter tone, and his brow descended over his eyes like a storm cloud. "Here's the deal, George. What I been thinking about. This son-of-a-bitch that did what he done to your wife...he needs to get his."

George swallowed hard. He frowned. "Why would you want to get involved in that?"

"Why?" Preston threw both hands in the air, turned to his two comrades, then back to George. "*Why*?"

George just looked at him.

"Because if he done that to her, he's bound to do it again. You've heard about this young girl that's missing, right?"

George nodded. A teenage girl from Lead had disappeared a week before, and they'd found her bloody dress in a gully.

"And you know there's going to be some that ain't got the courage your wife has...there's bound to be some that he done this to that aren't going to make a peep about it." He stared hard at George, who couldn't move. "Right?"

"Could be." George couldn't believe his ears. He wondered if he would have felt differently about this whole scenario a few weeks ago, before Jack was born. But he didn't think so. This was Preston, after all. The man was out of his mind with righteous anger.

"So what do you know, George? I know the papers said she didn't see the man's face, but is that true? Do you know who this son-of-a-bitch is?"

George shook his head. "No idea," he said.

Preston pounded the table. "Dammit. I was hoping that story was holding back on the facts."

"'Fraid not," George said. "She didn't get a look at him."

"So we're gonna have to find out who some of these other women are."

"How you propose to do that?" George asked.

"I don't know...I've been thinking..."

The waiter appeared with their dinners, balanced impressively along one arm, and he distributed them among the men with a graceful bend at the waist.

Preston chewed on the inside of his cheek, and George was thinking about the letters Catherine had received.

The five of them began eating, and Preston looked as if he was going to devour his steak in three bites. The nervous energy in his actions seemed to be contagious, as the other three men, glancing at Preston, also ate quickly, without manners, like coyotes over a fallen lamb. But George cut small pieces of meat and chewed deliberately, partly because his throat had closed up.

"What about that article?" Preston asked in a burst of sound. "Didn't your wife hear from anyone else after that article came out?"

George coughed on the juice from his steak.

"Ah ha!" Preston pointed at him with his fork. "She did, didn't she?"

George shook his head. "No, not at all."

"George." Preston lowered his chin. "Come on now."

"I heard she did," Bernie chimed in.

"Honestly," George said.

"You're nervous, ain't you, George? People are going to look at you...you're the husband. They're going to assume you should have done more to protect your wife. That's why we aren't asking you for nothing but information."

"Listen, Preston...I'm having a damn hard time understanding why you want to get involved. There's no reward. The sheriff didn't even investigate"

"See now, George...this is the problem with most people, and I thought you were different...you're just focusing on one thing..." Preston poked his fork at George again. "Money. Not everything is about money."

"No, just most things."

"Well you might be right about that. But every now and then, there's something that's too important to put a price on. Something that you know in your heart the Lord is calling you to do. Do you know what I'm talking about, George?"

George sighed.

"Oh bull, George. What about your work? You love working on a ranch, right?"

"Yeah, but I get paid for that."

"Sure you do...'course you do. But let's just say that one day ol' Dan Hardin shows up at your door and he says to you, 'George, I'm real damn sorry to tell you this, but we're in a hell of a bind right now, and we just can't afford to pay you for a while. As soon as we get out of this mess, we'll pay you everything we owe you, and I wish I could tell you when that will be, but I can't.' Would you stay if that happened, George?"

George nodded. "I think I would, yeah."

"'Course you would. Now see...that's how I feel about this. I'm not interested in the comforts of life...the things you can hold and feel...but that kind of inner satisfaction you get from doing what's right...doing what you know in your heart is going to make the world a better place...how can you put a price on that, George?"

George chewed on his steak.

"You can't, George. You can't."

George was surprised to see that his plate was clean. Preston's energy had clearly gotten through to him. His mind was spinning. What could it hurt, really, telling him that Catherine had heard from this woman.

"So let's hear it, George. She did hear from someone, didn't she?"

And without thinking, George nodded. "We don't know who it is, though."

"She thinks she knows who did it?"

George nodded. "Yeah. And she's scared he'll come after her if she tells."

Preston sighed. "Well of course she is. She's got every reason to be. And I'm sure your wife hasn't been treated real well, airing out her story. People don't like hearing that stuff."

George did not...could not, respond to this.

"Well, we know there are others out there. It's just a matter of finding them."

Now George didn't know what to say.

"Listen, George...is your wife still in contact with this woman?"

George nodded. "They been writing back and forth."

"Oh good...that's good." Preston scooted up until his stomach was pressed hard against the table. "Here's what we're gonna do. I want you to encourage her to keep doing that...and let her know you want to hear all about it...you want to know what this woman says, every word. And you pass that along to us, okay, George? Meanwhile, we'll be poking around for whatever we can find, too. Somehow we'll track this son-of-a-bitch down."

George nodded, but knew there was no way he was going to follow through with this promise. "Well, I need to be getting back home." George stood, stretching. "Thanks a lot for the supper, Preston."

But Preston made no move to stand. He sat looking at George with a strange smile on his face. "You know, George...you still have that quality...you don't say much, but you bring something to the mix."

Again, George was baffled. "Yeah. Okay, well...should I contact Bernie here if I have anything to report, or..."

"That's right. See...I don't have to spell everything out for you like I do a lot of guys. You have that..." Preston pointed to the side of his head. He wrote down a post office box number and gave it to George. "Just write to this box number when you hear anything."

George sighed. He still couldn't help from wondering whether he was going to get shot in the back as he walked away from these men.

"You didn't touch your drink, George." Preston pointed at his glass.

"I know...someone else can drink it...I'm not much of a drinkin' man."

Preston nodded to the other men, as if this was one more indication of George's gift. "You take it easy now, George," Preston said. "Take good care of that baby."

George tipped his hat, but this last statement stayed with him.

RO

I dodged mud puddles to get to the mailbox, where I was pleased to find another stack of letters. I tiptoed my way back to the house, avoiding the spots where the thick gumbo could pull me to the ground. Inside, I opened the envelopes one at a time, adding names to my list.

The first meeting of the Albion Women's Club had been a rousing success. Fourteen women showed up, and we talked for two hours, making plans about events we could organize for the community, and things we could do to help people in need. It was exactly what I needed, this connection to the people around me. It helped that another attack had been reported in Belle Fourche. I wasn't the only one any more.

Some of the women even talked to me in hushed voices about what happened. I was happy to be developing a circle of friends.

Now I had seven more women on my list. But the last letter was different. The last one was from my mystery friend. We had been writing for several weeks now, every few days.

I smoothed out the paper and laid it on my knee.

Dear Mrs. Arbuckle,

Thanks again for writing to me. I feel like we have almost become friends these past few weeks. I really haven't made many friends since we moved here a few years ago. My husband don't like to go out much, and when we do, he keeps me pretty close by. So I don't get a chance to visit like I would if I was by myself. As much as I love my husband, this has been the loneliest time of my whole life.

And I worry that it will never get any better. But I don't want to burden you with my troubles.

Wasn't that rain the past few days wonderful!! I sometimes want to just run out there and raise my arms up and let it wash over me, it looks so clean. And of course, the men are always in a better mood when it's raining, so that's good too.

I also want you to know that I think I'm ready to tell you who it was that attacked me that day. Thank you for being patient with me about sharing this man's name, because I am scared to death of him. And scared to death that letting it out will put both of us in danger. But I trust you, Mrs. Arbuckle. I think you're a good-hearted person, just like I think I'm a good- hearted person. And I don't think we done a thing to be treated this way.

I know you know who he is, too, because you have a history with him. Or at least your husband does. And his initials are PS. So I'm guessing from that you can figure out who I mean. My hand was just shaking like crazy and got all wet with sweat from writing those initials down. Nobody should have to live with this kind of fear.

Your friend

After this final salutation, there was a large blotch of ink, as if the woman had written her name and then blotted it out. I held the paper up to my lantern and peered at the blotch, but I couldn't make out any letters.

So....it was Preston Sanford. This wasn't a surprise. He had certainly been near the top of my list all along. But as far as I knew, there had still been no actual sighting of the man since he disappeared.

I wondered what this meant. Had he managed to be that clever about hiding for the past few months? Or had he just shown up long enough to get his revenge on a few people before disappearing back into the dark corners of the West?

For the rest of the afternoon, I went about my business wondering why I didn't feel more relieved. I felt as if I was wandering around in the middle of a cloud bank, my vision obscured and my senses dull. I leaned up against the woodstove and seared a silver dollar-sized brand into my thigh without realizing it.

By the time George got back from the fields, I had almost forgotten about the letter.

We sat up to the table, and the corn and mashed potatoes and fried chicken made their way from hand to hand. The men talked about how green the grass looked, so much greener than it was just a week ago, and how this was sure going to help the hay crop this year, and how the cattle would have twenty percent more meat on them because of it.

We talked about the next dance, and the boys talked about their next chance to get to town and get drunk and see their girls.

I ate without tasting my food, and the words from everyone's mouth seemed to gather in each ear, like cotton.

At one point, I felt a hand on my forearm, and looked up to see George looking right at me, with a question in his eyes.

"What?" I asked.

"I just asked if you wanted me to serve the pie...you seem a little distracted."

"No no...I'll get it."

I cut the apple pie and leaned each wedge onto a plate, serving it up to great compliments. The boys wasted no time finishing their dessert, then pardoned themselves to the bunkhouse after thanking me for another fine meal. They were nice boys, I thought to myself. There was never a night that they didn't thank me for cooking for them, and almost always added some special compliment about the food.

I wished it helped me feel better.

After the boys left, I prepared our boys for bed and thought about how I was going to break this news to George.

"You were sure quiet tonight," George said.

I pulled my frock over my head, then unlaced my underclothes and folded them over the chair. I lifted my nightgown above my head and let it fall around me.

"I have something to tell you, George."

George was just crawling into bed, but he sat up straight. "What?"

"I got a letter from..."

"From that woman?" He swung his legs over the side of the bed and was spring-loaded to come to his feet.

I sat on the bed next to him. "She told me who it was."

"She did?"

I nodded, and I suddenly felt so tired I had to lie down. I fell back against my pillow and closed my eyes.

"Well what did she say? Who is it?"

"Preston Sanford," I said. And then I waited for the response. And I waited. But there was nothing but an eerie silence. Finally, I opened my eyes and lifted my head from the pillow, studying George. He was standing five feet away, staring at the wall, his mouth open just an inch. He looked completely lost.

"George?"

His eyes moved to me, but his head didn't move at all. "What?"

"I know this is upsetting, but you're not really surprised, are you?"

His eyes returned to the wall. "That can't be right," he said.

I began to get a sick feeling in my stomach. "George? What do you mean?" I swiveled and dropped my feet to the floor.

George returned to the bed, sitting down next to me. He shook his head. "You know when I was in town for the auction the other day?"

"Yeah?"

George went on to explain the meeting with Preston and his men. I listened with growing irritation. After he'd finished, I held my tongue for as long as I could, absorbing the information. "George."

"I know...I should have told you."

I nodded. "Yes. Yes, you should have." My breath raced, and I clamped my mouth shut and let it flow freely through my nose until I had calmed down a little. "Okay, now that we've got that straight...let's talk about what we do from here."

"All right."

"So let's think about this...if this is true, that Preston is the one who did this...what could he possibly have to gain from pretending otherwise?"

"That's easy...he's trying to fool us into thinking it's someone else."

I nodded slowly. "And the letters?"

George held a hand to his chin. "He's hoping to find out who this woman is, so he can go after her."

"That sounds right to me."

"So we have to do everything we can to keep from giving him any information."

"We just need to stay away from the man and from anyone who knows him, including his brother."

George nodded.

I sighed. "This man is scary, George. He's a frightening, dangerous man."

"I know, Catherine...we knew that when I turned him in."

"And yet, it was still the right thing, George...you did the right thing."

George turned his eyes to me. "Do you really think so?"

I touched his arm.

"Even if he's the one who did this to you?"

I turned my face downward, moved by the fact that he acknowledged the rape. "George, I'm not sure how to explain this, but I decided a while ago that I need to figure out a way to turn this around....to make it positive somehow."

George took my hand.

"George, do you agree that this has gotten in the way of a lot of things?"

"I suppose."

"What do you think we can do about that?"

George shook his head. "I wish I knew, Catherine....I'm not good at this kind of thing."

I ran a hand along his shoulders. "I won't argue with that."

George smiled. "No, I don't suppose you would."

"Maybe neither one of us is very good at it."

George sighed. "I just keep wondering...there's got to be something I can do to make this right. There's got to be something I can do..."

I have never understood men. I guess I never will.

WHILE THE WORLD AROUND HIM WENT ON as if nothing had happened, George Arbuckle got stuck. For days, he thought of nothing but Preston Sanford. He slept in half hour bursts, thirty minutes of non-stop activity. He was either hunting, running, or wrestling some weapon from Preston's hand. Each morning, George would be so exhausted from fighting all night that he could barely pull his dungarees up to his waist.

The first morning, Catherine asked him how he was, and his answer was delivered with such extreme irritation that she didn't ask again. So his fight was a lonely one, a private battle against a foe that refused to show its face except in George's mind.

It had been nearly a week since the rain stopped, and the hay was dry enough to cut, so there was no break from hard labor, no leisurely days in the saddle. George dozed on his horse on the way to the hay field each day, and then willed his body to join in a different struggle, a physical struggle, walking along the rows of hay and pitching it into the wagon. His back went numb from doing the same thing over and over again. But every now and then, a spasm would hit that brought a groan to George's throat.

He didn't let it slow his progress, though. Each of the hands were in the same state, after all.

Through it all, George pictured Preston, his pitchfork driving into him, into his torso, into his leg, into his face. He thought about their trip to Deadwood the coming weekend. He knew it would be impossible for him to enjoy their stay, despite the fact that they were going for a celebration. He knew that all of this intense awareness of Preston's presence would only be worse in town.

The Days of '76 was the biggest event of the year in Deadwood. Between the rodeo, the market, the stock show, and the games and food, there was always something going on. It was two days of constant activity. And in spite of the crowds, which always made George uncomfortable, the Days of '76 had always been his favorite.

They arrived Saturday morning, after a quiet ride into town. Even the boys were quiet, which was especially unusual for that time of day. Catherine had brought the standard fare...a blanket to claim their spot on the fairgrounds, a picnic basket with food and plates and utensils, and toys and books in case the boys got bored. George was always amused by this, as the boys never got bored at the Days of '76. There were kids everywhere. Catherine also brought several pies for the bake sale her women's club was going to sponsor on day two of the festivities. She and the Albion Women's Club had organized the bake sale to raise money for the little schoolhouse they were building out near Alzada.

The Arbuckles claimed their spot, just under a nice big oak tree, and George's surveillance began. He knew even as he scanned the crowd that the chances that Preston would make his presence known in public were almost nil. But this didn't deter him at all from studying every group of people, double-checking each head of grey hair, each man taller than he. He wasn't about to miss the chance if it came. And yet...and yet...he had no idea what this meant. He didn't know what he would do if he saw him.

"George?"

George turned. Catherine looked worried. She tilted her head, and George pivoted in that direction. Walking toward him was Bernie Sanford. "I'll be right back," he said.

He heard Catherine say his name, but he pretended not to hear, moving to meet Bernie halfway. "What do you want?" he hissed. "Why you got to bother me when I'm with my family?"

"Well now, George...we haven't heard from you for a long time...we gotta take the opportunity when it comes along."

"You ain't heard from me 'cause I got nothing to tell you."

"You got nothing to tell us or nothing to report?"

"What's that supposed to mean?"

"You got something to hide, George?"

George just fixed a look on him. Bernie reached into his back pocket and handed George a folded piece of paper. "This is where you can find me if you decide to tell me the truth."

George glared at him then turned back toward his family.

"You better not be hiding anything," Bernie yelled after him.

"What was that?" Catherine asked the minute he was within earshot.

"Don't worry about it."

But Catherine pushed right up against him, without touching him. She moved into the space that filled the air around him and took it all for herself. "Don't you ever tell me that, George Arbuckle. We're in this together, good...bad...all of it. Now tell me what that piece of scum said."

George ran his palm over his eyes, back and forth, trying to scrub the worry away. He sank onto the blanket. "He just wanted to know whether we had any more information."

"And what did you tell him?"

"I told him we don't know any more than I already told them."

"Good." She sighed and sat down right next to him. "What are we going to do, George?"

George shook his head. "We'll just keep going along, Catherine...not much else we can do."

"What's that?" She nodded to the piece of paper.

"He just gave me directions to where I can find him."

Catherine took the sheet of paper from him and studied it. She started to hand it back to George when little George came barreling into her, crying about some kid that was calling Catherine names.

RO

I sat in the middle of a crowd of people I had known most of my life, in the country I called home, and tried not to think about how out of place I felt. I wanted to bundle up my boys, hold them as close as I could, and climb back into our wagon and go home. I wanted to be back in a place I knew. Even though I didn't always feel safe in my own home anymore, at least it was familiar.

George's muscle worked in his jaw, his eyes shifting back and forth. And I knew that neither of us was going to enjoy the day. But I also knew there was no way of admitting this, or even addressing it. No, we would stick it out. We couldn't hide forever. And I decided to make the best of it.

I dug into the picnic basket. "Do you want some cookies, George?"

"Cookies?" George frowned. "No...what's gotten into you? We haven't even had dinner yet."

"I know...I just thought it would be nice for a treat."

George shook his head. "Don't give those boys any either, or they'll never eat another thing all day."

"George...do you think I don't know any better...honestly."

George sighed, and I didn't press the issue. But the visit from Bernie had set the tone for our day. We bore our concern separately, focusing our attention on friends who walked by, or on the endless parade of entertainment. There were jugglers, musicians, magicians, and even a man who drew charcoal pictures right on the spot.

I was surprised to see George pull out his wallet and ask the man to draw a picture of Jack, who was fast asleep. The man pulled a folded canvas stool from his bag, set it up right in front of the sleeping baby, and started drawing.

"Boy, is that one beautiful baby...how old is he?" The artist had a nice face, and a calm presence. His beard was evenly trimmed, and when he smiled, his eyes closed almost completely.

"He's just a few months," I answered.

"He's kind of small, isn't he?"

"No he ain't," George answered.

"Yes he is," I said. "But just a little."

"Well now, I didn't mean to start a fight between you two." The artist smiled to himself, his eyes disappearing, as he continued scratching away at the sketch pad.

I looked at George, hoping we could share the joke. But he had turned away.

The artist continued to ask questions, and I waited for George to answer the first couple of times, but when he didn't show any interest, I carried the conversation. I found out that the artist had moved out from Pennsylvania just a year ago.

"That's a big move," I said. "Do you like it here?"

"I'm getting used to it," he replied.

"What's the hardest part?" I was pleased to hear this question from George.

"The hardest part? Hmmm." The man stopped drawing for the first time since he'd settled onto the stool. "Well, the easy answer would be that I miss my family...but I think the hardest thing for me has actually been making friends. I travel a lot doing this work, and I haven't stayed in one place long enough to get to know people."

"That would be hard," Catherine agreed.

"Well, you know...it could be a lot worse...I ain't complaining. I made the choice." He suddenly stood and flipped the sketch pad around. "What do you think?"

"Wow." George's smile spread wide, and he grabbed the portrait from the man. "That's really good!"

I laughed. I couldn't remember the last time I'd seen my husband so excited. He handed the pad to me and dug into his pocket for his wallet again. "I want you to do one of her, too." He tilted his head toward me.

"Oh George...no!" I started laughing. "That would be a waste of paper."

"We'll hear none of that," the artist said. "You have a wonderful face."

"You just want our money," I teased.

"Well, I never turn down business, it's true." He winked at me, and I was horrified to feel my face turn hot, a flutter rising up in my breast. I looked over at George, wondering whether it showed. But he was counting out his money, oblivious.

For the next twenty minutes, I had to endure the knowledge that this man who had suddenly lit a fire inside me was sitting there studying every part of my face, perhaps even the rest of me. My body. I felt the sweat gathering in every extra fold of skin and wished I hadn't worn a white dress. George stood by holding the baby, a slight grin on his face, as if he couldn't wait to see the final result.

"Surely you're almost finished...are you drawing the whole town behind me?"

"True art requires just the right amount of time," the man said, squinting at me.

Please don't wink again, I thought.

"Well look at this! A masterpiece in progress!"

"Lars!" Although I wasn't able to turn, I would know the voice anywhere.

"Are you sure you've got her best side there?" Lars asked the artist.

As he made his way around and appeared, I was pleased to see Addie clutching his arm.

They stood beaming, and after watching the artist sketch for a while, Lars laid himself out on their blanket and stretched out his legs.

"Join me, Addie." He patted the spot beside him.

Addie smiled and crouched down, then carefully tipped over onto one hip and curled her legs behind her. She propped herself up with one arm. She was wearing a beautiful dress, cream- colored with upper sleeves that puffed out, and a full skirt. I couldn't help but notice that Addie acted more refined than most women I knew. Even women who thought of themselves as refined.

George presented the portrait of Jack to Lars. "Oh, that's marvelous!" Addie said.

"Looks just like him," Lars added. "We should get one done," Addie said.

I was just about to ask for a break when the artist stood up with a flourish and whipped the pad in front of me. I took it in both hands and studied the portrait. And to my utter surprise, I started weeping.

"You don't like it?" The artist looked as if he was about to fall on his knees and beg for forgiveness.

"Oh no no no," I said, trying to gain my composure. "It's beautiful...much more beautiful than it deserves to be."

"Let all those among you who have sinned, and those of you who cavort with sinners, take the step today to repent and seek the Lord's forgiveness for your transgressions."

"What the hell..." George muttered as we all turned to see that Donald Smalls had set up his soapbox just thirty feet from where we sat. He stood directly facing us.

"The good book tells us that we must avoid the temptations of the flesh...that we must not lie down with members of the opposite sex before uniting as one in the eyes of the Lord. The good book tells us that..."

"The good book tells us that we should forgive those who sin...that we should not cast stones unless we ourselves..." The dissenting voice rose up above Donald Smalls', and I stood and gasped when I saw that it was my husband who approached the preacher, pointing and walking toward him with what seemed to be clear intent to hurt the man. He was still holding Jack.

"George, no!" I followed him.

"And just what do you know about the bible, my good man?" Smalls shouted. "When was the last time your shadow crossed the threshold of the house of the Lord?"

"You have no right!" Now there was another voice...and another figure approached, this one tall and foreboding and red-faced beneath the flowing yellow hair. "You have no right!"

Smalls was now laughing, his expression smug. "Listen to this, good people! This man, who has taken into his home a woman from the lowest of places...a woman who sold her very self, her most precious gift..."

Before I thought about it, my legs pumped hard, carrying me toward my good friend Lars, whom I could see was beyond angry. From the corner of my eye, George was still advancing toward Smalls, from a different angle. I experienced a moment of hesitation, trying to decide which of them seemed most at risk, before shifting direction toward George. I was relieved to see that someone had grabbed the baby from his arms, so at least Jack was safe.

Shouts from the crowd echoed in my ears as they came from every direction. I couldn't even interpret what they were saying...whether they were shouting their support or protest.

I barreled through people, nearing my husband, but just as George was about to reach Smalls, with Lars just a few feet further away, a third figure flew across my vision, like a blur, and stepped in front of Smalls, throwing arms into the air and screaming as loud as humanly possible. The crowd froze.

Standing between the onrush and the solitary figure of Smalls, Addie posed with her arms straight out. "Just because he can quote from the bible doesn't mean he understands it."

"Addie, let me at him," Lars said.

"No no, Lars...this man isn't worth the effort. He doesn't deserve to get beat up just because he's ignorant."

I slipped a hand into the crook of George's elbow. "Come on, George. She's right."

Smalls stood with a conflicted smile on his face, as if he wasn't sure whether he'd won or lost. The conflict seemed to reflect the mood of the crowd as well, as they glanced from face to face, looking for a hint of how to respond. Smalls made one final effort to renew his sermon, but the crowd had started to drift away, and the indifference visibly deflated him. He gathered up his box and merged into the sea of people.

"So are you folks still interested in a portrait?"

Everyone turned as one, and I was surprised to see that the artist was still there. He had been waiting patiently off to the side.

"Yes, absolutely." Lars jumped to his feet and offered Addie his hand.

"You can just lie there if you want," the artist said. "It will probably be more comfortable."

"All right." Lars stretched himself out again, and Addie plopped down next to him, grinning broadly but still looking somewhat tense.

The artist opened his little wooden case, studied the contents, and plucked a piece of charcoal from inside. He began to draw. And I was ashamed at how I could not stop watching him. I looked at my husband, hoping he didn't notice, but George was staring off across the prairie, a thousand miles away.

CHAPTER 28

GEORGE SAT ON THE GROUND, watching his neighbors enjoy their day. Even his closest friends took one look at him and kept walking, as if they didn't recognize him. And in truth, he wanted it that way. He didn't want to be approached. The thought of carrying on a conversation with anyone exhausted him.

So he was surprised to hear someone speak his name from behind. George turned, annoyed. Standing just a foot away, leaning close to his ear, Sheriff Pierre LeFont smiled an odd smile. "How you doin', George?"

"Fine," George answered, turning his back to LeFont.

"You need to come with me for a second, George."

"I do?"

"Yeah...I got something I got to talk to you about."

George sighed and shook his head. He leaned over toward Catherine, who also had a strange look on her face. A slight, dreamy smile. "You okay?" he asked.

She flinched a little and worked her mouth as if she needed moisture. "Yes...I'm fine."

"I'll be right back," George said.

"Where are you going?"

George tipped his head toward the sheriff.

"What is it?"

"I don't know, Catherine."

"We won't be long," LeFont assured her.

Catherine absorbed the information, but George could see the worry in her face. She nodded.

The Deadwood Jail was lousy with drunks and pickpockets. LeFont took one look around and grabbed George by the elbow. "Let's go somewhere else." He ignored the questions the deputies threw his way as they ducked out of the small stone building.

LeFont led George to a small house near the jail and opened the door. "Anyone here?" LeFont shouted. No one answered, and LeFont muttered "Good" before they entered.

"Is this your house?" George asked.

LeFont nodded. "Yeah, you thought I might have a mansion on the hill, huh?" He held his palm out. "Have a seat."

George sank into a chair at the kitchen table. "So what's this all about, Sheriff?"

LeFont remained standing. "You remember the last couple of times we chatted, George?"

"Those would be hard to forget," George said.

"A lot of water under the bridge since then," LeFont said, shaking his head.

George nodded.

"You know I never believed you shot that guy, don't you?"

"Yeah, I kinda figured that, but you had me going there."

LeFont pulled his mouth to one side. "Yeah, I know...I couldn't get nothing out of nobody about what happened out there."

George wasn't sure what to make of the difference in LeFont's attitude. He showed none of the cock-sure arrogance that made George so uncomfortable the first time they met. LeFont seemed resigned to something...some unhappy fact.

"Listen, George, I just want to let you know...this thing that happened with your wife..." LeFont shook his head. "I gotta admit, I didn't pay much attention at first. People were talking about it, and of course, there was talk about her just wanting attention...that kind of thing. I don't know Catherine that well, so I wasn't sure what to make of it..."

George held his breath.

"Here's the thing, George...we got several other women telling us the same story. And now this teenage girl...they found her body yesterday morning. So...I just wanted to let you know that we been trying to get to the bottom of this thing. I know it's probably been hard on you and your family, what with the talk and all. But we're trying to figure out who's doing this."

George was still having trouble breathing. He felt his face flush.

"Are you okay, George?"

George nodded.

"You got any questions?"

"So you have any idea who it might be?"

LeFont sighed, and George could see the weight of the whole question press down on him. "No idea."

George nodded.

"I'll let you get back to your family, George. I'm sorry to take you away from the party."

"Well, I think you should know something, Sheriff, since you brought this up."

"What's that?"

"We might know who this guy is."

LeFont propped his hands on his knees and leaned forward. "Oh?"

George nodded. And then he thought about the whole situation. How much could he really trust LeFont? He thought back to the day at Poplar's house, when LeFont questioned him, and it was clear that he knew about the vigilantes.

"Listen..." George stood and started walking a slow circle. "Maybe there's a way we can help each other out here."

George walked back to their little camp, his head hanging. Children raced in circles around him, and he nodded at a few people who said hello, but for the most part, George was unaware of his surroundings.

As he sank to the blanket, Catherine scooted closer to him. "What did he want?"

George shook his head.

"George Arbuckle, what's it going to take to get it through your head?"

"Catherine, I need to ask you a favor. Please don't ask any more questions about this right now. I'm sorry, but this time I have to insist."

Catherine's mouth had opened slightly, and it hung in that position for a moment. Then she let it close slowly, her eyes blinking in rapid succession. "All right, George."

RO

For the rest of the day, I felt as if George and I had been lost in the crowd and replaced by total strangers. We ate and played games and visited the booths where award-winning arts and crafts were on display. But there was no joy, no real interest in any of it. Something had happened to George, and I felt as if it was contagious. I also knew George well enough to suspect that he was trying to figure something out. But this insistence on keeping it to himself was new.

"Do we hafta go to the dance, Mom?" Little George tugged at my hand.

"Yes we do...but we probably won't stay for long." This was my hope anyway. George looked as tired as I felt, and it seemed as if it had been several hours since we talked. Once the band started, George led me to the dance floor, and we whirled wordlessly through the crowd with the easy grace of a couple that has covered many miles of dance floor together.

After a few songs, I told George I needed a rest. But as we left the dance floor, I felt a hand on my shoulder. The burn came back to my face when I saw the amiable smile of the sketch artist.

"May I have this dance?" he asked.

I could hardly answer, I was so surprised. I looked at George, who also appeared to be surprised. It was the most life I'd seen from him all day.

"Okay," I finally blurted, and the artist took me by the elbow and led me to the dance floor.

His arm wrapped around my waist, and our opposing arms jutted out in ready position before we began rocking to an easy waltz. As our bodies tilted back and forth, I felt as if the artist was moving closer with each step.

"You enjoy dancing, don't you?" he asked.

I nodded. "I really do."

"You're very good at it."

I could hardly stand to look at him. "Oh, come on...it's not that hard."

"No, really...you have a grace that's very natural."

I was just getting comfortable with being so close to this man when I felt a hand on my shoulder again.

"I think maybe I should cut in here." George's eyes looked cold and intense as he glared at the artist. I had never seen this expression on his face before.

"I think you're right," the artist said.

George said nothing more, continuing to stare the man down. The artist sloughed away, and George watched him, his eyes narrow and mean. He reached down and wrapped his arms around my waist without looking at me, and I settled into our familiar two-step position, but it felt different. He was clutching me, pulling me tight against his torso. But not too tight. Holding me very close so that I felt every movement he made as if I was helping him move. As if our muscles were connected in some silent, invisible way. I followed along as George dipped and swayed, his natural rhythm, which had always impressed me so much, taking me right into the heart of the music. For the first time in many months...maybe years, I felt the full heat of being close to him. And I closed my eyes and let it happen.

With both of us exhausted, we didn't stay long. I saw no sign of the artist after George cut in. I had brief chats with old friends and danced a few times with Lars. But when George suggested we call it a night, I was happy.

"I got us a room," he said.

"What?"

"I got us a room at the hotel."

"You're kidding. How did you manage that? They're usually booked for weeks before the fair."

"Yep."

"You reserved it before?"

George nodded.

So I followed as George led me to the hotel where we had spent his days recovering from his wounds, checked in, and situated little George in a bedroll on the floor, and Jack in his basket in the corner, before peeling off dusty, sweaty clothes and sponging ourselves off from the wash basin. We donned our night clothes and slid under the clean sheets, and I reveled in the feel of the thick cotton, and the smell of soap.

I was just beginning to drift off when I felt something squeeze my thigh. I jumped, and even let out a small yelp.

"Sorry," George muttered.

And I suddenly realized that my husband was touching me. His hand moved from my thigh, slipping between my legs, and a moan rose from deep within me. With no thought or plan or specific intent, I rolled against him and pressed hard into his hip, kissed him with sloppy intensity, then situated myself more directly above him. His hand escaped just before I rolled over onto him and began grinding. George grasped my breast, and another moan escaped, but this time it unleashed a flood of tears. I held my cries back, but my eyes gushed, drenching the sheets and George's chest as I slid a hand inside his underwear, pulled him out and wrapped my hand around him. I stroked twice, and then rose up and slipped him inside. I laid my body against him, and his arms wrapped around me just as we had done on the dance floor. George thrust, and he cried out, and then it was over, and George was snoring.

I wept for a long time after that, as if something inside had burst, my body convulsing on top of my husband, who never woke. I cried because I realized how much I missed having this in my life, and how I had been working so hard to convince myself that it didn't matter...that having a husband who was good and mostly kind was enough. And I cried because even now, we had come together without any conversation, without any indication of what had changed, or shifted. I felt as if George and I had lived through these past two years in parallel lives that never intersected. And even now, the coming together had been almost accidental, like a collision on the dance floor. And I cried because I knew this was probably as good as it was going to get with the man I married.

I finally rolled off him, and adjusted my nightgown, and eased up against him. And I started to count the months backward to the day I was raped.

GEORGE WOKE UP EARLY, pulled on his clothes, and kissed his boys on their foreheads. He stood over Catherine, who was still deep in sleep, and thought about touching her face, but he didn't want to wake her.

Outside, there were already a few people out and about, and it wasn't hard to tell which of them were still up from the night before, and which were up early for the new day. George stepped over a couple of cowboys who had passed out on the sidewalk. But he was too focused on his mission to pay attention to anyone else.

Halfway down Main Street, he reached inside his pocket for the directions to Bernie's house, and realized they were gone. He thought about going back to find them, but he didn't want to wake Catherine. So he turned right and strode with purpose right up to the front steps of Mrs. Tilford's Boarding House, where he took the stairs two at a time. Inside, he poked his head into the parlor where Mrs. Tilford spent her spare hours, and was relieved to find her awake, sitting in her usual spot, drinking a cup of tea.

"Good morning," George offered in a near whisper.

Mrs. Tilford stood. "Well, Mr. Arbuckle...what a surprise!" She crossed the room and took his hand in both of hers, squeezing. "How are you?"

"I'm doing well, Mrs. Tilford...it's good to see you."

She stepped back. "And you as well...are you interested in joining me for tea?"

"Oh...thanks, but no...I really need to get going."

"But Mr. Arbuckle, you just got here."

"Yes, well...the reason I'm here is because I need to ask you something..."

"Oh?"

George nodded. "I wanted to know whether Mr. Sanford is still living here in your house."

Mrs. Tilford face turned sour. "Mr. Sanford?"

"Yes...Bernie Sanford...he was here when Catherine was here."

"Oh believe you me, you don't have to remind me who Mr. Sanford is. Yes, I remember Bernie Sanford all too well."

George nodded. "So he's not here anymore? I heard he got married."

"That's right." Mrs. Tilford sighed. "Poor girl."

"Well do you know where they live?"

"I do." Mrs. Tilford walked across the room to a roll-top desk, slid the top open, and pulled a small book from the shelves. She opened it, flipping through the pages, and slid her finger until she found what she was looking for.

"Are you going to get out and celebrate today, Mrs. Tilford?" he asked, tucking the directions into his jacket.

"Oh no...I used to love going to the fair, but all those people..." She waved a hand.

"Well thank you very much," George said.

"My pleasure, Mr. Arbuckle. I hope he doesn't owe you money."

"No, not exactly."

"Well be careful...I don't trust that man."

George knocked on the door of a house that showed very little sign of care. The outside was littered with food scraps, as if they'd thrown them out for a dog they didn't have, and two of the front windows were broken, then covered on the inside with wood. The front door was warped so that it didn't quite fill the frame. When the door swung open, the woman who answered glared at George. "You got any idea how early it is?"

"Yes, ma'am."

"What do you want?"

George wasn't surprised that Bernie's wife was pretty, but she also looked like the type of woman whose focus on her appearance took up time that should have probably been devoted to other things.

"I think you better tell Bernie that George Arbuckle needs to talk to him."

"You gotta be kidding me."

George shook his head.

"You honestly think I'm gonna wake up my husband at 5:30 in the morning after he was out drinking until 4:00?"

George nodded. "Tell him George Arbuckle is here, and I think he'll be out of that bed before you know it."

Mrs. Sanford tilted her head. "You're sure."

"Positive."

She pushed her mouth into a point. "If you're wrong, there's gonna be hell to pay."

"You can tell him it's my fault."

She disappeared, not inviting George to come inside. And sure enough, Bernie dragged himself to the door just moments later. He tugged his suspenders up over his shoulders, trying to tuck his shirt in his trousers with his other hand. "George...good to see you."

Bernie was carrying his boots, and he dropped to one knee and pulled one on, then switched position, and pulled on the other. "What can I do for you?"

"I need to see your brother."

"Yeah?" Bernie stood, adjusting his shirt.

George nodded.

"Good! He's going to be happy to hear that. What do you got for him?"

"I think it would be best if I told him directly."

Bernie nodded. "All right...okay...well, I'm not sure when we'll be able to get in touch with him."

"You don't know where he is?"

"That's not what I said, George...I'm just not sure what he's got going on today."

"Well I suggest you take me there and we can find out together."

"Oh? That good, huh?"

George nodded.

Bernie studied him, one eye narrow. "All right...I'll be right back."

George positioned his horse just behind Bernie's as they rode. Bernie had loaned him one of his horses, telling him it was too far to walk. He memorized the cut of Bernie's jaw, the way his mouth pulled to one side when he was thinking. He watched Bernie's hands, their sudden, nervous movements.

They did not speak for the twenty minutes they were on horseback. And finally, Bernie led them into a slight draw, where the shade of the trees brought a slight chill to George's skin. The shade seemed to run along his arms like a cold, wet cloth.

Tucked away in a thick cluster of pine was a very small cabin...a shack, really. It was made of rough-cut logs, and covered with a sod roof. Bernie shouted Preston's name as they approached, and a dog barreled from the house, its teeth bared in direct threat of murder.

Bernie pulled a pistol from his saddle bag and pointed at the dog, and for a moment George was convinced he was going to shoot him. But a head poked out of the shack's single window, shouted "Buckshot" and then "Halt!" The dog stopped running, but didn't let up on the barking, its mouth a fountain of spittle.

"Stupid dog," Bernie muttered.

"Just doin' his job," George said.

"What do you want, Bernie?" Preston shouted, his head still poking out of the window. "I can hear that squeaky voice of yours."

"I got Arbuckle with me."

"You do?"

"Sure do."

"Well I'll be damned...prodigal son and all."

Preston Sanford welcomed George into his house as if he was some kind of royalty. "How have you been, George?" Preston pressed a cup of coffee into George's hand, clapping him on the back.

"I'm okay," George answered.

"Good...good." Preston held out a palm toward two rickety chairs made from wood with the bark still on. George sank into one of them cautiously, and sure enough, it tilted to one side with his weight.

"Sorry about that...carpentry isn't one of my strengths," Preston offered.

George shrugged.

"So you got some news for us?" Preston asked.

George took a deep breath. "I might."

"You think you know who it is?"

"I might," George repeated.

Preston laughed. "You know how to keep a guy on pins and needles, don't you, George? So what's it going to take? You want some money, 'cause I got nothing."

George shook his head. "Naw, I'm not interested in money...not for this."

"Well what is it then?"

George cleared his throat. "We're going to need more men."

Preston sat up. "Really?"

"What for?" Bernie asked.

George lowered his chin and looked at Bernie from the top of his eyes.

Preston started laughing. "Come on now, Bernie...our friend George here has finally come around to our way of thinking."

Bernie raised his brow, looking back at George, as if for confirmation.

George didn't give him any indication, but turned his attention back to Preston, whose enthusiasm had brought him to his feet.

"This is perfect!" Preston said. "We can just go to the fair and round up the men we need."

George nodded. "That's what I figured."

"You mean *I'll* have to round them up," Bernie said.

Preston frowned. "Bernie, what the hell's wrong with you? Of course George can help you out...plus you know I can't go showing my face around town...they'd string me up before I could say a word." Preston didn't even pay attention to Bernie's response...he started pacing around, rubbing his hands together. "Let's see...who can we get?" He started naming names, ticking them off with his fingers.

And then he stopped in front of both of them, legs braced, and said "What the hell am I thinking? Let's get going."

After scanning the area as they approached Deadwood, Preston found a suitable spot to hide. He tied his horse to a cottonwood tree and settled on a fallen log.

"All right, now here's what I want you to do." Preston collared Bernie and gave him specific instructions about who to approach first, and what they should bring...where they should meet. Bernie absorbed the information with a serious look, but it seemed to George as if his patience with his brother's instructions had run out a long time ago.

George and Bernie started down the mountain, leaning back in their saddles to compensate for the steep slope.

"We need to break up when we get down there," Bernie said. "I know."

"Act like you don't know me if we see each other."

George bit his lip, trying not to say what he was thinking. "So where should we meet up? And when?"

Bernie answered George's question, and then veered off in another direction. And once he was out of sight, George continued his descent, wondering how he was going to explain all this to Catherine.

R⦻

I finished nursing Jack and tucked myself back into my clothes. "Come here, George...bring your shoes over here."

"Where's daddy?" little George asked.

"He'll be along," I answered.

"But when?" George asked.

"Just get your shoes on, son." I wrenched George's feet into the tiny shoes. George grimaced from the force. "Let's go." I bundled Jack against me, picked up the picnic basket, and grabbed George by the hand, pulling him toward the door. But as I was leaving, I noticed a piece of paper lying on the floor and picked it up. I unfolded the paper, recognized it, and suddenly realized something that brought me up short. The handwriting. I opened my bag, and sorted through, pulling out the bundle of letters I carried with me everywhere. I unfolded the most recent one and held it side by side with the note.

I pulled my son behind me, out the door and down the stairs. And I moved with purpose, leading George, Jr., who stumbled and trotted behind, directly to the same spot where we'd spent the day before.

And then I began the nervous surveillance, searching for my husband. Friends of the family walked past, and I nodded and smiled as if everything was perfectly normal.

My breath didn't come all the way back until thirty minutes after I'd settled, and I spotted George striding through the crowd. When he approached, I tempered my urge to grab him by the throat.

"Where were you?" I hissed.

"I have to ask you again not to ask any questions about what's happening today."

"What does that mean?"

"I mean...I might end up disappearing for a while."

"George, no! No, you can't tell me that."

"Catherine...I'm serious...this is not a discussion we're going to have. I can't tell you anything."

"In that case, you can just go off and enjoy the day on your own then."

George nodded. "All right."

I glared. "I'll be busy with the ladies' club bake sale anyway, so that's just fine."

George took a deep breath. "Okay, that's good, right? So you won't worry."

I scoffed. "George, what on earth has gotten into you..." I thought about the previous night...and now this.

"Just trust me."

I shook my head, bending to pack our basket. "How long will you be gone?"

George stared off. "I don't know."

"George, before you go, I have to tell you something."

George looked nervous. "What is it?"

I crouched down and dug through the picnic basket, pulling out two sheets of paper. I handed George the directions to Bernie's house and the letter.

George looked puzzled. "Yeah?"

"Study them, George."

He focused on the two documents again, and his eyes suddenly grew. "The handwriting."

I nodded. "The other woman..." I made quotation marks with my fingers.

GEORGE WALKED THROUGH THE DAYS OF '76 crowd with a narrow eye. He wished he had a better memory for faces. He didn't think he would recognize a single man from the day they had gathered around the rustler and strung him up. But it didn't stop him from trying. He studied every man in the crowd, hoping to spot someone he recognized from that day. He thought about the many days he'd wandered through these same grounds through the years, half-bored. He looked forward to days like that again. But today, the world around him was a small, dangerous place.

He spotted Bernie a couple of times, and followed his instructions, as ridiculous as they were, acting as if he didn't know him. And he tried to figure out how this new information was going to affect his plan for the day. He checked his pocket watch every fifteen minutes, counting down until their appointed meeting time of 6:30. Just as the previous day, he hardly heard the greetings that were offered, but even the people that knew him seemed to pay little attention, as if everything about him told them to stay away. He made a quick trip to Pierre LeFont's office to inform him of what he had learned, and they discussed how it would change their plan.

"George!" A voice from behind made him jump, and he turned to find Lonnie Spicer jogging to catch up.

"Hi Lonnie."

"Where's your family?"

George did not alter his stride. "They're around."

"Yeah? Where? I haven't seen them for a while."

George stopped. He turned to face Lonnie directly. "What do you want, Lonnie?"

Lonnie moved uncomfortably close. And then he leaned even closer. His breath was atrocious. "I want to help," he muttered.

"What?"

"You know what I'm talking about, George...I want to help."

"Really?"

"I'm dead serious, George."

George kept his face still.

"Listen, George...please. I know who it is, and that's why I want to help. I know I ain't the most trustworthy guy in the world, especially with the history I got with your wife. But I'm telling you...this is one situation where you can believe that I'm only interested in one thing. It's personal."

George studied Lonnie's face, and saw nothing to make him suspicious. "All right, Lonnie. Okay."

"What do you want me to do?" Lonnie asked.

George told him where and when to meet him. Lonnie looked at his watch. "That's in fifteen minutes, George."

George dug out his pocket watch and studied it. "I'll be damned. All right. I'll see you then."

Lonnie's face reflected confusion as George walked away. But George had one more stop to make. He made a quick round of the grounds, found who he was looking for, and shouldered his way through the crowd. He approached the soapbox, sauntering up to Donald Smalls, and mumbled, "Can I talk to you for a sec?"

Smalls blinked his surprise, then said, "Of course" before climbing down from his box.

George approached the grove of cottonwood trees with a familiar, cool feeling in the pit of his stomach. He could hear the chatter of the men who had already gathered, broken by occasional bursts of laughter. Cigarette smoke drifted, the blue cloud patched by the thick green leaves.

When George appeared in the midst of the group, Preston Sanford immediately moved toward him. "George! We wondered where you were. We're ready to go."

"Good." George nodded. "That's good."

George took a quick glance at the circle of faces around him and couldn't believe how many of the men he knew. How had he not noticed this the first time?

"This fella said you'd vouch for him," Preston said, jerking his thumb toward Lonnie Spicer. "A couple of the guys got nervous about him being here, though, I gotta tell you."

"He's okay." George looked at Lonnie, who nodded his thanks. The circle kept their gazes fixed on George.

"So, George..." Preston's expression was just as expectant as it had been hours before. "Where we goin'? Show us the way."

George gave a quick nod. "This way." He tipped his head toward the south, and the men all made their way to their horses and mounted. George craned his neck to make sure everyone was in their saddles before nudging his heels into the borrowed horse's flanks.

Once they started their ascent up the mountain trail, George glanced behind him from time to time. He looked for subtle changes in positioning, or possible alliances. Although there was very little conversation going on, George took note of who was talking to whom. He wondered whether men who traveled in criminal gangs experienced this same paranoia. It irritated him.

The closer they got to the appointed location, the worse it got. George was turning to check on the men every five minutes.

The further they moved into the woods, the more intense the smell of pine became. The air felt cooler, thinner, and tighter against George's skin. Like a shirt.

One last glance back, and George was relieved that they had reached the appointed area without incident, but the nervous energy in this crowd was palpable. His breath caught in his throat, and he coughed it loose, drew his reins across his horse's neck, and turned around. "All right, this is good."

The others looked confused. Preston stared up into the trees, and George wondered whether he was looking for a suitable tree for a noose.

"So where we headed, George? Where's the culprit?" Preston asked.

"Well, that's the thing," George said. "We don't need to go any further, 'cause he's right here with us."

There was no response for a moment as the men looked around at each other. Preston chuckled. "What the hell, George? Who is it?"

"You got any guesses, Preston?"

Preston craned his neck, scanning the crowd of anxious faces. "Now how the hell would I know?" he asked.

George felt his breath catch in his throat thinking about what he was about to say. This was where the plans had taken a strange twist with Catherine's news. "Well, he's your own flesh and blood, Preston."

"That's right!" Lonnie shouted with such force that it made George flinch. "It's that son- of-a-bitch brother of yours."

"Bernie?" Preston frowned as if this was the most absurd thing he'd ever heard. "Bernie wouldn't hurt a lady...Bernie loves the ladies."

"This is pure bull and you know it," Bernie said.

Lonnie and another man nudged their horses right up next to Bernie, and Lonnie threw his leg up and off his own horse and onto Bernie's, launching himself so that he was sitting right behind Bernie. The other man grabbed the horse's reins while Lonnie wrapped his arms around Bernie, pinning his arms to his ribs.

"Are you sure about this?" Preston asked.

George nodded. "And in case you want some more proof, Preston, I got somebody here to help get it out of him." George slid his thumb and forefinger between his lips and let out a shrill whistle.

Donald Smalls appeared from a small grove of trees, cradling a bible in the crook of his arm.

"He's wrong," Bernie announced. "He's got nothing."

"Shut up, you scum!"

George was struck by the power of Lonnie Spicer's rebuke. He studied Lonnie's face and wondered whether allowing him to join the gathering had been a mistake. He didn't need anyone overreacting. He needed everything under control.

"What did I ever do to you?" Bernie asked Lonnie.

"I been hearing rumors about you for years," Lonnie said. "And I know one young lady that knows you attacked her."

"Well she's lying," Bernie said flatly. "I never touched a woman that didn't ask for it."

"See there." Preston pointed at Bernie, as if the evidence was clear from his appearance.

"He says he didn't do it."

"And why do you believe him?" George asked. "Why do you believe him when you didn't believe that rustler?"

"I know him," Preston said.

"That ain't enough," George said. "People hide their real selves from other people all the time."

"I still say we can't prove anything...we don't know for sure."

But George nodded to Donald Smalls. "Just wait a second," George said to Preston. "We did it your way last time. This time we're going to do it my way."

"Who's this?" Preston nodded toward Smalls.

"My name is Donald Smalls, Mr. Sanford." Donald stood close enough to Preston's horse to reach up and shake Preston's hand. "And I am a man of the cloth."

Preston turned to George and frowned. "What's this about?"

"You'll see," George said. He nodded toward Smalls, who returned the gesture.

Through all of this, Bernie Sanford had shown no sign of resistance, or made any move to escape. He appeared entirely unconcerned about the proceedings. And now he looked at Smalls and smirked, then started laughing. "What are you going to do, save me?"

"Only God can do that, young man," Smalls said.

Bernie shook his head. "This is stupid."

A loud smack sounded, and a verbal response rose up from every man there. "Shut the hell up." Lonnie Spicer had punched Bernie in the ear, and now had his arm wrapped around his neck like a steer wrestler. "You obviously don't realize how serious this is."

"Easy, Lonnie," George said. "No more of that."

But Lonnie glared at Bernie, whose eyes were big. At the same time, Bernie was still smiling, as if the whole proceedings continued to amuse him. Blood trickled from his ear.

"I'd kill you right now if it was up to me," Lonnie said.

"No more violence," George repeated.

"Good thing you're not in charge," Bernie muttered as Lonnie unwrapped his arm from his neck. He embraced him again, pinning Bernie's arms.

George nodded to Smalls again. Smalls cleared his throat and faced Bernie. "I'm going to ask you a few questions, Mr. Sanford."

"What makes you think I'll answer?" Bernie answered.

George was beginning to get nervous. He couldn't tell whether the men believed him or not. And he knew from experience that once they took a side, the mood of this crowd could shift in a second.

"If you don't answer his questions, we'll know you're guilty," George said.

"That ain't right," Preston said.

"Let's just see." Again, George nodded to Smalls.

"Mr. Sanford, have you accepted Jesus as your personal savior?"

Bernie's mouth hung open, his expression incredulous. But George noticed that Preston was intently focused on him, waiting for his answer.

Bernie shook his head.

"Well?" Preston asked.

"'Course I have," Bernie muttered.

Preston nodded, looking at George as if this was just as he suspected.

Smalls held his bible up to Bernie. "As a Christian, Mr. Sanford, you are obliged to tell us the truth then...you realize this, right?"

Bernie bristled, coughing and adjusting his collar. "I know all that."

"Do you know a woman named Catherine Arbuckle?"

"I'm not going to answer any more of these questions," Bernie said. "This is stupid."

"No it's not," Preston said. "Come on, Bernie...you got nothing to hide, so just answer the questions."

Bernie took a quick glance at Preston. He looked away, off into the trees, and at that moment, George knew he was guilty. He was now convinced.

"Yeah, I know her....everyone knows who Catherine is," Bernie said. "We used to live in the same boarding house."

"Why are we even bothering with these questions?" one of the men shouted. "Let's get this over with!"

"Get what over with?" another replied.

"That's the whole point," George said. "We need to figure out what we're going to do, and we can't do that until we get some answers."

"You're not going to get the answers from me," Bernie said.

"Keep going," George instructed Smalls.

"Mr. Sanford, do you know a woman named Sheila Kraut?"

"Why?"

"Answer the questions, Bernie." Preston's face darkened, a vein swelling in his neck.

Bernie glared at Preston, and the expression on his face showed the first sign of fear. But he gathered his composure and frowned himself back into the angry defiance. "Yeah, I know her. She's a whore."

"Ask him about Priscilla Hayes!" Lonnie shouted.

"Who is she?" Smalls asked Lonnie.

"She was my niece. She's not with us anymore. They found her body this morning!"

"What makes you think he had anything to do with that?" George asked Lonnie.

"He was the last one to see her. And she told her mother she was afraid of him."

George could feel the momentum shifting, building, creating a wave of accusatory emotion. It was starting to feel a lot like the night of the hanging, which was just as he'd hoped. But it also scared the hell out of him.

"What about Allison?" someone asked.

This name drew the biggest response from Bernie. His head jerked toward the speaker. "I didn't do nothing to her."

"Bull shit," George said. "I was there the night of the dance. I saw you leaving with her."

"That doesn't prove nothing," Bernie spat. "So we left together...that don't mean a thing."

"She got pregnant!" George said.

This seemed to surprise Bernie. But he didn't miss a beat. "That don't mean it was me."

"You really are a heartless bastard," George said. "That poor girl is dead."

"What would you do if you were surrounded by everyone you thought was your friend?"

"Most men would tell the truth," Smalls said. "If a man has nothing to hide, then he has no reason to lie."

"Is that from the bible?" Bernie asked.

"It's just a fact." This statement, delivered in a calm, sad voice, came from Preston Sanford, and it drew the attention of everyone else present. Did this mean he was convinced?

"What do you mean by that?" Bernie asked his brother.

"It's fact...if you got nothing to hide, then just tell them the truth, Bernie. You got nothing to hide, right?"

Bernie nodded. "That's right...I got nothing to hide."

"This is a lot harder when it's someone you know, isn't it?" George directed his question to Preston. "It's not so easy to condemn someone when you got something at stake."

"Hey, I'm just trying to give my brother a fair shake here," Preston said.

George nodded. "All right...that's exactly what I'm trying to do...not like you did with that poor bastard out in the prairie." George gauged Preston's reaction to this, but Preston showed almost nothing.

"So let me ask you this then." George dug in his pocket, pulled out a sheet of paper, and held it out toward Preston. "You recognize this handwriting?"

Preston studied the paper briefly, frowning, then nodded. "Yeah. I know that writing...that's my brother's hand...that's directions to his house." Preston looked proud, handing the paper back to George. "That don't prove nothing."

"No, that doesn't...but what about this?" George pulled out the final letter Catherine had received, the one fingering Preston, written on the same kind of paper. He held it out to Preston. This time Preston read the words carefully, and his face took on an expression of recognition, then confusion. "What the hell is this?" He held it up to Bernie. But he quickly shifted his burning glare back to George. "What are you up to, Arbuckle? This is some kind of trick, isn't it? Bernie wouldn't write something like this...it's a trick."

"No it isn't, Preston. My wife got that letter just a few days ago...she's got a whole bunch or letters just like it."

Preston turned to Bernie with questions in his eyes. "Bernie, what's this all about? Someone held a gun to your head?"

"What's it say?" one of the other men shouted.

George explained to the men what happened...how Bernie posed as another rape victim and pinned the blame on Preston. He watched a quiet glaze wash over Preston's eyes. Bernie's chin fell a little lower with each fact.

"Bernie, this ain't a Sanford thing...we don't do this kind of thing," Preston pleaded.

"Let's string him up!" someone shouted.

"Yeah, let's hang him!"

A noose appeared, and one of the men tossed the rope over a tree branch, where the noose hung like an omen above Bernie's head.

"You won't be hanging nobody today!" Preston shouted, his face turning red.

"You got no say in this, Sanford," Lonnie said. "This is no longer your show. This is our show!"

"Nobody's hanging my little brother." Preston, in a nimble move that surprised George, pulled himself up on his feet, standing on his saddle, and reached for the noose. He wrapped it up in his hands and pulled himself up. His horse moved a few strides away, leaving Preston hanging.

"Let's hang them both!" Lonnie shouted, and shouts rang out as the men started to crowd around Bernie's horse.

"No!" Smalls stepped into the middle of the fray, holding up his bible. "This is not the right thing to do."

One of the men knocked Smalls to the ground with the butt of his gun. And that was when George decided it had gone far enough. He slid his fingers into his mouth again and the shrill whistle echoed through the pines.

From every direction men on horses emerged from the thick stand of trees, their guns drawn and aimed at the gathering. The men continued shouting, calling for a hanging, but as they realized they were surrounded, they quieted down one by one. George watched each of them consider their own survival and decide.

Preston lost his grip on the rope and fell to the ground.

From the middle of the trees, Pierre LeFont pushed into the crowd, right up to Bernie's horse. He turned in every direction, taking in the faces around him. "I hope you all realize that you're gonna get yourselves arrested today."

"Oh come on, LeFont...we're trying to do something good here," one of the men proclaimed.

"I'm sure that's how you see it," LeFont said. "The law has a little different take on things like this."

"The law doesn't get everything right," someone said.

"That's right! Sometimes the law is just as dangerous as the criminals."

"I know that," LeFont says. "You've all seen that happen."

"It's all we got, though," George said.

"That's right," LeFont said.

And then a sudden motion disrupted everything. A thump, a kick of boots into the air, and the digging of hooves into the thick ground. By the time everyone figured out what happened, Lonnie was lying on the ground, and Bernie had spurred his horse into the trees. "Get him!" LeFont shouted. George and several of the deputies started after him, their horses muscling into the steep incline, throwing dirt and leaves and pine needles into the faces of those left behind.

George's heart rose up and bobbed in the top of his chest as he guided Bernie's own horse after him, ducking branches and still getting swatted. And he realized as he chased that his heart tasted the thirst for murder, that he wanted to catch this man and push a gun against his head and fire. That the taste of blood had filled his mouth and was now running down his throat, filling him up with the desire for more.

But of course...he had no gun.

One of the deputies had managed to race ahead of Bernie's horse and cut in front of him. Just as Bernie approached a narrow path, the horse appeared, and the deputy jumped off just in time to avoid getting rammed by Bernie's horse. The horses collided in a clash of muscle and bone and power and speed. Bernie flew over his horse's head, flipping in the air, and landing like a sack of feed on his back. George caught up to him as Bernie was still trying to catch his breath. George swung from his saddle, and without a thought, he jumped on top of Bernie and straddled him, holding his arms down with both knees. He bent down close to him until his face was inches from Bernie's.

"You havin' trouble breathing, Bernie?"

Bernie just stared at him, his eyes huge.

"Now you know what my wife felt like when you done what you did to her." George reached down and held a fist against Bernie's throat, further blocking the flow of air. "You feel that? Does it scare you?"

Bernie still didn't respond.

"Damn right it scares you. That's what you did to these women, you selfish bastard. And that's what you did to their families, too. Because it didn't stop after you left. It didn't stop when you went on your way, you understand? It kept on rushing through our lives like a river. You understand that?"

Bernie's face started to turn blue, and George felt the desire to press even harder. He wanted to block the air forever. But the thought came to him, and he knew it was true, that this would turn him into one of them. That he would be just like them. So he eased up. But not completely. He kept just enough pressure to make sure Bernie didn't know which direction he would turn.

"Remember this feeling...remember that this is what you did to people."

Moments later, George sat on his horse watching the deputies round up the vigilantes, and he wondered how much of what happened in this world was a replacement for words. The slam of fist against flesh, or the blast of a bullet. Even the unwelcome thrust of a man inside a woman. How much of this was just a way of saying something that men couldn't seem to find the words to speak out loud. Men trying to reach deep down and touch some wordless place inside of them. It all seemed so senseless.

George heard something from behind him. When he turned, a furry back wound through the trees, probably a fox, or a coyote. And George became aware that there was a whole world behind him. A cattle trail led down the mountain, away from what was happening in front of him, back to civilization, where people were dancing and drinking good whiskey. And beyond that, the land unfurled around him like every dream he'd ever had. George pictured Catherine and his boys, sitting in the small house George had built with his own hands, on the ranch they called their own, and it occurred to him that wherever she was, Catherine must be scared to death.

George turned away and started down the hill.

"Where you goin', George?" He turned, and Preston looked at him with a sad smile. "You lose your nerve?"

"Nope...just found it."

RO

I sat in front of a table of pies, my heart thumping against my ribs. The rumors had been galloping around the grounds of the Days of '76, wild stories about why so many of the men had suddenly disappeared. And I was afraid of what this meant. Afraid that my husband's desire to help me had led him to some kind of ridiculously manly solution to the problem. I was worried he'd been sucked into the seduction of violence.

People stopped and studied the baked goods on the table and made the same noises they would be making if the food was in their mouths. They pulled coins from their purses and pockets and handed them to me, then pointed to the item they wanted. I went through the motions of being present for all of this, saying the right things, laughing at their jokes, shaking the hands of friends and neighbors. I laughed at my kids, scolded them, fed them and held them when they hurt themselves.

I studied the trees, trying to will the appearance of the man I married. I thought back to the night he'd appeared at my window, and I asked him to surprise me one more time.

And then he was there, walking toward me through the crowd. My legs felt weak, but I rushed out from behind the table, straight to him, and threw myself into his arms.

"I'm so sorry, Catherine," he said. "I know I've put you through a lot this past year."

"Stop...don't talk for a minute." I held him at an arm's length, checking for bullet holes or broken skin of any kind. "You didn't get shot?"

"I didn't even sprain an ankle."

"George, what happened?"

George pulled me to him, completely ignoring the strange looks we got from the people around us. "I'll tell you all about it later...right now, I just need some rest."

We pulled into our yard around midnight, milling blue and cumbersome under a very thin sliver of moon. George carried his namesake and I carried Jack, and then George went back out for the picnic basket, which had no more food but might still attract varmints with the lingering odors.

We tucked the sleeping boys into their beds, and then I held onto my husband after we slid under the quilts. And in a whisper, he told me what happened. I didn't interrupt or ask questions until he told me the whole story. I was amazed how wide awake George was with it being so late. He gestured with his hands, and even in a whisper, his voice was expressive and full of emotion.

"So you asked Donald Smalls to come and help out?"

"Yeah. I thought it might help sway Preston."

"That was a great idea, George."

He lifted his head. "You think so?"

"Yeah, I really do. And I'm sure it made Donald happy to be asked."

"Right up until he got knocked in the head," George joked, and we chuckled quietly.

I rolled toward my husband, lay my head against his shoulder and rested a hand on his chest. "What made you think to do all this, George?"

"I don't know, honey...it just came to me there in LeFont's house. I knew those guys would be thrilled to get a chance to string another poor guy up, so I figured getting them all gathered in one place would be the easy part. But...well, I wasn't so sure about the rest of it."

I thought about how much he'd risked, how easily it could have gone wrong. And about the price George would have paid for that. I couldn't help but be a little irritated that he'd risked his life that way. On the other hand...

"George, the next time you want to save the world, just give me a little more warning, okay?"

George chuckled. "All right...I think that's fair enough."

He turned his head toward me, and then the rest of his body, and we pressed against each other, and then together.

I HANDED A BIG BOWL OF GRAVY to my youngest son Bob and told him to 'very carefully' carry it to the dining room table. As my ten-year-old walked in measured steps toward the table, his two younger sisters bounced around him like puppies, their bodies wriggling with the excitement of life. Katie, who was eight, was trying to get her four-year-old sister Muriel to sing "In the Good Old Summertime" with her. But Muriel was much more interested in telling her sister about the big snake she and Bob had seen earlier in the day.

"He was longer than any snake you ever saw in your life!" Muriel insisted. "And he had a head like a spoon."

"Oh, he wasn't that big." Bob placed the bowl of gravy in the center of the dinner table as if it would break at the slightest touch. "We've seen a lot bigger snakes than that one, Muriel."

"Well I never have," Muriel insisted. "Never in my whole life."

"Sing with me, Muriel...come on!" Katie took her sister by the hand and nearly jerked her into the living room, spinning her around.

"Did you girls wash up yet?" I asked.

"Yes, Momma," Muriel said.

"What kind of snake was that, Bob?" Muriel asked.

"It was nothing but a little ol' garter snake," Bob said.

The back door opened, and George entered, stomping the mud from his boots. He bent over and pried them from his feet, propping them against the wall.

"You kids sit up to the table," I shouted. "Your father's here."

George limped over and kissed me on the forehead. "Where's the boys?"

"No sign of them yet."

George nodded, scrubbing his hands in the wash basin. "Must have had to pull a cow out of the bog. It's muddy out there."

I watched my husband as he cleaned up. I had often noticed that the labor of our lives had affected us so differently. The constant work kept George thin and sinewy, his muscles sharply defined. For me, carrying water buckets, churning butter, and slinging children and food around had resulted in a squat, solid figure that tested the seams of most of my dresses. It seemed unfair somehow.

"How are the Glassers?" I pulled the roast from the oven and set the pot on top of the stove. I lifted the lid and smelled.

"They're doing fine. Said to tell you hello."

"Did they have any potatoes?"

"Oh hell...I left them in my saddle bag...I'll have to get them after supper."

I forked the roast out onto a platter.

"Or do you need 'em now?" George asked.

"No no...they're for tomorrow."

"How do the cattle look?" I asked George as we sat down to supper.

"Fatter than ever. We're going to do well at auction."

"Can I go this time, Dad?" Bob bounced in his chair.

"We'll see...we might just be able to take you along this year."

"Really! Will Blake be there too?"

"I bet he will," George said, reaching out to pinch Bob's nose.

I had insisted that our third son, Blake, move into Belle Fourche to attend school there. Neither George Jr. nor Jack had been interested in continuing after the small one room school in Albion, which only offered the first six grades. Blake was now an eighth grader and got high marks from his teacher.

As the meal continued, and the older boys still didn't show up even as the light faded, I thought about an incident I'd been trying to forget for several days.

That previous weekend, we had gone to Belle Fourche to stock up on food and supplies. We picked up Blake from the house where he boarded, and the whole family went to a musical production at the Belle Fourche Theater. After the show, as we walked down the street, George Jr. began talking about the show, and in his usual fashion, started to act out one of the scenes.

Everyone was laughing, including the people passing by, when Jack suddenly said to him, "Why can't you keep quiet for once?"

George responded as he always did, laughing at Jack and giving him a gentle shove. "Don't worry, Jack...no one believes you're with us anyway."

It was a joke George made frequently, teasing Jack about the fact that he wasn't as social as the rest of the kids, but it made me cringe every time, knowing Junior had no idea about the implications. Oddly enough, as Jack grew older, he was the one who looked most like George Sr. But the joke always got to Jack, almost as if he knew, which was why George repeated it, of course.

Jack usually kept his anger bitten hard inside his mouth, then tamped down inside. But for some reason, on this day, Jack responded, loudly and immediately. "If you ever say that again, I swear to God...."

"Oh come on, Jack." George just held his arms out, a big smile on his face. "You know I'm kidding."

"Stop it, George," George Sr. barked.

Junior's arms dropped, and he shook his head. "Why are you always defending him anyway? Why does he always get special treatment?"

"He does not," I butted in. "Your father and I treat you all the same."

And it was the next statement that came as the biggest surprise. Blake, who never joined into arguments if he could possibly avoid it, stated in his reasonable, factual way, "Yes he does, Mom. We all know it. Dad always treated Jack different."

I wouldn't easily forget Jack's response to all this. He glared at Blake with a look that sent a shimmer through my spine.

As we finished our dinner, George looked at me with his brow raised and asked, "We got anything sweet?"

"Well, I made a pie...does that count?"

George looked around at the children, rubbing his hands together. "Ooooh, a pie!! You kids think it's okay if we have some pie?"

The children all shouted their approval, and I laughed. George's playfulness with our children had come as a surprise at first. He always seemed so serious. But his willingness to get down on the floor and wrestle with the boys or swing the girls around the floor in an exaggerated form of dance, had started to emerge after the events of Deadwood, and it now delighted me.

For a few years after the events in Deadwood, I had watched my husband reject the efforts of many well-intentioned people to make him into some kind of hero. Although the vigilantes were barely punished, and some folks didn't support any punishment at all, George was considered a hero for his efforts to bring them to justice. Many people had urged him to run for public office, a suggestion he never seriously considered. It didn't suit his personality or his ambitions, and I was glad I didn't have to tell him that. He knew.

But he was uncomfortable with the attention for another reason, and it was just one more thing I knew we would never talk about. But he had alluded to it once, when he looked at me one night, and in a moment of sudden softness, said quietly, "I'm sorry I didn't do something sooner..."

"I know," I told him before he even finished. And for a moment, I thought about telling him what bothered me most about it, but I couldn't say it, and I probably never will. Because itis just one of those rules that never seems to be broken in this vast, quiet place. But it is still with me, the fact that it took more women coming forward for people to finally believe me. And the worst part of it all was the fact that I knew this kind of skepticism was exactly what killed my friend Allison. She knew that if she told people what happened to her, the consequences would be more than she could bear. I could certainly vouch for that. I had decided to take that risk. She couldn't, and it cost her.

I cleared the table while George kept the children entertained. I cut wedges of apple pie, tipping them onto plates. I was just beginning to pour a little cream onto the pie wedges when someone came in the back door.

"Finally," I said to myself. "Dinner is still on the table, boys!"

A slow stride echoed through the room, and I looked up. Jack stood in the doorway, his head bowed.

"Is Junior feeding the horses?" I asked.

Jack shook his head. Jack didn't make a move to the dinner table and hadn't spoken since he entered. There was something about this quiet that got my attention. I glanced at him again.

"Is everything all right?"

Jack shook his head again.

"Jack, what's going on?"

And Jack crumpled. His knees thumped against the floor, followed by his elbows. And he stayed that way, his body hunched, and convulsing.

"Oh god...George!" I called.

George appeared, the smaller children gathering around him, the girls hiding behind his bandied legs, fear draining the color from their faces.

"What's wrong, Jack?" George asked. "Where's Junior?"

"He's in the river," Jack finally mumbled.

"He's what?"

Jack turned his head to the side, looking up at his father. "He went down, Dad...he went under."

George crossed the room and grabbed his boots. "Where?"

"Just north of the crossing."

I listened to this exchange as if it was happening in another life.

"Come on, Jack," George said.

I watched my son rise slowly to his feet, and I thought to myself that there was obviously some mistake here. George was the best swimmer of all the kids. Plus he had no reason to go into the river this time of year. This made no sense. George Jr. would most certainly walk in any minute, smiling, wondering why Jack had left him behind.

Jack and George headed out the door.

RO

George's horse shook its head, balking at George's effort to push him.

"Come on, boy...I know you just got back to the barn, but this is an emergency."

The horse eventually responded to his prodding, and he and Jack arrived at the crossing. "Where did you last see him?" George asked.

"Right here, Dad....he came over to water his horse. And it took a lot longer than it should, so I rode over, and his horse was here, but no sign of George."

"God dammit," George muttered. He climbed from his horse and started downstream, bending over, studying the water for anything at all...any sign of motion or breath. Jack followed closely behind.

About fifty yards down, George noticed a swirl, and he dove in without a thought, the cold water bringing a gasp and a shout. George planted his feet, and began wading through the river, waving his arms under the water. His hands found branches, bunches of grass, a clump of sagebrush, and finally something smooth. George's breath caught in his throat as he tugged at the leg-shaped item. It didn't give, and it didn't give. George pulled harder, and finally it came loose, and George groaned as he leaned toward the shore. George drove forward with his legs, and when he found dry ground with one foot, the broken corner of a dining room table emerged.

George tossed the table leg to the side, then started downstream again.

"Dad," he heard.

George peered into the dark and found Jack striding toward him. "What is it?" he asked.

Jack held something out, and George reached for it. The item was wet, but he recognized Junior's hat.

"How far down did you go?" he asked Jack.

"All the way down to the bend."

"Is that where you found this?"

Jack nodded.

"Let's go a little further."

Jack nodded, and they rode their horses another hundred yards downstream, where they dismounted and searched for another two hours. But the sky was cloudy, hiding the half moon, and it was almost impossible to see. George shouted his son's name over and over, his own name echoing out into the clear night in his own voice, and he couldn't overlook the fact that his other son, this son he had tried too hard to treat as his own, was not calling George's name. Was not getting into the water. George's heart ached as he scanned the inky flow and realized how futile this search was.

George laid a hand on Jack's shoulder. "We'll try again tomorrow."

He looked for some sign of something—anything—in Jack's expression. But there was nothing he could read in him at all. And he wondered whether this was what his years of experience as a solid, pragmatic rancher had passed along to his boys, or if there was something else.

On the ride back, George fought the growing feeling that there was no hope. He thought about the possibility that George had been washed downstream and crawled out and walked back to the house. Yes, he was there right now, warming himself by the fire, laughing about the two of them wasting their time looking for him. That would be just the right way to end the day, laughing about their concern. Then they would return to their usual routine and get up early the next day and be back in the fields, doing what they did every day.

RO

I waited, sitting at the kitchen table, my stomach in a knot. When I heard the men come in, I jumped to my feet and met them at the door. But I could tell by the look on George's face that they hadn't had any luck. The first thing George did when they entered was look around, and I could see he was hoping to find George there.

Jack sat silently for a while, staring at the fire.

"We'll look some more in the morning...it was too dark to see much of anything," George finally said.

I nodded. But the feeling was so strong I couldn't squelch it. I knew there was no chance. I knew that Junior would have found his way home if he was alive. I knew that George knew it too. I kept waiting for Jack to say something.

"Did you hear him go in?" I finally asked.

Jack's small eyes seemed to get even smaller as he looked away and shook his head. "I was too far away, I guess."

"He must have just gone in to cool off or something," George said, and I bit my tongue, wishing my husband wasn't always so eager to answer for Jack.

"I better get some sleep," Jack finally said.

We went about our nightly routine as if it was just another day. And I was certain that no matter what happened tomorrow, or the next day, or any day in their future together, that this was how it would always be. If our son was tangled in the weeds at the bottom of the Little Missouri River, we would never talk about what it meant, or how it felt. Just as we had never talked about what happened fifteen years ago, when Bernie Sanford was found guilty of raping me and several other women and hanged. Just as we had never talked about everything that led up to that.

And I knew the reason we would never talk about any of that was because it would interfere with what really needed to be done. I knew that anything that got in the way of work would be ignored. And more than anything, I knew that if I was going to survive in this isolated world, this world where the truth was avoided even when it was known, this world where the space between people was deliberate and vast, I had better not expect anything more from the people around me, especially the man I married. I knew that, whether I liked it or not, the secrets we kept from each other served a purpose, and that the best way to get through each day was to simply do the things that were necessary to make our life comfortable. And I knew that I would do that. I knew that this was a good life. I knew that I had a good man in the bed beside me. And I knew that I would do whatever it took to keep what I had.

Lying next to each other, George and I stared up at the ceiling. I could tell he wasn't asleep by his breathing, and by the occasional shift in his position. I took his hand, and he squeezed, and because I knew I couldn't ask the question that was rattling around in my head, I instead rolled over and pressed myself against him. I knew the answer anyway. But the question stayed firmly lodged in my mind, as it would for many years after. And I wondered whether the answer to this question had anything to do with everything that had come before. Of course, I knew the answer to that, too.

But I couldn't stop thinking about the fact that when he came back the first time, Jack's clothes were completely dry.

Books by Russell Rowland:

In Open Spaces
The Watershed Years
High and Inside
West of 98: Living and Writing the New American West, co-edited with Lynn Stegner
Fifty-Six Counties: A Montana Journey

CPSIA information can be obtained
at www.ICGtesting.com
Printed in the USA
FSHW020951100719
59878FS